A Long and Winding Road

Also by Win Blevins

Stone Song

The Rock Child

ravenShadow

Give Your Heart to the Hawks

RENDEZVOUS SERIES

So Wild a Dream

Beauty for Ashes

Dancing with the Golden Bear

Heaven Is a Long Way Off

A Long and Winding Road

*Dreams Beneath Your Feet**

*forthcoming

A Long and Winding Road

A Novel of the Mountain Men

WIN BLEVINS

A Tom Doherty Associates Book

New York

A LONG AND WINDING ROAD

Map by Mark Stein

A Forge Book
Published by Tom Doherty Associates, LLC
175 Fifth Avenue
New York, NY 10010

www.tor-forge.com

Library of Congress Cataloging-in-Publication Data

Blevins, Winfred.
A long and winding road : a novel of the mountain men / Win Blevins. — 1st hardcover ed.
p. cm.
"A Tom Doherty Associates book."
ISBN-13: 978-0-7653-0577-0
ISBN-10: 0-7653-0577-1
1. Trappers—Fiction. 2. Indians of North America—Fiction. I. Title.
PS3552.L45L66 2007
813'.54—dc22

2007026500

First Edition: December 2007

Printed in the United States of America

0 9 8 7 6 5 4 3 2 1

To Meredith:
You make the world go round.

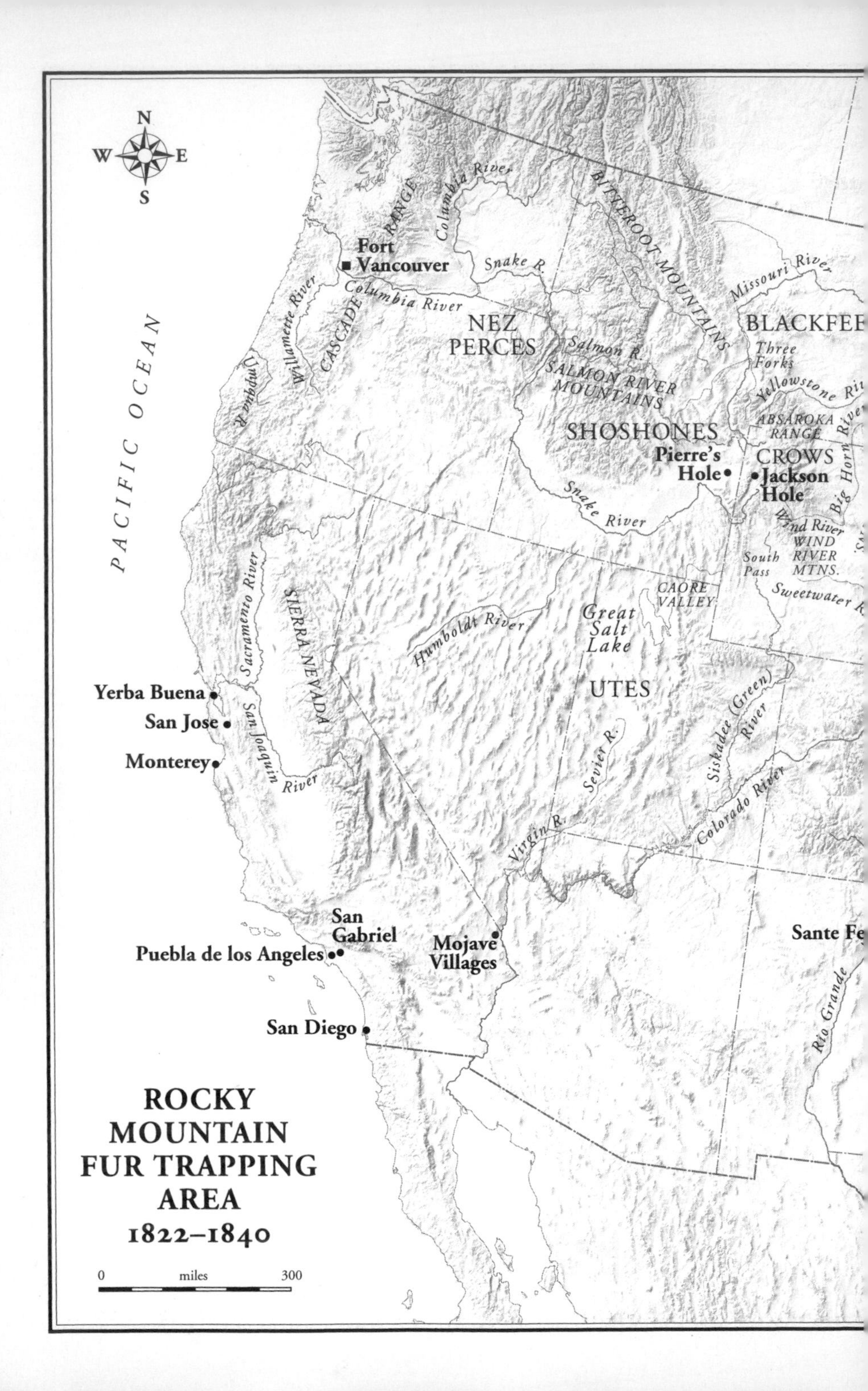

N
W
E
S
PACIFIC OCEAN
Columbia River
CASCADE RANGE
BITTEROOT MOUNTAINS
Fort Vancouver
Snake R.
Missouri River
Willamette River
Columbia River
NEZ PERCES
BLACKFEE
Umpqua R.
Salmon R.
Three Forks
SALMON RIVER MOUNTAINS
Yellowstone Ri
ABSAROKA RANGE
SHOSHONES
CROWS
Pierre's Hole
Jackson Hole
Big Horn River
Snake River
Wind River
WIND RIVER MTNS.
South Pass
Sweetwater R
CAORE VALLEY
Sacramento River
SIERRA NEVADA
Humboldt River
Great Salt Lake
Yerba Buena
San Jose
UTES
San Joaquin River
Monterey
Sevier R.
Siskadee (Green) River
Colorado River
Virgin R.
San Gabriel
Mojave Villages
Sante Fe
Puebla de los Angeles
Rio Grande
San Diego
ROCKY MOUNTAIN FUR TRAPPING AREA 1822–1840
0
miles
300

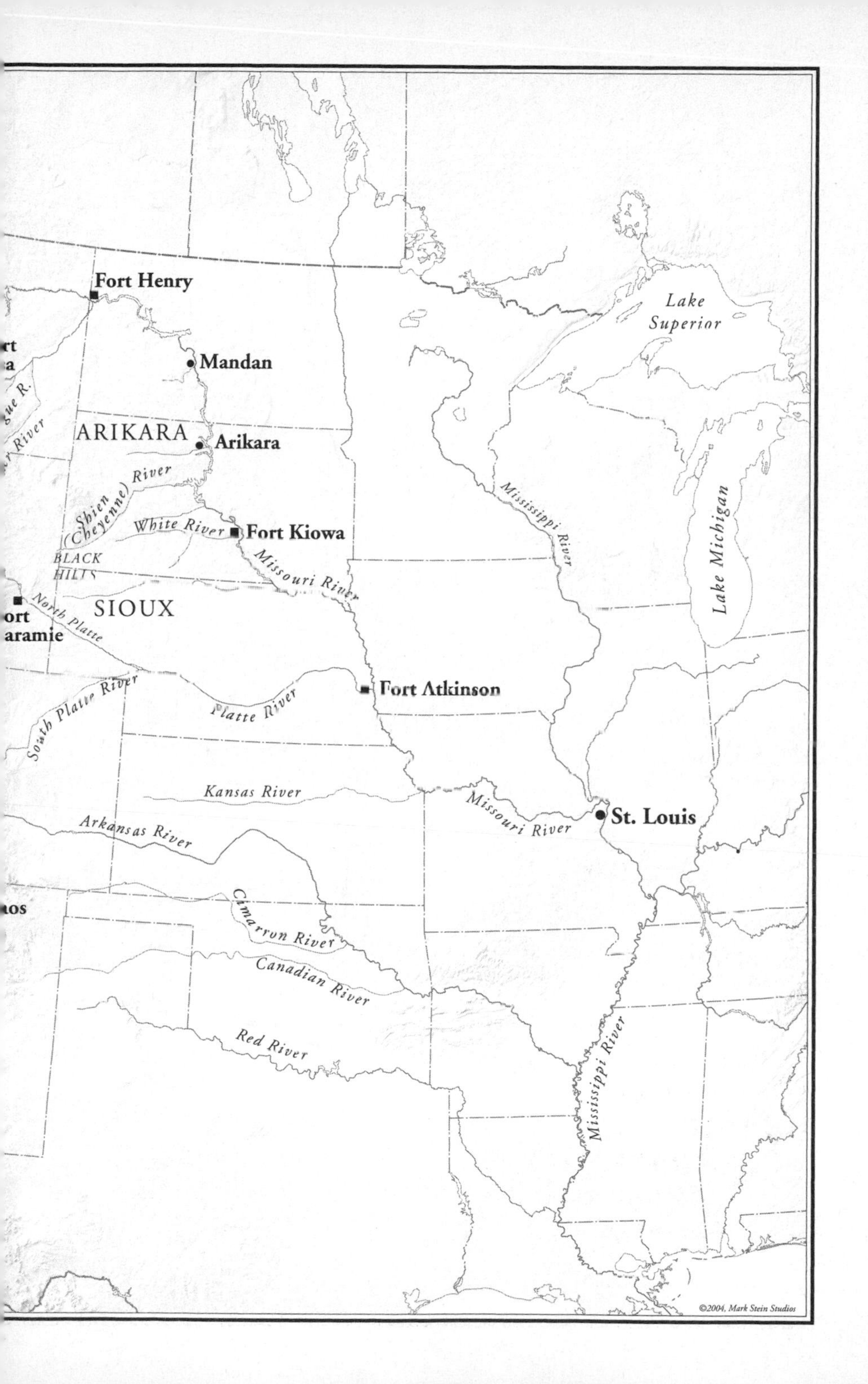
Fort Henry
Mandan
ARIKARA
Arikara
Shien (Cheyenne) River
White River
Fort Kiowa
BLACK HILLS
Missouri River
SIOUX
North Platte
Fort Atkinson
South Platte River
Platte River
Kansas River
Missouri River
St. Louis
Arkansas River
Cimarron River
Canadian River
Red River
Mississippi River
Lake Superior
Lake Michigan
©2004, Mark Stein Studios

Synopses of the Previous Volumes, 1822–1828

In *So Wild a Dream*, challenged by the half-breed Hannibal, Sam follows his heart west. After traveling to St. Louis with the con man Grumble and the madam Abby, he goes to the Rocky Mountains with a fur brigade and begins to learn the ways of the trappers and the Indians. At the end he is forced to walk seven hundred miles alone, lost and starving, to the nearest fort.

In *Beauty for Ashes* Sam courts the Crow girl Meadowlark. Helping Sam attempt a daring feat to win her hand, her brother is killed. Seeking reconciliation, Sam goes through the rigors of a sun dance, and Meadowlark elopes with him. Her family takes her back by force and kicks Sam out of the village. But Meadowlark runs away to join Sam, and at the trapper rendezvous they are married.

Dancing with the Golden Bear launches Sam and Meadowlark to California with a fur brigade. After terrible hardships crossing the desert, they reach the Golden Clime and the ocean. But Meadowlark dies in childbirth. On a harrowing journey across the Sierra Nevada and the deserts beyond, Sam passes through the dark night of the soul.

In *Heaven Is a Long Way Off* Sam returns to California for his daughter, only to discover that she, her uncle Flat Dog, and her aunt Julia have been kidnapped. He brings off harrowing rescues and makes a wild escape on a river in flood. On the way back to the Crows, he becomes deeply involved in rescuing teenagers from slavery. Finally he returns his daughter to her village, and finds his rival waiting to kill him.

Cast of Principal Characters

SAM MORGAN, a Pennsylvanian who left home for the Rocky Mountains. When he lived with the Crows, he acquired the name Joins with Buffalo.

PALOMA LUNA DE OTERO, owner of Rancho de las Palomas in Santa Fé and Sam's lover.

HANNIBAL MACKYE, a scholar and an Indian, born to a Dartmouth professor and a Delaware woman. Once a trainer of circus horses, he's now a trader.

TOMÁS, a Chihuahuan boy taken as a slave, then freed by Sam and adopted as a son by him.

LUPE and ROSALITA, slaves, then adopted sisters of Tomás.

JOAQUIN, a slave, then husband to Lupe.

SUMNER, a slave who claims his freedom and follows Grumble into the con life.

HOSTEEN TSO, a leader of the Navajo.

NEZ BEGAY, a war leader of the Navajo.

FLAT DOG, Sam's Crow brother-in-law.

JULIA RUBIO, daughter of a California don, Flat Dog's wife.

ESPERANZA, Sam's daughter.

PEANUT HEAD, a fledgling trapper.

BELL ROCK, a Crow medicine man.

GRASS, a slave, then fiancée of Tomás.

COY, Sam's pet coyote. In a huge prairie fire Coy led Sam to safety inside the carcass of a buffalo, and they've been inseparable since.

PALADIN, Sam's medicine hat pony, trained in the skills of circus horses.

HISTORICAL CHARACTERS

JEAN-BAPTISTE CHARBONNEAU, son of Sacajawea, a trapper.

PEGLEG SMITH, trapper and trader.

KIT CARSON, trapper.

MANUEL ARMIJO, former governor of Nuevo Mexico, a player in the Indian slave trade.

NARBONA, a headman of the Navajos.

WALKARA, a headman of the Utes.

TOM FITZPATRICK, an Irishman who becomes a brigade leader, later an owner of Rocky Mountain Fur Company.

JIM BRIDGER, trapper, brigade leader, and yarner extraordinaire, later an owner of Rocky Mountain Fur Company.

JOE MEEK, Virginian, trapper, child of nature.

CAPTAIN WILLIAM DRUMMOND STEWART, lord of Murthly Castle, Scotland.

OLD BILL WILLIAMS, free trapper and free spirit.

JIM BECKWOURTH, a mulatto and a trapping companion of Sam's.

WILLIAM BENT, fur trader, builder of Bent's Fort.

A Long and Winding Road

One

A WEDDING PROCESSION delighted Santa Fé as much as anything except, maybe, a fandango. Old men and women, young boys and girls, courting teenagers, couples with the responsibility of families, the sober, the drunk, people who were happy, or habitually unhappy—everyone turned out to see the bridal party parade toward the church. People lifted their flasks and cried *"Hola!"* The town was celebrating.

In that spirit Sam Morgan breathed in the clear autumn air, looked around at his fellow riders, hoisted his jug, and took another swig. He knew it was too early to get swoopy, but this was a great day. He reached from one jouncing horse to another and handed the Taos lightning back to Pegleg Smith.

Kit Carson grabbed the jug from Pegleg, gurgled deep and long, and passed it on. Smith, who seemed to be drunk every day, growled at him. Carson answered by glaring back comically. "Coy!" said Carson. "Bite that man's peg leg!"

Coy, Sam's pet coyote, gave Carson a disgusted look.

Pegleg had a reputation for fierce and wild. Once when he got wounded, the man cut off his own leg. Now he wrenched the whiskey away from someone and chugalugged. Then he fired his rifle into the air and roared, "I am a one-legged, whiskey-drinkin', woman-chasin', alligatin' son of a mountain lion and a grizzly b'ar!"

Coy barked. Sam often wondered what the coyote's commentary meant.

"Ye-e-e-ha-a-w!" whooped Hannibal MacKye. Hannibal liked to act drunk when he wasn't—a safer way to go, he said. For good measure he fired his rifle into the air. *KA-BOOM!*

All the boys fired their rifles and hollered. Carson pulled his pistol out of his belt and shot the handgun off too. Sam grinned—both weapons were now empty. "Kit," said Sam, "if the Comanch hit us now, you got no pecker in your pants pouch."

"Then piss on 'em," said Carson.

The boys laughed loudly and roughly. Coy yipped.

Sam looked back to make sure Paloma wasn't close enough to hear the rough talk. He wouldn't have talked like that if he wasn't a little light in the head.

There was no danger of Comanches hitting, not here on the narrow, twisty river road that ran between Santa Fé's adobe houses, and certainly not on this warm autumn midday when the mountain men were leading the bridal party in a fine procession to the Church of the Virgin of Guadalupe on the plaza.

Eight or ten mountain men headed the parade on their horses, colorful in their beaded buckskins and bright sashes, looking rough with their beards and wind-whipped faces. One of them had switched professions, and looked it. Sumner, a black man turned professional gambler, wore a tailored suit of lilac wool. In his opinion gambling was a much better job than standing in cold creeks and skinning stinky beaver.

Close behind walked the two brides and two grooms, dressed in the best clothes they could borrow. Paloma had improved the teenage brides' outfits with every piece of lace, embroidery, and fine fabric she could find. Lupe wore a full-skirted dress in broad bands of violet and white, with butter-colored lace on the bodice. Rosalita's bodice was emerald, above a flaring skirt of light green and gold, each broad stripe pointed at the bottom. The brides had also tied rosemary to their sleeves, a traditional herb used to spark love.

All four of the betrothed were former slaves, stolen in Chihuahua and brought to this far northern province of Mexico. All of them had been bought out of slavery by Paloma. So this was a special occasion for Señora Paloma Luna, owner of Rancho de las Palomas, who for a decade had conducted a quiet campaign against slavery.

Behind the nuptial couples strode their families, which were makeshift, and tiny. Paloma herself acted as adopted mother to the brides and grand dame to the whole affair. Tomás, another teenager bought out of slavery, stood in as the brides' brother. Sam Morgan, Tomás's adopted father, rode ahead with his fellow mountain men. Stolen by Apaches, none of the slaves had ever seen their blood families again.

At the rear came Manuel Armijo, one-time governor of the province of New Mexico, and several of his drinking partners. By no means part of the family, Armijo was former owner of both grooms. Somehow Paloma had twisted his arm until he agreed to lend the proceedings some social sanction. Sam turned on his horse and eyed Armijo. The former governor sat his ornate saddle with casual arrogance, and gazed with open lust at the women who lined the streets.

Paloma kept her eyes on the two couples. She was proud, and not thinking of the cretin behind her.

As the wedding procession passed, people from the narrow *calles* and low adobe houses ran out to watch and then fell in behind. Boys called to Coy, "*Hola*, Señor Coyote!"

Suddenly one of the horses unloaded a pile from beneath its tail. Kids tittered. Middle-aged Joaquin, the betrothed of Lupe, was looking at the crowd, head high, beaming at all the attention.

"Cuidado!" called one of the boys to Joaquin. Watch out! The groom-to-be didn't pay any attention, and put the toe of his boot right into the pile.

Everyone laughed. The bridal party stopped, and Lupe said several choice words to Joaquin. The graying man stooped, whipped out a handkerchief (perhaps the only one he'd ever carried), and wiped off his boot. Then he walked over to the boy and presented him the handkerchief with a flourish.

The crowd roared.

"Amor y mierda," said Hannibal, *"una pareja rara."* Love and dung, an odd couple. People laughed at this witticism, and the boy waved the handkerchief and grinned.

At the front, immediately ahead of Coy, walked Fiddlin' Red, along with Mexicans playing guitars and the bass *guitarrónes.* Red bowed out one dance after another, and the guitarists surrounded him with a cloud of sonorities. No one was dancing, but everyone in the procession felt as if they were.

Sam's attitude was, *Why not?* It was a beautiful afternoon, and his friends were getting married. Then he had to correct himself again—not friends, daughters. Lupe and Rosalita had asked him to act as their father and give them away. Sam was glad to do that, because his adopted son Tomás called the girls his sisters. Torn away from their homes to a faraway land, they had formed a bond, and that was plenty for Sam.

More and more people thronged around or fell in with the parade. Santa Fé was in a festive mood.

Fiddlin' Red switched to a march. He arched his back, lifted the fiddle high, and bowed mightily. He was determined to be heard above the clopping of horses' hoofs, the shouts of children, and the hubbub of adult talk.

Watchers babbled and bobbed their heads. The town had buzzed about this wedding since the banns were posted. Most people said it was marvelous. Some of the rich called it an embarrassment. Sam wished he could hang these last folks up and quirt them.

The procession came into the plaza, the Palacio de los Gobernadores on one side and the church at the far end, its spires pointing to a gorgeous sky of the blue particular to New Mexico. People called it Franciscan blue, after the robes the priests wore. Many homes in Santa Fé and Taos featured doors and windowsills painted this hue.

Sam Morgan loved New Mexico. Now he looked hard at the spires. The priests said they pointed to heaven, but all he knew of heaven was the love of a man and a woman. As a very young man he had been married for one year. He and Paloma had spent five winters as lovers.

As the wedding party marched across the plaza, Sam took his mare Paladin to the fore. Hannibal came along with his stallion Brownie, and they sprang a little surprise. Fiddlin' Red launched into a bouncy old Irish tune, "Mairi's Wedding," and the two riders lifted their voices. Sam had made up new words for the song.

Mountain men in Santa Fé
Young and enthusiastic
Dance we on our merry way
Trip the light fantastic

As trained, Paladin and Brownie began to dance to the lively tune. They pranced forward four steps ahead, then shuffled four to the right and four to the left. On the last line of the verse, the horses did two curvets forward, leaps which took all four feet briefly off the ground.

The mountain men cheered, and the crowd roared.

Plenty liquor, sweet café
Eyes upon the lasses
Fun for all and all will play
Trip the light fantastic.

As they moved in their saddles, dancing along with the horses, Sam and Hannibal reveled in the moment. The words meant something special that only they knew. Sam's mountain friends had sung "Mairi's Wedding" at the rendezvous of 1826, when he married Meadowlark. Then his wife died of childbed fever the next spring. All the years since, he'd struggled with that. Paloma told him he sometimes lived in the dark corners of the past. Today, for special reasons he'd told only Hannibal, he was emerging from those shadows forever. So now, for another wedding, he gave the old tune bright new words.

On went the song, each verse ending with "trip the light fantastic"—and on went the dance. With the sun, the mild autumn air, song, dance, and the applause, the day was perfect.

When the music ended, Sam spoke to Coy, and the coyote bounded high onto his lap and let out an arching howl. Everyone laughed and cheered.

When they reached the steps of the church, the mountain men rode off to one side and let the brides and grooms come forward to the base of the steps. Sam dismounted and came alongside Rosalita, who was round and sweet-faced, and Lupe, whose visage spoke always of drama.

"I'd say Lupe's betrothed is in for a wild ride," Hannibal said.

Carson and Pegleg looked at him, putting together what "betrothed" meant. Sober, they might have been quicker.

"Ernesto got the sweet one," said Carson.

None of the mountain men knew Joaquin and Ernesto well—they were Armijo's field hands.

Sam stepped forward to join Paloma and Tomás at the front as the brides' family.

Father Reyes smiled down on everyone from the top of the steps and motioned them close.

Hannibal smiled to himself. Now was the time Sam would have to control his anger. And look at Paloma—her eyes lightninged fury at the priest.

When Paloma made the request of the priest weeks ago, he had consented to marry these couples. Yes, they were freed slaves, near the bottom of New Mexico's social order, but Paloma argued that they were also Catholics, baptized and raised in the church. They had a right to all the sacraments, including marriage.

The priest had agreed. This was a breakthrough—no slave marriages had been sanctioned so publicly before.

"We will conduct the wedding on the steps of the church," added the priest, "and then we will enter the church for the mass."

Paloma was irked. "I was married in the church, in front of the altar. Why are they not treated the same?"

Since he was new to Santa Fé, perhaps Father Reyes didn't know about Señora Luna's battle. Slavery was accepted comfortably in New Mexico. All the rich had slaves, except for a few families, and some Americans. But Paloma Luna fought the slave trade and the holding of slaves passionately. Whenever she could afford it, she bought a slave girl and freed her. Her own household help at Rancho de las Palomas consisted of former slaves who chose to work for Paloma for wages. Among the wives of her field hands were slaves she had liberated. So when two of her girls wanted to marry men owned by Gobernador Armijo, Paloma had splurged—she bought the men and freed them.

"Why?" repeated the padre to Señora Luna lightly. "Because it's traditional. Always the better families have been married near the altar, the poorer ones on the steps. In the old days, the higher your station, the closer to the altar your wedding was performed—"

Paloma interrupted him. "This is the *New* World, and *New* Mexico."

The priest smiled and shrugged.

When Sam got back to the rancho from his fall beaver hunt two weeks ago, Paloma told him about the wedding, and added, "The priest is an ass."

Still, she prepared for the weddings in a flurry. She worked feverishly and spent her money wildly. Sam was impressed—Paloma was determined to make this ceremony beautiful.

Now the priest proceeded to make the formal declarations and ask the required questions: "Does any man know of impediments to these marriages?"

From the back the boy called, "*Amor y mierda . . .*"

The mountain men laughed, the bridal party smiled, and the priest scowled.

One by one he asked the brides and grooms if they consented freely to this marriage.

"Do you want this woman?"

"I do."

"Do you receive this man?"

"I do."

The eyes of the brides glistened, and Joaquin of the dirty boot wept openly.

Father Reyes now spoke of the marriage bond lasting forever, of the importance of fidelity, the importance of conformity to the laws of the church, and of marriage as a reflection of God's love for mankind.

At last he came to the marriage vows. One by one Father Reyes led them through them, the marriage candidates repeating after him:

"Lupe," said Joaquin, now blubbering, "I take you to be my wife and I espouse you, and I commit to you the fidelity and loyalty of my body and my possessions, and I will keep you in health and sickness and in any condition it please our Lord that you should have, nor for worse or for better will I change toward you until the end."

Since Joaquin had done the crying for them, the others just spoke softly. Everyone was touched by their sincerity.

When the vows had been pronounced, the priest took the rings (Paloma had paid for them to be made of gold) and put them on the fourth fingers of the left hands of the brides. "Isidore of Seville," he said, "writes that we put the ring on the fourth finger because there is a vein there connected directly to the heart."

At this Hannibal led the mountain men in a rousing cheer, and they all fired their weapons again. Coy let out a fusillade of yips.

"On that note," said the priest, "let us enter the church for the mass."

Hannibal and the other mountain men filed into the church behind everyone else. Sam had talked them into it. They weren't

Catholics, or at least were too sinful to take communion. What they wanted was a blowout. And that was coming—after the wedding, everyone would ride downriver to Rancho de las Palomas for a feast and plenty of Taos lightning. But Sam had convinced them that as free men—"Wild men," put in Hannibal—they should stand up for these freed slaves.

The buckskinned figures stood at the back of the church. Sam and the two brides waited at the rear. When the priest began to chant the entrance antiphon—"May the Lord send you help from His holy place and from Zion may he watch over you. May He grant you your heart's desire and lend His aid to all your plans"—Sam stepped forward with a bride on each arm, beaming.

Two

SAM AND HANNIBAL wandered around the party, Coy tagging along. Sam wanted to be with Paloma—to talk and drink and dance with her—but she'd asked the two men to play the convivial hosts. Sam looked at her across the courtyard. "She's acting a little distant," he told his friend.

"You going to let that stop you?"

Sam shook his head. "This is our big night." Hannibal was in on the secret of the gift.

They checked on Red and the guitarists in the courtyard. Three more players wandered around performing serenades—Armijo had hired these others spontaneously. The governor loved a *baile*.

Sam, Hannibal, and Coy stopped to greet a merchant here, a tradesman there. Several times Hannibal poured from decanters, wine Paloma produced here on the rancho. Occasionally Sam accepted a sip himself, and he was pleasantly tipsy.

Couples moved rhythmically to the music in the courtyard. Some of them were Santa Fé married couples, others young people courting, others American mountain men swinging any willing women. The custom was that no trapper spent the night alone after a blowout. Some married pairs huddled here and there, talking and drinking Paloma's wine. They didn't entirely approve of the libertine ways of the young women with the Americans.

"There's none of the big families here except Armijo," said Hannibal.

"The rich don't like the way Paloma sees things."

"The anthropophagy wouldn't," said Hannibal agreeably.

Sam wasn't sure what that meant. His friend liked to use big words sometimes. He was the son of a Dartmouth professor of classics and a Delaware woman, fluent in English, backwoods American, Greek, Latin, and other languages. For a decade he'd been like a big brother to Sam, or a wise uncle.

They went looking for their friends the beaver hunters.

"I haven't seen Paloma for a damn," said Sam. "One night here, then she sent me and Tomás to Taos."

Coy growled.

Hannibal knew Sam's mission had been to get some fine embroidery from a merchant. Tomás's was to flirt with a certain waitress, Xeveria. While there, Sam enticed Carson, Pegleg, and a couple of other mountain men to ride down from Taos with him just for this event. His promise had been all the whiskey they could drink and a chance to taste the women of Santa Fé.

The buckskinned men and two gamblers were sitting cross-legged around a keg on the grass in the last of the sunlight. Even on a mild evening like this one, people would soon move inside to the fireplaces.

"It's not the same," said Sumner, "not at all." The black gambler had a sunny disposition, and the gold and jeweled rings on his fingers flashed. But now he was looking at Tomás beetle-browed.

Sam paused to hear what this was about. The lingering sun caught Tomás's agitated face.

Sumner went on, "If you think Indians treat slaves the way white people do blacks—"

"Funny," said Tomás, "I thought losing your family was losing your family."

Sumner gave him an exasperated look.

"I thought being hauled to another country," Tomás proceeded, "was being hauled to another country."

Sam felt for his eighteen-year-old son. The boy was proud, he was smart, and he wasn't about to be one-upped by Sumner. In fact, being short and scrawny, he refused to be one-upped by anyone.

"Listen to me. I am not talking about what was done to you. You know Narbona, that headman of the Navajos, was born a Mexican?"

"To hell with that," interrupted Tomás. "When the Navajos come raiding, point a gun at your head," said Tomás, "you gonna go with them, or you gonna fight?"

"I kick they ass," said Sumner in slave talk.

Coy got to his feet and sent up a peal of yips.

"Me too," said Tomás. "What happened to me, I never fortheget it."

Sam smiled. Tomás had some oddities in his English, like *fortheget* for *forget* and *me* for *my*. When Sam tried to correct him, Tomás just said, "I'm smart."

Now the debaters all simmered down, happy. Until Pegleg spoke up. "I don't cotton to it," he said. He put on a big grin, but he was drunk and slurring his words.

He got up slowly on his wooden leg and lifted his cup, sloshing whiskey out of it. "I done bought Indian women for my bedroll. I've had 'em from this here country, and"—he flashed his eyes at Tomás—"and I've had 'em from way south. And I've done traded both kinds, from above or below, to the next man."

He grinned broadly, looked around at his fellows, and seemed suddenly to take thought about what he was saying. He lifted his cup in a toast, losing more whiskey. "From what I've learned," he said less raucously, "Joaquin and Ernesto look fair to have some fine tumbles around the bed."

He lifted the cup as high as he could and poured whiskey straight into his open mouth. After one dribble it was empty. He banged the cup on his thigh and peered around the circle. Then he pounded on his chest. "This here man"—it sounded like he wanted to say *white man*—"does as he likes, and don't you fortheget it, boy. Gimme some *aguardiente*."

It was one insult too many.

From a sitting position Tomás bulled forward and plowed his head hard into Pegleg's gut. Youth and older man went sprawling onto Kit Carson, who thought he was having a peaceable evening.

Tomás whacked at Pegleg's face.

Carson grabbed both the young man's fists.

They glared at each other.

Pegleg grabbed for his knife, but Sam was quick to put a foot on his hand.

"Idiota!" Tomás barked in Pegleg's face. Whenever he was angry, he lost his English.

Sam and Hannibal pulled the one-legged man a few steps away. "Let's go somewhere and find you another drink," said Sam. The thought of Pegleg passed out on the grass seemed good to him.

"Idiota!" Tomás yelled again at their backs.

When they'd found Pegleg a bottle of his own, Sam and Hannibal ambled on with Coy. They saw the two bridal couples, clinging together, holding hands shyly, conversing politely when they wanted to be elsewhere. They watched Paloma chatting with some of her guests. She was gravely beautiful, this woman. Sam had met her when he first came to Santa Fé five years ago. Then she was thirty-three and a wealthy, widowed ranch owner, and he twenty-three, a poor trapper, a widower with an infant daughter. Despite these differences, she had seduced him immediately.

For the last five years they'd had an improvised life together for half of each year. From May to November Sam traveled to rendezvous to spend time with his six-year-old daughter Esperanza and then hunted beaver. The rest of the time he lived with Paloma at the ranch, training her horses by day and loving her by night. Then back to trapping and to rendezvous.

Paloma spent each year nurturing her ranch. Unable to bear children, she cultivated her lands and animals with a passion.

Now he was almost twenty-eight, she approaching thirty-eight.

"You still thinking about how different you two are?"

Sam looked at Hannibal. Age, social class, money, language, culture, nationality—all had looked like obstacles. "Not anymore," said Sam. He tapped his shooting pouch and smiled at Hannibal. That was where he had the surprise tucked away.

He sighed and reminded himself of the new song he sang today. "I'm ready."

"Let's drink to the New World." They did.

He pictured Paloma and thought of the bond of their passion, and their other ties. Days they spent with the horses, riding, training, and breeding them. In the evenings she read to him classic Spanish love poetry. The poetry became part of their heart life.

Still, their commitment was partial, half of each year. As far as Sam was concerned, all that was past now. It would change tonight.

As he looked at her, as he saw the grace with which she raised a wineglass to her lips, heard her soft, throaty laughter, and admired the loveliness of her form, he felt his love like a warmed stone against his chest.

"Excuse me," he said to Hannibal.

He walked to Paloma, acknowledged her friends, and took her aside. He said to her, "I think we'd better rescue the wedding couples."

She looked at him quizzically. Coy rubbed up against Paloma's legs.

"Fiddlin' Red," said Sam, "has been dedicating one song after another to each of the four. They're trapped."

Paloma laughed gaily. That felt good to Sam. She wasn't withdrawn now—probably had just been preoccupied with the wedding, anxious about it.

The two of them stepped forward. "Señores and señoritas," said Sam loudly enough for all the courtyard dancers to hear, "we hope that Fiddlin' Red keeps your toes tapping until dawn. It is time, though, to excuse our new brides and grooms. I think they have other hopes for the evening."

The dancers tittered.

"So if you'll play a processional, Red . . ."

To some tune Sam didn't know, he and Paloma led Lupe and Joaquin, Rosalita and Ernesto, toward their *casitas*. The women knew these homes well—they'd cleaned them thoroughly during the last few days, decorated them a little, and filled them with many candles provided by Paloma. But these domiciles were only temporary. Both couples had accepted the government's invitation to start a new village on the edge of Navajo country. They were starting their married lives as landowners, and were thrilled about it.

"Good night," said Sam.

"God bless you and your unions," said Paloma.

Coy mewled.

The unmarried couple watched the newlyweds disappear into the darkness.

"I'm still worried about them out at Cebolleta," said Paloma.

It was a big volcano, a sacred peak far to the west, that marked the eastern boundary of Navajo land, Dinetah. The government had offered a score of families plots of land in return for moving there. Thus issued forth a political statement to the Navajos—this is *ours*—and the families got to own land, a rarity for peasants.

But Cebolleta was far from Sam's mind. "I want you."

She smiled and kissed him lightly. "I have many duties tonight," she said. "Right now I want to talk to my sister, alone."

Rosa Luna Salazar de Otero was the wife of one of the other *ricos* of Santa Fé.

Sam frowned at his mistress.

"Meet me in the courtyard in half an hour, and we'll dance." She gave him another peck on the lips and ran off.

"I wish she'd given me that kiss," came a voice from the darkness.

It was Baptiste, sitting in a cottonwood.

Sam barely knew this trapper, and was curious. He laughed. "Even a peck?"

"Todo en amor es triste," said Baptiste, *"mas triste y todo, es lo mejor que existe."*

Sam had to laugh—a French Canadian sitting in a tree, probably half-drunk, quoting a Spanish proverb. It meant, "Everything about love is sad, but sad and all, love is the best thing in life."

"I don't think you'll have trouble finding love tonight." Of all the trappers Baptiste was the only one who was classically handsome, and he spoke elegant French, elegant English, and as Sam had just discovered, beautiful Spanish.

Now Sam said to Baptiste, "You're a mystery man to me."

The French Canadian jumped out of the tree, shifted his wine bottle to his left hand, and extended his right. "My full name is Jean-Baptiste Charbonneau."

Sam grasped the hand. "Charbonneau," he said. "I know your father."

"The whole world knows him," said Baptiste. Sam couldn't tell whether the French Canadian was pleased about this.

Old man Charbonneau and his young wife Sacajawea had tramped along with Captains Lewis and Clark on the best-known expedition in the history of the half-century-old United States of America, to the Pacific Coast and back. Sam had heard some of the expedition's stories from General Clark himself, in St. Louis. The stories made Sacajawea sound useful, but her husband was a braggart, a drunk, and half useless.

Sam shook his head, looking at the handsome son of the drunk. "Well, I'll be damned. So how did you get your beautiful Spanish?"

"I lived in Europe for six years," he said, "and traveled in Spain."

Sam nodded. He took another swig. "Lived in Europe six years. Amazing for the son of a slave woman."

"Sometime I'll tell you a little of the story," said Baptiste. "Right now I want to find a dancing partner, and you must attend the beautiful Paloma, as you promised."

Sam walked, Coy at his heels. Now he was fascinated.

Baptiste went through the gate and within seconds was dancing with a young woman Sam knew as a seamstress. Sam hoisted himself onto the wall and watched the couples swirling. Fiddlin' Red's music pranced through his head. He looked around for Hannibal but didn't see him. Had his friend already found a woman to entrance him?

Through a window Sam could see Paloma in the *cuarto de recibo*, the room for receiving guests, in urgent discussion with her sister. He felt lonely.

"NOT THE BEDROOM, not yet," said Sam, pulling Paloma toward the kitchen. There he had already made their favorite midnight snack, chocolate milk spiced with cinnamon and sugar, piping hot. He poured them each a cup. He gave Coy a few meat scraps, as he usually did when they had a midnight snack.

"I am tired," Paloma demurred, "and I want you now." She rubbed against him and kissed him.

Sam knew they would make love tonight. Six months apart, and only one brief night last week. Then Paloma had seemed distracted—she did not even shed her nightgown—yet she had been physically voracious. Now he felt the need for her strongly.

"First I have something to give you and something to say," said Sam. They sat at the kitchen table, and Paloma sipped at the chocolate.

Sam took the gift, wrapped in a beautifully tanned piece of white sheepskin, from his shooting pouch and put it in front of her. "For you."

He watched her open the wrapping. Sam had written to his old trapping partner Gideon Poorboy for this extravaganza. Gideon had become a very good silversmith. Sam had sent a letter months ago via New Mexican trappers going to California, and had picked up the finished piece only last week.

Paloma gasped. "It's gorgeous," she murmured.

From a gold chain long enough for her slender neck hung a large golden ring. Encircled by the ring was the figure of a dove, a *paloma*, pictured in flight. Its body was silver, to suggest the dove's gray. Chips of sapphire edged the widespread wings, where they would catch the air. The pink and violet of a dove's neck were ingeniously wrought in chips of amethyst and rose quartz. And the bird's single eye was a large, beautifully faceted sapphire.

"I've never seen anything so beautiful," said Paloma.

"Gideon Poorboy made it for you," said Sam. Paloma had heard many stories about Sam's friend, even the tale of the terrible night Sam had to amputate his leg.

"It's too extravagant," she said.

"I asked Gideon for his best work and sent him gold coins," Sam said. "He sent the coins back. This is his wedding present to us."

Her head snapped up. "His what?"

"Paloma Luna, will you marry me?"

She looked at him long, and he saw grief in her eyes.

"I would love to be your wife, Sam Morgan," she said.

But something was wrong.

"Come with me to the bedroom, please."

In front of her full-length mirror she undressed completely. She was lovely, her body lithe. Coy sat and looked at her in the mirror too.

She put her hands on her left breast and squeezed. An odd-looking fluid oozed, not milk, but something thinner and clearer.

"Touch it," she said. "It itches all the time."

The flesh felt hot to Sam, and hardened and thickened. The breast was red, in places even purple. There was one reddish area, and in another what looked like a bruise. The aureole was dark. With a sharp pang Sam understood why she had kept her nightgown on last week, why she had seemed remote.

He looked into her eyes, and saw it all.

"Breast cancer, the doctor says," she mumbled unnecessarily.

He kissed her, and then kissed her again fiercely. They stumbled backward, fell on the bed, and ravished each other.

Three

THEIR EMOTIONS SPENT the winter in sunlight and in storm.

Sometimes Sam and Paloma talked for hours at the dining table, and felt as much intertwined as two human beings in love can be. Sometimes they spent days barely speaking. Sometimes they had loud, passionate sex. Sometimes they slept on opposite sides of the bed. Their best times, often, were riding the countryside on bright winter days, drawing the cold air into their lungs and gazing at the snow-and-sun-spangled Sangre de Cristo Mountains, or riding on the mild, spring days, seeing the cottonwoods bud and leaf and the wildflowers blossom. Often they raced their mounts wildly, splashing through creeks, tearing through meadows, leaping gullies. Paloma was absolutely reckless, and for the first time often beat Sam and Paladin. She whooped and hollered when she won.

On quiet days she made her plans. She decided to make the long journey to see the shrine of the Virgin of Guadalupe in Mexico

City. She would leave in May with the trading caravan led by Hannibal MacKye. For the last several years Hannibal had trekked livestock from the ranches of New Mexico to the mining towns of the Sierra Madre, bringing back the kinds of goods manufactured there and in the city of Chihuahua. Paloma chose this trading outfit not only because Hannibal was a friend, but because he did not trade in slaves. Virtually all the caravans, or *conductas,* did.

She insisted from the beginning that the trip was hers alone. In the spring she would travel to the mining regions, and during the summer, with a caravan carrying copper and silver, to the national capital. Unspoken—she hoped to live long enough to reach Ciudad de México.

Once Sam hinted at a miraculous cure and a return to Santa Fé.

"I seek only to pray before the Virgin," she answered, "and ask her to give succor to my soul." She said nothing of her body.

She had willed Rancho de las Palomas to her sister.

When he was alone, Sam roamed through the rooms of the main house, thoughtful. Most often he sat in the library. Five years ago he had learned to read and write English mostly in this room, and to read Spanish. From English at first he got practical advantages like being able to make a list of trade goods he was taking to rendezvous. Later he came to love the plays of Shakespeare and the poems of Lord Byron. In Spanish his favorites were *Don Quixote* and Lope de Vega, and the love poetry he and Paloma read to each other in bed. Sam admitted to himself, now, how much books had come to mean to him, how much learning to read helped his life to open up.

But he didn't like being alone these days, not to read or do anything else. Half the time he and Paloma talked and played and roamed and loved. Half she stayed to herself, face pensive and dark.

In this way they came inevitably in late April to their last night together. She sent the servants away and cooked supper for the two of them herself, an old standby that was Sam's favorite, shredded pork in a sauce of green chiles and onions, with goat's cheese on the side. She got out a bottle of the brandy brought from El Paso del Norte, the region's finest, and got an early start on it. She set the dining table with her best china and silverware, and they sipped brandy while supper simmered.

Paloma said to him, "Don't act like this."

"Like what?"

"Long-faced. Not tonight."

She looked directly into his eyes. "You know what I want on this night of all nights?"

"No."

"Dumb jokes. Good stories. Maybe a silly game. And love, lots of love."

The love of the body, he thought, *when your body is dying*. "It's hard—"

She interrupted. "Nonsense! I will do the hard part tomorrow. Leave what I love most in this world, and my land, Rancho de las Palomas, and my lover, Sam Morgan. But tonight!" Her eyes were wild. "By all that is holy we will have tonight!"

She danced around the kitchen, skirts whirling. Sam almost believed he heard music.

Coy gave a little yip. Paloma circled the table, took up the brandy bottle and poured for each of them again. "*No sombrío!*" Nothing somber!

"I offer a toast! To everything that is bright, gay, and beautiful!" They drank. Then she began to tell stories of her childhood—not stories that were touching or splendid, but silly ones. The time her mother dressed her beautifully for Easter mass. Then her father took her and Rosa outside to see the new buds of the cottonwood trees, and Paloma slipped in pig shit and sat straight down in it, silk skirt and all. About how her sister, though older and bigger, could never win at king of the hill. About her father's fondness for puns, and how he embarrassed her mother by making them in front of company.

To Sam the stories may have been ordinary, but her rapture in telling them wasn't. After half an hour and three glasses of brandy, she wasn't telling the stories but acting them out.

She took a break to stir the *chile verde*. Then, suddenly, she whirled on him and shoved him halfway across the room. Crash! He landed backward on the dining table. Glasses and dishes flew to the floor. The brandy bottle toppled, shattered, and splashed the tiles. Sam's back and butt told him some silverware or broken china had not, unfortunately, fallen off.

She jumped on top of him and glared into his eyes, grinning and wild-eyed. "I want you now!"

They squiggled against each other. She kissed him hard, and he gave her full measure back.

Paloma reached down, unfastened the belt that held up his breechcloth and leggings, and flung it against a wall. Coy howled.

She seized the breechcloth and quickly tied his hands with it.

She looked eagerly at what she'd exposed. Then she jumped him.

A few minutes later they stopped crying out, quit moving, and cuddled up on the table.

"Enjoy yourself?" whispered Paloma.

"I think my ass has been tomahawked."

She looked under him and found two forks, tines up. "Whiner!" she said, and snuggled back up to him.

Later they untangled, and she served dinner. He loved the chile, the cheese, the tortillas, and the flan and strong coffee afterward. He quaffed another glass of brandy and held the liquor on his tongue. But he could feel his mood changing. Tomorrow gnawed at him.

"Bedtime?" she asked.

"Yes."

She picked up the bottle of brandy, and they headed down the hall.

They undressed silently. When they crawled beneath the covers naked, he spooned up behind her.

Mechanically, he caressed her right breast, the one that was healthy, with one hand.

She wiggled her tail against him. "If you think I'm going to let you get away with this, you're crazy," she said.

"This?"

"Sam, turn me over, or I'm going to fart on your cock."

He was stunned—she had never said either of those words before.

She twisted her face toward his. Her eyes wild, she made a buzzing sound with her lips.

He started laughing.

She flipped over completely, trapped him with arms and legs, and glared into his eyes. "Ravish me!"

He was frozen.

"I'm warning you!" She made the buzzing sound again.

I'll play!

He made the same sound; they both burst out in laughter. The laughter bubbled like a creek. Then it sang like a river. Finally it roared like a waterfall.

As the water sailed into the sky and fell glistening through the air, Sam fell upon her and kissed her in every imaginable way. She kissed him back hungrily. Then she bit him in several places. He took her fiercely, and at the great moment they howled, both of them, mad with passion, wild with love.

Sometime between midnight and dawn their bodies softened. She put her head on his shoulder. After a while they slept sweetly.

Sam's last thoughts were the words to a song he might write, about fixing the stars in the heaven, stopping the moon in its arc across the sky, and making one moment last forever and ever.

Four

THE NEXT MORNING Hannibal's caravan stopped at Rancho de las Palomas. This time the train picked up not only sheep, cattle, and grains, but the proprietress herself.

Sam rode along with them for half a day, to the Rio Grande. When the carts turned south along the river, the shrieking of their dry wheels seemed to speak for his soul.

Sam and Paloma stopped their mounts and watched the sheep plod by. He held her hand, thinking, *This is the last time.*

"Let me go now," she said, taking her hand back. Everything was in her eyes, more than any words could express, his or hers. She stroked his hair and gave him a light kiss. "My beautiful, white-haired lover. Your gift, the silver dove in flight, it will always be around my neck."

He looked at it now. Then he spoke the last words he would ever speak to her. "I love you." He was surprised at how light they sounded.

She returned the words she had never said to him. *"Te amo."* And in memory of last night, or of all they had meant to each other, there was a wild gleam in her eyes. She said, "We did something great. We stole happiness away from time."

Then she touched her heels to her mare and moved along with the caravan. She did not look back.

Hannibal turned and rode back to Sam. For several minutes they sat their horses, side by side, silent. Coy sat beside Sam, fidgeting.

"I'll take good care of her," Hannibal said.

"I know." Paloma's enemies were inside, not outside.

They watched her get smaller for a while.

"Down in Chihuahua I found something I thought you'd like." Hannibal handed Sam a small, wooden box about a foot long.

Sam lifted the lid. "A telescope?"

"No. Have a look through it."

Sam peered into the eyepiece and saw . . . He gasped. The world was an amazing geometrical design in six-sided shapes and an amazing array of bright colors.

"Turn it."

He did.

An entirely new world of shapes and colors dazzled his eyes.

"Turn it again."

Another world! He turned the cylinder again and saw a fourth world.

"Unbelievable," he said.

Coy whined, as though he wanted to see.

"It's called a kaleidoscope," Hannibal said. "From the Greek words *kalos*, beautiful, *eïdos,* form, and *skopeïn,* to view."

"Incredible."

"Optical mirrors reflecting bits of colored glass, not that it matters how it works. Here's what does matter. Regardless of how many times you rotate it, the design never repeats itself. Every image is entirely new. And when you turn the kaleidoscope"—Hannibal pantomimed a turning motion—"the last design, that piece of beauty, is gone forever."

"My God. I don't know what to say."

"Thanks will be enough."

"Thanks."

"An old Mexican gentleman gave it to me, an extra after a big trade. Here's what he told me: 'The meaning of life is hidden in there.'"

Hannibal reined his horse Brownie away.

"Whoa!" said Sam.

Hannibal stopped.

"The meaning of life?" called Sam.

"That's what he said. I thought such a thing should be passed around, so I gave it to you."

"The meaning." Sam couldn't help smiling a little.

"Yep."

The friends looked into each other's eyes.

"Next time I see you, tell me what it is."

Hannibal waved and touched his heels to his horse.

Sam lifted the kaleidoscope and held it where he thought his friend might be. Only bright colors. He turned it further, in the direction of the love of his life. Bright colors, and no meaning he could see.

Five

SAM MORGAN SAT on the bank of the Rio Grande, looking into the water. He didn't see the light glittering off the swift, faceted waves. He didn't notice the delicate new leaves of the cottonwoods above his head. He cared nothing for the balmy spring day. The kaleidoscope lay behind him, forgotten.

He jerked a leaf of sagebrush off a bush and ground it with his molars. He loved the smell of sagebrush and hated the bitter taste. The juice went down his throat and burned. He spat the pulp out and stared at the river.

The water churned past his feet, making whirlpools and suck holes.

"Everything is whirlpools and suck holes," he said to Coy.

The coyote squealed.

"You miss her, too, don't you?"

The mare Paladin, staked on nearby grass, turned her head and looked at Sam. She was big with foal, and beside her grazed one of her colts. Now larger than his mother, he belonged to Tomás and was named Vici. Tomás took the name from a phrase quoted by Hannibal MacKye, *"Veni, vidi, vici"*—I came, I saw, I conquered.

For Sam the coming birth was bitter irony. Six winters and springs with Paloma. Now she was gone to Mexico City to pray before the shrine of the Virgin of Guadalupe and die.

"I hate the Virgin of Guadalupe," he told Coy.

Coy panted.

"Why hate?" he asked himself.

"Why not?" he answered.

"Who are you talking to?"

Sam jumped at the voice behind him. Then he recognized it—Tomás.

"Nobody. I'm sitting here until my ass grows a taproot."

The boy didn't sit down, so Sam turned his head curiously. Tomás was one roiled-up, pint-sized eighteen-year-old, but right now his face was twice as angry as usual.

The river still sucked and twisted at Sam's feet. Coy rolled over in hopes that Tomás would scratch his belly. "Sam. Dad. You can't mope any longer," said Tomás. "Lupe and Rosalita, they've been kidnapped."

Six

Sam looked over Paladin's neck at the little village. It was still smoking. The raiders had set fire to the shacks along the water. The ruined buildings smoldered, and the grass around them was blackened.

"One of the four sacred peaks of the Dinetah," said Baptiste. Meaning land of the Navajo. Sam was surprised at how many languages this French Canadian spoke, or knew a little of. "The New Mexicans call it Cebolleta. The Navajo call it Turquoise Mountain."

"Ought to be called Bloody Mountain," said Sam. A generation ago the Spanish had put a military post and a mission on the east side of the peak, and were forced to fight a big campaign to keep them. This village, on a lake fed by a warm spring at the southern base of the peak, was a much bigger intrusion into Navajo country. The Dineh knew this place as Tosato, a place celebrated in their sacred stories.

To the government of New Mexico Tosato was a place to make a declaration. We thumb our noses at you, we claim the land this far west.

"Bloody Mountain," Sam repeated.

He looked at the three riders with him, Tomás, Baptiste, and Sumner. Baptiste and Tomás were veteran trappers, good men to ride the river with. Sumner was far better at dealing from the bottom of a deck than hitting what he shot at.

"In an affair like this," Baptiste said, "extra rifles are always good."

Shaking his head, Sam said, "I like my men few, hard, and sly."

Sumner put an end to the discussion. "This here, it's about slavery. I'm coming."

Sam knew it was a bond. What an irony. Freed slaves everywhere in Sam's life. Even Baptiste was the son of a slave woman, Sacajawea. *My father always said slavery is a curse.*

Now he clucked to Paladin. Coy and three mounted men followed him into the small village.

So tempting. Offer a plot of ground and a few sheep and goats to the peasants. Make them bait.

Now Lupe and Rosalita were kidnapped, Joaquin and Ernesto probably dead.

The four rode into the single lane between the swatch of a dozen huts and the lakeshore. The black and crumbled ruins of the buildings looked the way Sam felt.

"Probably drove off the sheep and goats too," said Baptiste.

They clopped the length of the lane, and there—

Joaquin, Lupe's middle-aged husband, sat propped against the wall of a shack. Sam couldn't believe the rest: a naked infant sucked on Joaquin's dry nipple.

Sam swung out of the saddle, went to the man and child, and squatted, wordless.

The black-haired baby turned its head and whimpered.

Sam shook the man's arm.

Joaquin's face was blank. If he had shed tears over his wife, they were dried and gone. He made no acknowledgment of Sam.

Sam took the baby. A girl, he saw. His mind flashed to Esperanza, his own daughter, living far to the north with her Crow relatives. *It's best for her,* he told himself for the thousandth time.

"Joaquin."

Nothing.

"It's Sam Morgan."

Nothing.

"We've come to help," he said in Spanish.

The wrinkled face contorted into a bitter smile. "Too late."

"Your daughter?"

"No. Francesca was born to Ernesto and Rosalita."

"Where's Ernesto?"

"Dead."

"Where are the other men?"

He shrugged. "Mostly dead."

Sam knew one had escaped and ridden to the military post at Cebolleta, probably on a burro, maybe the only burro in the village.

"Where are the men who are alive?"

"Walking to Cebolleta. They said they would send someone back."

"Why didn't you go?"

"I sprained my ankle."

"Where are the women?"

"Taken, every one."

"The children?"

"All taken but Francesca." His mouth contorted again. "She's too young to trade for pesos."

"Navajos?"

"Sí."

Sure, this would be Navajos. Their land.

Sam looked at Baptiste. Utes, Apaches, New Mexicans, Chihuahuans—all of them stole women and children, all of them sold human beings, all kept them as slaves. Each tribe's story was, "They started it, we only do it to get even."

The New Mexicans, who were Catholics and regarded the Indians as barbarians, took slaves from every tribe and believed they were elevating them to civilization.

"Tell me what happened."

Joaquin's lips barely moved, and the words sounded neutral, numbed. "When the Navajos came, some of us men were gone with the sheep and goats. Others were close by, working in the fields. The raiders came very fast, mounted. They grabbed the women and children. Our men, they ran in from the fields, but they had only hoes and knives against bows and arrows, spears, war clubs, and one or two rifles. Now they're all dead."

Sam couldn't say a word.

"Those of us out with the herds, we're alive. Isn't it wonderful? They left us alive, with nothing to live for." Joaquin's emotions were always all over the place.

"Help will be here soon. Your man got the message through. We just moved out quicker than they did." It was Sam's opinion that a handful of mountain men could act faster than any government, with its rules and rigmaroles, and get more done.

"And why," said Joaquin theatrically, "should I care?"

Seven

The government of Nuevo Mexico decided to send a treaty delegation to the Navajos. The delegation, well armed, would be led by former provincial governor Manuel Armijo.

Sam and Baptiste rode out to Armijo's rancho to see the great man. Sam left Coy with the horses, and the men trod softly, in moccasins, into the office where Armijo waited.

Sam's first words were blunt. Leaving out the friendly greeting *Don Manuel,* he said simply, "We're going with you."

The ex-governor pursed his lips into a half-smile and came out from behind his desk. "Greetings, my friend Sam Morgan." He spoke in English, a gracious gesture. Armijo accepted an introduction to Baptiste Charbonneau. Baptiste's elegant Castilian Spanish made El Gobernador's sentences sound unrefined.

"You are new to our province, and you wish to go with us to the

Navajo. I believe that to engage an enemy successfully you must know him. Do you know the Navajo, Monsieur Charbonneau?"

"I hope to learn, Gobernador." Baptiste spoke politely, without detectable sarcasm. He did not mention that he spoke Navajo.

"Have you seen these beautiful blankets?" Armijo picked up a large weaving from the back of a sofa. The ex-governor had a fleshy face with drooping eyelids and a sensuous mouth. "This one is what is called a storm pattern."

Sam decided to try politeness. "What is its symbolism?"

"Please. That's foolish barbarism. I collect them because they are beautiful." With a sweep of one arm he indicated the room full of weavings.

"Beautiful they are," said Baptiste.

"They are called slave blankets," Armijo went on. "An irony. They are woven by women captured from the Navajos, women we hold as slaves. They produce much beauty for us."

He looked at them with an expression Sam couldn't have described. He detested the man.

"For two centuries we have stolen their women and children, and they have stolen ours."

"Actually," Sam said, "they have stolen the women and children of the Christianized pueblo Indian people. Your own Nuevo Mexicano women and children mostly stay safe in your cities."

Armijo inclined his head in acceptance. "That, I think, is greatly to our credit." He smiled and sneered at once. "I was only reflecting that it is a shame that peoples treat each other so, people who are capable of creating great beauty."

Sam kept himself from snorting. He knew that Armijo had a dozen slaves right on this rancho, several of them Navajos, and some of those were forced to produce these blankets. He said again, "We're going with you."

"Naturally, my friend, you are welcome. With your rifles we will be even more formidable."

"When?"

"We must wait," Armijo said. "We have sent a messenger to their headman, Narbona, and suggested terms. If they accept our proposal, a place and a day will be appointed to sign the treaty and return the captives."

Sam glanced sideways at Baptiste, who looked perfectly composed.

Armijo sat down again. "I know you are impatient with our methods, Señor Morgan, but we have dealt with these savages for two hundred years. You must be patient for a few days."

Sam eyed the governor across the desk. *Two hundred years and not a week when you didn't rob and kill each other.*

"You would have no chance, bounding out there to search for your friends on your own. The Navajo nation is huge, almost as big as New Mexico itself. So I will send you a message when the time comes."

Sam nodded at Armijo. He looked at Baptiste. They left without another word.

"Tell me about Armijo," Baptiste said when they were mounted.

"He's just what you see, a man who will seize wealth and power by any means available." Sam smiled and tasted his brandy. "Then he'll give you a wink that says, 'You'd do the same, if you could.'"

"I have known his like," said Baptiste.

"He's a monstrous child," said Sam.

"We may be late to rendezvous," Baptiste told Sam and Tomás.

"Let's forget our troubles with something to drink," said Sumner. The four were gathered at a table in the cantina where he made his living at card games. "Pass brandy," he called to the man behind the bar, "two bottles." When the man brought the brandy from El Paso, he put down meat scraps for Coy.

"I have to be at rendezvous," said Sam.

"Our trading venture," Sumner said. Sam customarily carried goods to supply trappers at rendezvous. Sumner financed Sam.

"We all need to make a Yankee dollar or two," said Baptiste.

Sam nodded. "For me the big part is personal reasons."

"And it's a long ride." Baptiste's speech was always easy and unruffled.

"Wherever we go," said Tomás, "is no Yankee dollars. Is to get Lupe and Rosalita back."

"Es la verdad," said Baptiste.

"Damn *verdad*," said Tomás.

"There's no saying no to my son," Sam told Baptiste with a smile.

"Damn not," said the teenager, with a dark look at Sam. "Don't fortheget it."

"I'm going to tell Baptiste the story," said Sam. "He needs to understand why."

"This makes me uncomfortable," said Tomás.

"Five years ago," Sam began, "I saw my first *conducta*. Like all of them it brought expensive manufactured goods—iron tools, weapons, domestic and imported fabrics, all that stuff." Sam paused. "And slaves. The next day, at Armijo's rancho, I saw my first slave auction."

"Me too," said Sumner, "first and last. Goddamn."

Coy growled.

"Tomás was one of the boys auctioned," Sam went on.

"Wasn't no boy," said Tomás.

"You were thirteen."

"I never fortheget, I was sold for thirty-six dollars," said Tomás.

"Sam and I bought him," said Sumner. "The trader Cerritos got drunk later and told me that with our money he got one *fanega* of corn, six blankets, three mares, and one buffalo robe to take back down the trail and trade."

"We're the ones to go get Lupe and Rosalita," said Tomás. "We been slaves."

Baptiste ventured dryly, "Three of the four of you."

"That's it," said Sumner.

Coy whimpered.

"Back to that day," Sam said. "The auction. We saw something horrible." He looked gravely at Tomás. "First off, Cerritos led out a beautiful teenage girl in chains, hand and foot, and put her up for auction. Her name was Maria."

"One day I kill that bastard," said Tomás.

"Enough," said Sam. "Cerritos told the crowd, all men except for Paloma, that Maria wasn't yet good enough for us. Then he stripped her naked and raped her."

Sam watched Baptiste and saw his lips stiffen and his eyes flash.

"'Now,' Cerritos told us, 'she's good enough.'"

"Merde," said Baptiste.

"I kill—"

Sam shushed Tomás with a hand and despite an evil look pushed on. "The story has just begun. Sumner and I took Tomás back to Rancho de las Palomas and told him he was free."

"All the way free," said Sumner. "Do whatever you want, go wherever you want. 'Course, he was too young—"

"What we didn't know yet was that Maria was Tomás's sister."

No one at the table seemed to be breathing.

"The next morning Tomás was gone. When he came back, he'd killed the man who had bought his sister."

"Estupendo!" said Baptiste to Tomás.

"Except that Don Emilio lived. Tomás's cleaver took a fine portion of scalp, but it bounced off the don's hard skullbone." Sam and Tomás smiled at each other. "After that, Tomás had a little trouble with the law in Santa Fé. That's why he stays down at the rancho and comes to town damn seldom, and why we'll winter in Taos from now on."

Before Baptiste could speak, Sam added, "The host of the slave auction that day was our ex-gobernador. I took Tomás to the mountains, taught him the beaver man ways, and ended by taking him as my son."

Sumner said, "I offered to teach him everything I know about gambling. That way he could reach into the chests of the oppressors and grab what they keep hidden in their hearts, their money."

"We talk about that," Tomás said, "when we finish taking me sisters back."

Eight

THE SPRING WAS in a nowhere place, below an outcropping of ocher stone. Trickling away, the creek was lined by willows and a few cottonwoods in new leaf. Around it for as many miles as the eye could see were broken desert cliffs studded with cedar trees. Only Mount Cebolleta to the east rose high over the horizon, pointing in the direction of the New Mexican settlements. Sam wondered if the water ran all year round, or only when the snow was melting. Turkey Spring, they called this place.

Coy sat and sniffed in the direction of the Indian camp.

"Anything could happen here," warned Baptiste.

It was true. Sam used his field glass to study the Navajo encampment at the spring. "No more than twenty," said Sam. Which meant they could honestly be a delegation sent to Armijo to give formal approval to the treaty and exchange captives.

"A hundred could be in the next valley," said Baptiste. A band of warriors to wipe out the New Mexico party.

"It wouldn't be the first time," said Sam. He didn't distrust the Navajos, particularly. He was damned leery of both sides.

Armijo touched his spurs to his mount and pussyfooted down the soft slope toward the creek. Sam, Baptiste, and Tomás flanked him. The soldiers bearing the flags of Mexico and New Mexico fell in behind.

"We'll camp below those rocks," Sam said, indicating with his head.

Sam wanted a place he could defend. To Armijo's credit he turned that way.

Sam, Baptiste, and Tomás put their bedrolls a little apart from the tents of the soldiers and other official representatives. They hadn't brought Joaquin, because every time they saw him he was drunk. As the three went through the routine of setting up camp, Sam kept an eye on the Navajos upstream.

Coy padded to the creek and lapped for a long time.

"Is this going anywhere?" Sam said to Baptiste, half idly. He meant the proposed exchange of captives and treaty-signing.

"I doubt it."

Sam led Paladin downstream and let her drink. Baptiste and his mount came along.

"When you glassed the camp, did you see any captives?"

"No."

"If Lupe and Rosalita are here—if any captives are here—they're being held somewhere away." Within half a day's ride, near water.

"Let's ask Enrique where it would be." Enrique was the messenger originally sent to make contact with the Navajos and set up this meeting, though he did not speak their language. In their arrogance the Nuevo Mexicans expected the Navajos to conduct all business in Spanish.

Enrique's answer wasn't helpful. "In springtime like this," he said, "all the washes, the ones that are usually dry, they run with a little water. More Navajos, they could be anywhere."

"And we're on their ground," Baptiste said.

"*Sí.*"

Sam looked across at El Gobernador, busy making motions and giving directions. "I think we're wasting our time."

"As long as we're not wasting our scalps," said Baptiste.

Within half an hour the Navajos sent a man to say that they wanted to meet this evening.

Armijo raised an eyebrow at Sam. "You are my majordomo," he said.

El Gobernador had sense enough to know that the mountain men would be better protection than his soldiers.

Sam considered. On Navajo land he would not know what was around him. But the evening light would last. The meeting might be mostly ceremonial, and Sam was impatient—he wanted to get Lupe and Rosalita and be gone.

"We will come soon," Armijo told the messenger in Spanish.

"You, Enrique, me, and Baptiste," said Sam.

Armijo nodded.

"Nearby," said Sam, "four of your men, armed, and Tomás."

Baptiste spoke decent Navajo, but Sam said nothing about that to Armijo. It was an advantage he and Baptiste would keep to themselves.

In a hour they sat in a circle, a dozen men in the inside ring, a good many Navajos behind, opposite the Mexican party's backup. No one in the circle was armed. In theory. Sam knew that the blankets of the Navajos concealed knives and tomahawks. He and his party had their hidden weapons as well. One of his was a belt buckle that popped out and became a knife.

Sam eyed the old man who led the Navajo contingent, Hosteen Tso. His body was scrunched with age, but he had a striking head of silver hair tied into a bun with white cloth and brightly intelligent eyes. He reminded Sam of a wise lizard, at home in the desert, a survivor. Sam felt a flicker of hope.

On Tso's left, in a position of seniority, sat a tall, beautifully muscled man in his twenties. He was as fine a physical specimen as Sam had ever seen, with the predatory eyes of a hunting bird.

Enrique spoke some initial courtesies, and on behalf of the generous government of New Mexico he made some gifts to its friends the Navajo people. He introduced El Gobernador and his companions, White Hair Morgan and Baptiste Charbonneau. A young man on Tso's right murmured a translation into the leader's ear.

At length Governor Armijo rose to his feet. Young Piercing Eyes frowned, but Tso's face was neutral. Sam wanted to say, "This *gobernador* doesn't know it's rude to put his head above yours," but he kept his mouth shut.

As an amanuensis recorded his words, Armijo proceeded to state the four main points of the proposed treaty in a florid and ceremonial way:

"The Navajo nation will turn over all captives which you may have made of our people and return them without hiding any. The same with the fugitives, if there are any."

Armijo gave the old lizard Tso what was meant to be a commanding look. Tso glanced briefly at Sam and Baptiste, and his eyes seemed to smile. There was no hint of a smile on Piercing Eyes' face.

"The government of New Mexico will return to the Navajos those people who fled to us. That is, we will return them provided they wish to go back. However, if they should wish to receive the saving waters of Baptism, it is the desire of Catholics to favor them with the Sacrament and exhort them to the end that the number of faithful adoring the True God of the Christians is multiplied."

Sam kept his eyes down. He didn't want to see Hosteen Tso's ironic amusement, or Piercing Eyes' anger.

"You will return all that you have stolen in the Province of New Mexico, since the date of the last peace celebrated, giving back to the injured parties what was taken, in its entirety.

"Last, and a point of importance, you will give great consideration to allowing priests of the most Holy and Apostolic Catholic Church to come among you, as the people of the Pueblo tribes have done, and like them be converted to belief in the One True God. After that, you will live as the Pueblo tribes do in fixed settlements.

"When you have agreed to these stipulations, we will exchange captives and fugitives here tomorrow, so that they may return to their families."

Sam concentrated on looking at the red sand in front of his legs. He knew Armijo's dirty little secret.

El Gobernador sat down.

Hosteen Tso, Piercing Eyes, and the other Navajos gave Armijo the courtesy of waiting quietly and at least appearing to give consideration to his words.

Sam and Baptiste looked sideways at each other. *Will we have to run for our guns?* Or would Hosteen Tso somehow be accommodating?

After what seemed too long, Tso spoke quietly and easily in the Navajo language, his eyes fixed on Armijo. "My good friend El Gobernador," Tso's translator began, "we are glad to return to you people taken from your settlements, or from the pueblos. But we ask, what of those who do not want to go back? What of those who prefer the Dineh way of life? What of the women who have married our men, borne their children, and prefer to stay with their families? What about children who love their new mothers and fathers?"

Armijo coughed. Sam knew he was not about to admit, in a proceeding being recorded for posterity, that some captured Christians might prefer the barbarous Navajo style of living, might put Navajo gods before the One True God, might choose nomadic life over civilization. After all, was not civilization the path of righteousness? The governor blinked rapidly at Tso.

"Perhaps you are not ready to answer these questions yet," Tso went on smoothly. "We can discuss them tomorrow. In the meantime, I will put a few more questions to you.

"Why are the people held by the Dineh said to be 'captured' and those held by the New Mexicans described as 'fled to us'? You know well that you sent men from the pueblos along with your own soldiers and took our women and children by force. Just as we did to yours. If we are to be friends, does not friendship begin with candor?"

Now it was Armijo Sam couldn't look at. But he felt a heightened respect for Tso.

Piercing Eyes wore an air of triumph.

"You say you will give us back our women and children, except those who want to be baptized, who prefer your Christianity. In that case, are we permitted to keep those New Mexicans and pueblo people who want to walk with us the path of harmony between the four sacred mountains?"

After a brief pause he went on smoothly. "You propose that we give back whatever we have taken from your people. Do you then intend to give back the sheep, goats, and horses you have seized from us? Do you intend to pay us for the fields and orchards you burned? The hogans you destroyed?"

Tso spoke slowly, as Armijo had, and probably with words equally ceremonious, perhaps even beautiful. His tone held no rancor, his eyes no anger. All the anger was on the face of Piercing Eyes.

"As for the suggestion that we welcome your priests, accept your gods, and take up life in pueblos, I know I speak for my people when I declare that we are content with our own path. Since we came to this glittering fifth world, we have lived as we do, growing a few crops, grazing our herds wherever the grass is good, hunting where the game is abundant, and setting our feet on the path of beauty and harmony. We wish to continue in our own way."

He let a moment go by, evidently so Armijo could absorb this point.

"Our last statement, like yours, is an important one. We will never accept a settlement of your people at Tosato. You have your soldiers at Cebolleta, on the east side of Turquoise Mountain, where your lands are. But that is as far as you may go.

"Perhaps one day, if you are interested, during the winter, when it is time to tell stories, we will tell you the tale of how Turquoise Mountain was created, and how Boy Who Carries One Turquoise and Girl Who Carries One Grain of Corn came to live there, or even how the Hero Twins slew the monster at that special place. But that story is not for today."

Sam looked at Armijo. The man had gotten bored and distracted just when he should have paid attention. If Armijo believed in understanding his enemy, he'd missed his chance.

Tso gave Sam an ironic glance. He had seen it too.

"Men of good will may disagree on some matters and still cooperate," Tso continued. "We would like to give you the people of yours we have brought to this place, if you will in return do the same."

Sam gave Baptiste a sharp glance. Here was the tricky edge of trouble.

"We will be glad tomorrow to discuss all of what you said earlier, and to seek common ground, if you like. Then you will give us the people born to us, and we will give you yours."

On the way to the little camp, Armijo told Sam, "Something is not right. If he meant to negotiate a treaty, Narbona would be here."

Nine

A FIRE, A coffeepot, the first glow of light in the east. These small things brought solace to Sam's heart. He liked to get up early, while others slept, with only Coy for company, and drink coffee. Not to think, especially, but just to take in the beginning of the day.

This morning, though, he was thinking. He was wondering what would happen when Hosteen Tso found out Armijo's secret. He was wondering if he and his friends would have to fight Navajos for the sake of the cheating New Mexicans. *Hell,* he thought, *maybe we should switch and fight against the New Mexicans.* Except for Tomás and Joaquin, why not?

He grinned. He'd been thoroughly a Crow once. Took a Crow name, Joins with Buffalo, carried the sacred pipe (as he still did), became a member of the Kit Fox Society, went to war with Crow comrades, and married Meadowlark. Without hesitation he would have fought Blackfeet or Californios or New Mexicans shoulder to shoulder with Meadowlark's brothers.

But then it all went wrong, and he wasn't going to dwell on that.

He poured coffee and pulled down his first swallow of the day, strong and hot.

Tomás materialized, reached for the pot, and poured for himself. They sat together without a word. Coy rolled onto his back and scratched himself on the seams of Tomás's moccasins. He liked Navajo footwear, with the red tops and white soles.

Silence was good. Sometimes father and son were good together. Not always. Tomás was hot-blooded, self-conscious about being short and skinny, and never quite satisfied that he hadn't killed any of the men who took his sister's life.

For sure Cerritos and Don Emilio did exactly that. The day after she was sold at auction, still in Don Emilio's bedroom, Maria's despair led her to hang herself.

Sam couldn't imagine, didn't want to imagine, what it was like for Tomás to walk in on his sister like that. Coming to rescue her, he found her body at the end of a noose. Then he lashed out at one source of her agony, Don Emilio.

Tomás stirred a second spoonful of sugar into his cup. He liked it sweet, the way Indians drank it.

Not that anger about being enslaved and about Maria's death were the whole story. Tomás was a teenager and full of hot teenage juices. He and Sam had their spats. But Sam was glad every day that he had a son.

He grinned and looked sideways at Tomás. *Life would be easier if I stopped thinking of my son as a boy.*

And then Sam thought of his daughter, far away in Crow country.

THE ONLY GOOD part of the morning conference was that it started early.

Armijo spoke first, and he talked in circles. His answer to Hosteen Tso's questions—Tso's objections, really—was to spin out a lot of words, float them around everyone's heads, and then smile like he'd actually said something.

Not that anything Armijo could say would matter. The treaty was tilted steep as a sitting dog's back to the advantage of the New Mexicans. Outrage was written all over Piercing Eyes' face.

Finally El Gobernador ran down. There was silence. Then Hosteen Tso said, "Do you want to exchange captives now?"

Big, heavy silence. When Armijo opened his mouth to speak, Sam could see the lie ready to dart out of his mouth.

"Tell him the truth," Sam said in English.

Armijo flinched. Sam wondered whether it was because of the switch in language or because Armijo couldn't stand to be given orders by an inferior.

The governor gathered his breath, turned to Hosteen Tso, and started to speak again.

"Tell him your dirty little secret," said Sam. "We've ridden all the way out here on a fraud. We haven't brought a single captive to exchange for theirs."

Now Armijo stared at Sam.

"We don't have one member of a family of any Navajo to give them."

The two men stared at each other.

"If you don't tell him, I will."

That made Armijo recover. "How dare you?" he growled in English.

"I dare to save your goddamn life."

"To save all our lives," added Baptiste.

"I want to know what White Hair has to say," said Hosteen Tso.

Sam let this sit for a moment. Then, to Armijo, "Suppose you go through with this. Suppose you ask them to bring their captives in, and you turn up with none. They'll know you for a cheat and will figure you intend to take their captives by force."

"Which damn well would be the only way you'd ever get them," said Baptiste.

Sam went on, "And they will attack." He eyed Armijo with heat.

"We have no idea how many warriors Tso has holding the captives. How many warriors he has just two or three hills over. How much we're outnumbered. But you can bet he has enough to get the job done."

Enrique spoke up. "Gobernador, Señor Morgan speaks the truth."

Sam couldn't help smiling. So Enrique spoke English too.

"I'm going to count to ten," said Sam. "By ten, if you haven't started telling Tso the truth, I will. My first words will be, 'Hosteen Tso, we are sorry. Gobernador Armijo was unable on short notice to find people captured from you who want to be returned. However, I know there are many who long for their families. Perhaps we can make an exchange in, say, one moon from now.' "

Sam laid one finger on his thigh, then two. On finger five El Gobernador began, "Hosteen Tso, we are sorry . . ."

Ten

PIERCING EYES SPOKE quietly but vehemently to Tso.

Baptiste translated for Sam in a whisper, "Hosteen, why should we not kill these men?"

Unable to hear Baptiste, Armijo smiled at Tso fatuously.

His eyes on Armijo, Tso spoke to his warrior.

"We don't kill people for being fools," Baptiste translated softly, "or everyone would be dead. And we may yet get some women and children back."

Sam suspected that the hosteen knew Baptiste understood his words.

"What you suggest is good," Tso said to Armijo. "We will meet you at this place at the next half-moon. We will bring captives." He paused. "And so will you."

Tso rose abruptly, turned his back on the New Mexicans, and strode away.

Sam wondered if Armijo knew he'd just been insulted. If he knew that this affair was not over, and blood might yet spill onto the sand.

Piercing Eyes, with his magnificent physique, stood up and glared. Then he stepped toward the creek, perhaps to get a drink. As he passed by Tomás, the youth said, "Thank you."

Sam thought, *Strange thing to say.*

Piercing Eyes' reaction was stranger.

"Fool!" he exclaimed in Spanish. "Idiot!" His look of contempt erupted like lava in Tomás's face.

Sam spoke to defuse the situation. "You speak Spanish," he said.

"Since childhood," snapped Piercing Eyes.

Piercing Eyes turned back to Tomás. *"Diablo."* He uttered the insult calmly. "A Navajo does not say or accept *thank you.* Unless it means that someone has performed such a service that he is indebted to you for life, those are the words of a beggar, or a slave."

Tomás colored. Then he slapped the Navajo's face.

SAM AND BAPTISTE both grabbed Piercing Eyes instantly, one on each arm.

The man screamed and exploded upward, and both of them flew like dolls. With an unforgettable war cry the Navajo dived at Tomás.

The youth dodged with amazing swiftness.

Before Piercing Eyes could recover and change direction, half a dozen men grasped him.

"Amigo!" said Sam, holding tight. "Amigo! We understand. We will make this right."

The Navajo lunged like a bull at the end of a rope.

Tso spoke sharply in his language.

Piercing Eyes visibly willed his body to relax.

Hosteen Tso walked back to the group, and Sam saw a glimmer of pleasure in his ancient eyes.

He asked Piercing Eyes something in Navajo. "What has happened?" Baptiste translated to Sam in a whisper.

Piercing Eyes answered, "The bastard slapped me in the face."

Tso considered. Then he turned to Armijo and said through his translator, "That is a grave insult. This man must answer for it."

Sam heaved out the biggest breath of his life. A fight, not a war.

"My son is called Tomás," said Sam. "Will you tell us the name of the man he will fight?"

"Nez Begay," said Hosteen Tso. It was not a proper introduction, with the name of the mother's clan and the father's clan. Another slight.

Sam's chest constricted violently. *My son . . .*

Eleven

SAM SAID TO Tomás, "I understand your rage at being called a slave." He added not a word about the youth's foolishness.

In the little time available he talked gently to Tomás about fighting without weapons. He reminded him of the techniques they'd worked on, and mentioned what he might be able to use. Not that he really thought Tomás could use anything. He said the obvious: "You must not let him get his hands on you."

Tomás could survive a blow, maybe a lot of blows. But not a neck twisted until it broke. Nor could he afford an arm wrenched out of its socket, an eye gouged out.

Both parties, Mexican and Navajo, were circled around a big space of red sand. A few greasewood bushes grew here and there, and there was one rock as high as a man's waist. Not much to use.

The terms were simple. They were to fight until one man admitted defeat. No weapons and no killing.

Sam had no confidence in the no-killing provision. And he didn't think Tomás would quit, ever.

Sam fixed his eyes on Tomás's and made a hard decision. "Listen to me," he said, "I know you've got those blades on your waist cord."

"What?!" These were strictly secret.

"If you go for them," Sam said, "we're all dead. All of us." He was so scared it hurt his belly.

Tomás nodded, turned, and walked away.

Sam thought, *You are the sacrificial goat for all of us.*

He called after his son, "You're only trying to satisfy him."

"I will kill him with my bare hands," said Tomás.

AT FIRST THE antagonists circled, eyes on each other.

The Navajo suddenly strode to the middle of the ring and stood stock-still. It was an invitation: *Attack me, little man.*

Tomás circled. He shook his head, grinning. His message was, *The first move is yours.*

It came so fast Sam missed the start. Nez Begay dived at Tomás and seized an ankle.

Tomás kicked wildly and got loose.

Nez Begay had intended mostly to intimidate. But he was on his face in the dirt, and Sam heard a few titters.

Like a cougar, the Navajo sprang back to his feet and charged head first.

Tomás rolled, and the Navajo missed again.

Tomás bounced to his feet. For a youth trained to do somersaults on a horse, rolling was no great trick.

Now Tomás attacked. To Sam's astonishment, while Nez Begay was recovering, Tomás took two quick steps straight at him, flew into the air, and lashed a foot at the Navajo's head.

Nez Begay dodged the kick.

Tomás landed on one foot and one fist.

"Crow-style kick," Sam murmured. He couldn't help being proud.

Nez Begay charged.

Tomás got balance enough to roll.

The Navajo turned, bellowed, and sprinted at Tomás.

The boy ran ahead of the warrior.

Several times they repeated this—the Navajo would scream and run at Tomás, the boy would dash away. He was taunting the warrior.

Suddenly Tomás ran behind the waist-high boulder, jumped onto it, and in one instant threw himself feet first at the Navajo.

Nez Begay shifted to one side and grabbed Tomás's legs. It was one of the quickest, most athletic movements Sam had ever seen.

With the ankles in his grip Nez Begay whirled Tomás's body full circle and hurled him back at the rock.

Tomás splatted into the boulder. He collapsed to the ground and lay limp.

The Navajo pounced on him.

Before the warrior could twist off an arm or a leg, Sam and Baptiste seized him.

Nez Begay froze, his eyes furious.

Sam appealed to Hosteen Tso. "The fight is over. Our man is knocked out. The fight is over. That's what we agreed."

Hosteen Tso stepped forward and looked at Tomás's crumpled form. His forehead was bleeding, his nose bleeding, his lips bleeding. Sam had no idea whether his son would live or die.

Ignoring Nez Begay, Hosteen Tso looked at the circle of Navajos and Mexicans. "Honor is satisfied," he said.

Sam knelt by Tomás. He felt his head gingerly. For several minutes . . .

The youth's eyes blinked open. Sam smiled.

Twelve

THE NEW MEXICANS put their horses to a lope for a mile or two and then walked them fast.

As they rode, Sam and Baptiste told Tomás what was going to happen.

"We're going to follow them," said Sam.

"No, you're not coming. You can barely ride."

"No you're not," said Baptiste.

"I'm very proud of you, but you can't come."

"You were incredible, but you can barely ride," said Baptiste.

"If you come, it will inflame Nez Begay," said Sam. "You'll put all our heads on the block."

Finally, Sam and Baptiste simply galloped off. Luckily, Tomás stayed where he was.

Back near Turkey Spring they staked their horses on some grass, crawled to the top of a hill, and found the Navajos with the field glass. The Indians rode northwest. Sam and Baptiste followed at a distance, being careful not to skyline themselves.

After about an hour the Navajos rode into a small, grassy valley. Ponies grazed, and two dozen people moved around two hogans on their daily chores.

"The captives," Baptiste said.

As tight-throated as he had ever been, Sam glassed the camp. "I don't see Lupe or Rosalita, but they might be inside."

"Getting caught now," Baptiste said, "would be a very bad idea."

"So let's do the opposite of getting caught."

Sam spurred Paladin at a gallop toward the Navajo camp.

On the next-to-last rise he saw riders whipping their horses out toward him. He hoped Tso would be one of them. Sam and Baptiste stopped their horses on the hill, dismounted, and waited.

"We are calm," said Baptiste with a half-smile.

"Naturally," answered Sam. "Mountain men have buttermilk for blood."

They both laughed, and Coy gave a little bark.

"He agrees," said Baptiste.

A dozen warriors galloped up, bristling with weapons. Sam was relieved to see only one rifle.

He set the Celt on the ground butt down. This rifle, his legacy from his father, had gone with him everywhere between Pittsburgh and California.

The warriors charged up face-to-face with the mountain men. Nez Begay came to the front. Tso wasn't there.

"White Hair," said Nez Begay, "what do you want?"

"We have come with gold. We want to buy two women back. Relatives. Women from Tosato."

The warrior slowly took in the several meanings and smiled. "And why shouldn't we kill you and take your gold?"

"Because you don't know where the gold is," said Sam.

"Also," said Baptiste, "your lives are more valuable than coins."

The Navajo regarded Baptiste coolly.

Sam slid one hand down the barrel of the Celt, and with the other touched the pistol at his belt. He smiled at Nez Begay. He didn't have to say, "Four of you will die, maybe more."

He did say, "Let us talk to Hosteen Tso."

After a long moment, Nez Begay nodded, and led the way to the camp.

SAM HAD NOTHING to go on but his appraisal of the Navajo leader, which was based on very little.

They sat in a circle. The afternoon had gotten hot, and a gusty wind kicked up dust devils.

"You sure like to live on the edge," Baptiste had said as they dismounted.

"Every year I like it less."

Hosteen Tso welcomed them to the sheep camp of the Etcitty family, and introduced Hosteen Etcitty, a very elderly man.

Old enough not to be bloodthirsty, Sam hoped.

Sam thanked Hosteen Tso for his courtesy and hospitality and for hearing his request. Then Sam spoke in a direct way, and what he said would have been honest in the Navajo way of understanding blood relations. "Two women taken from Cebolleta were my daughters. They are also the sisters of one of the young men with me back at the spring, Tomás. We want to give the Navajo people whatever is right for the return of these women, especially because one is with child and one is the mother of an infant. Their names are Lupe and Rosalita.

"Some gold is hidden back near the spring, two thousand pesos. In return for my daughters, we will give it all to the Navajo people. And I will give you the gratitude that only a father can feel."

Sam could feel Baptiste's wariness next to him, like heat. Before walking into camp, they had told each other about their hidden weapons.

Tso was equally direct. "White Hair, we do have here people

who were willing to go back to the New Mexicans. But we have no women of child-bearing age, and none from Cebolleta." He looked at Nez Begay. "Bring all eight of them."

In a moment the warrior was in and out of a hogan, followed by six women and two small boys. Half the women were elderly, half middle-aged. One of the boys walked on a crutch, and the other had a deformed spine.

"Do you want to buy any of these people?"

Sam was tempted, but he shook his head no.

"You are not New Mexicans," said the hosteen, "I know that. I do not trust the New Mexicans."

Sam knew well that Tso didn't trust anyone who wasn't Navajo.

"It is so crazy for you to come here alone that I can see only one explanation, that you are speaking the truth." He gave a big lizard smile.

"So, White Hair the brave and foolish, I will make you an offer. If you want to come to my home in Canyon de Chelly, we may be able to discover where your daughters are."

Sam looked at Baptiste. Both of them understood. Hosteen Tso was offering them his protection. They didn't know why. They would be volunteering to go very deep into Navajo country as outsiders. It was probably dangerous to refuse the invitation.

Sam said to Baptiste in English, "No choice."

Baptiste gave an imperceptible nod.

Sam said to Tso, "We accept."

The hosteen's smile got broader. "Then would you like something to eat?"

It was good to be crazy.

Thirteen

SAM WAS MESMERIZED by the beauty of Canyon de Chelly. They rode on a carpet of green grass beside a meandering stream the color of the sky, and were walled in by vertical slopes that were sometimes a deep, burnt red, sometimes lustrous ocher. When they neared either side, here and there they could see the ruins of ancient pueblos.

"The Anasazi," said Tso. Sam had heard of the ancient people who had lived here, in pueblos like those along the Rio Grande. He knew that the Navajo would not go into these shattered buildings. They had an aversion to places of the dead.

"Look," said Baptiste, "above the kiva."

The art of the dead ones—handprints, animals, and strange shapes Sam couldn't make out, painted on the rock or etched into it.

"I'd love to get a close look," he said.

"When the time is right."

Coy gave a little yip.

They turned a corner and saw a wonder. From the valley floor rose a slender pair of stone fingers, touching, and perhaps a thousand feet tall.

"Spider Rock," said Tso.

After a long look, Sam said, "The taller finger, it's white on top."

"Those are the bones of children," Tso said with a chuckle. "We tell our little ones, 'If you don't behave, Spider Woman will catch you in her web, and your bones will decorate her home.'"

They rode, and Sam turned in his saddle to keep watching the spire.

He also kept being aware, on every plop of every hoof, that Nez Begay was watching him with hostile eyes. He ignored it.

"Ahead," said Tso, "is the hogan of Hosteen Narbona."

Sam looked at Baptiste. Maybe this was why they'd been brought on this journey, to see the Navajo headman.

Nez Begay glared at them and smiled, as though satisfaction was at hand.

Narbona's place was in fact several hogans, in both the male and female shapes of Navajo dwellings, some fruit trees, and clumps of sheep.

As they dismounted, a handsome man apparently in his sixties watched them. He had a glance like a blade. The party walked up to where he sat cross-legged. Tso introduced Sam and Baptiste to Narbona.

After a long look the old man said in unaccented Spanish, "You are not Spaniards."

"No," said Sam.

"You are men who hunt the beaver."

"Yes."

"Then sit. We are friends of beaver men. I am Narbona."

"I am White Hair."

"I am Baptiste."

Coy trailed Sam to the council and started to sit. "Go away," Sam said, pointing. "Lay down."

"Let him stay," said Narbona. "The song dog has a sweeter voice than ours, and he may be wiser."

He repeated the little joke in Navajo and got a few chuckles.

Sam sat in the circle. He looked over the men who sat there, without the rudeness of gazing directly into their eyes. He guessed all were warriors except for Narbona and Tso, who were leaders. All their faces were impassive except for Nez Begay's. This enemy stared aggressively at Sam and Baptiste.

"Would you like some water?" said Narbona.

They accepted, and dippers were passed.

"In a few minutes one of my wives will bring some coffee."

Sam and Baptiste breathed easier. Hospitality meant safety.

"You are surprised that I speak Spanish. In fact," said Narbona, "I am by birth one of the Spaniards I hate. I was taken as a child from their country and brought to the land between the four sacred mountains. It was the luckiest thing that ever happened to me.

"White Hair, I wish you could see the expression on your face. Tell me what you are thinking."

Sam decided to take a chance. "What sense would it make to return all captives to the Spaniards, when some are like Narbona, sixty years among the Navajo, and passionately one of the Dineh?"

"My opinion of you," said Narbona, "just went up. I think you also enjoy the fact that life, which brings us to these strange corners, is amusing. Ah," he said, reaching for a pot, "let's have some coffee."

Narbona passed the pot, and all drank in a silence that seemed easy enough. Then for a while the old man spoke of his sheep, his orchards, how cold the winter had been, and how unruly his grandchildren were. Finally, he said, "We come together here with different purposes. You want to ask me some questions. I want to tell you some things. My friend Hosteen Tso thinks maybe you have ears to listen, and that is good.

"So. I suggest that I speak today, and you ask your questions tomorrow."

The friends said yes, not that they really had a choice.

"When we are finished, I will ask you to carry a message to the Spaniards. Tell them exactly what I have to say."

"We will," Sam said.

"Good." Narbona looked at them with eyes like lightning. "I spit on the Spaniards." He reflected for a moment. "It is for their practice of slavery most of all that I despise them. Oh, you say, Navajos also take slaves. Apaches take slaves, Utes take slaves, Comanches take slaves—all the tribes do. So I will tell you the difference. No, I will show you."

He spread his arms wide.

"Myself. I am the difference. Many decades ago I was taken from my family and brought to the land of the Dineh, to the ways of the Dineh. Now I am a headman. That is because I was invited in—invited into a family as a son, invited into the ranks of the young boys learning to be men, into the ranks of the warriors. Eventually I became a leader.

"Yes, I was brought here by force. Yes, I wept hot tears for my mother and father. But the Dineh gave me an opportunity to earn a place, and I did.

"All the tribes I am acquainted with are this way. A man is invited to fight shoulder to shoulder. A woman is welcome to become a mother, and a sister to other married women. A slave for a day, perhaps, but a brother for a lifetime."

Narbona looked off toward the canyon walls, as though seeing something there.

"The Spaniard does things differently. A slave is a slave forever. A man may be a peon, that only. And the Spaniards own—this is rank in my nostrils—the fruits of their loins. The children are *born* slaves."

Sam thought of Sumner and said to himself, *We Americans do it the same to blacks*. He felt profoundly disgusted.

Narbona waited, just looking at them. "This is the first great reason I despise the Spaniards. The second, unfortunately, involves me personally. Do you know the story of Massacre Cave?"

"No."

Narbona nodded. "Almost thirty winters ago, the Spaniards built the fort at Cebolleta, the one which is still there. You have seen it?"

"We know about it," Sam said.

"It almost touches the slopes of Turquoise Mountain. This is the boundary of the lands given to the Navajo, the edge of our land closest to where the sun rises. The Spaniards built a settlement on the margin of our land, like a dare.

"We took up their challenge. I was even then head of the Tachi-i'nii clan. I gathered together about a thousand men and attacked Cebolleta over and over. We taught them some hard lessons."

His eyes changed. "However, they sent word far to the south for more soldiers, and the soldiers came from Chihuahua, where they live as many as ants. They attacked us. Not only near Turquoise Mountain did they strike us, but far into country they knew was ours, where soldiers had never marched. During that next winter they even came here."

The old man took a moment to look into the past. "I wanted to draw the soldiers away from our hogans, our fields and orchards, our sheep, goats, and horses. I was glad to fight them, and whip them, young warrior against young warrior. Not trusting the Spaniards, I sent more than a hundred of our old men, women, and children into a cave in the place people now call Canyon del Muerto. Then I asked some of our young men to lure the soldiers onto the mesa above, where we would fight them like men."

He sighed. "A foolish old woman, one who had been a slave among the Spaniards and hated them, she could not keep quiet. As their soldiers passed by the cave, she taunted them.

"The Spaniards ordered their troops to shoot against the sloping walls of the cave and make their bullets bounce down into those who were hiding. When they had finished this shooting, which wounded many people, they marched their soldiers up the wall and into the cave. There they finished the job. They shot all our people. They knifed them. And with their rifle butts they bashed their skulls in. Not one old man, woman, or child survived. That is why we call it Massacre Cave."

Narbona didn't speak for a long time. "I was a young leader, and I had failed my people. Also, I was stupefied at what the Spaniards had done. At the time I was ashamed that the blood of such men runs in my veins. What kind of men, I asked myself, make war on women, children, and old men? What honor do they find in that?

"Now, White Hair and Baptiste, brave men, I ask you the same questions. What kind of men kill the defenseless?"

"There is no answer," said Sam. He and Baptiste both thought the old man was right, and both knew the New Mexicans would tell similar stories about the Navajos.

The old man coughed and went on. "I have one. Crazy men, men who have lost their way utterly, only they do such things. The best thing to do with crazy men is stay far away from them.

"So for thirty years I have kept my people away from the Spaniards. Sometimes young men still make raids—young men are wild, and no one can control them. For thirty years I have raised my sheep, eaten my peaches, made love to my wives, walked the path of Hozhoji, and kept the peace."

He gave a half-smile and looked directly into Sam's and Baptiste's eyes. "So, White Hair, this is the message I want you to carry to my relatives and enemies, the Spaniards." He took a moment to think. "'If you come no further than Cebolleta, I will stay at home. But if you send a single soldier beyond that point into my country, I will unleash thirty winters of fury upon you. I do not forget. The Dineh do not forget. We will come as a storm of red sand and black wind. We will destroy you with arrows of lightning.'"

And he laughed.

Fourteen

FOR A WHILE they all looked at the words Narbona had thrown out before everyone. Then he said, "I understand that you have questions for me, and I am glad to receive them. However, my wives say it is time for us to begin our feast—we have butchered a sheep. I will discuss other matters with you tomorrow."

Sam and Baptiste looked at each other. Stymied for the moment.

"Thank you," Sam said to Narbona. Everyone rose and wandered away. Sam said to Baptiste, "Damn if we aren't guests of honor."

Later, when Sam was stuffed and twilight took over the deep canyon, Sam said in English to Baptiste, "Is Narbona the wise old man, the genial host, or the fierce warrior?"

"All three. Bet on it."

"And how does Nez Begay fit into this?"

"Whenever I look at that son of a bitch, the skin on my back gets squirmy."

"I prefer either of them to Armijo," Sam said. "He is a shrewd politician who cares for nothing and no one."

Sam fed Coy scraps of mutton. None of the Navajos seemed taken aback by a pet coyote, but they watched curiously when Sam fed him meat by hand.

"Let's put out our bedrolls," said Sam.

"Take turns at watch?"

"We're safe here tonight. If we aren't, we'll never get back to Santa Fé anyway."

Baptiste rummaged in his possible sack. "People say you play the tin whistle." And he held up a harmonica.

In a few minutes Sam knew that Baptiste was a terrific musician. He bounced nicely along with Sam's Irish jigs and crooned sweetly with his ballads. But he knew all sorts of other songs—German folk tunes, French ditties (genuinely French, he said, not French Canadian), Hungarian songs, Spanish songs, and even a Gypsy melody.

Sam liked the Gypsy one a lot, and they worked out a pretty way for Sam to play melody while Baptiste made the harmony.

Sam watched Coy scrunch in the cottonwood leaves at Sam's feet, and a special feeling came to him. The sun was down in the northwest, below the rim. Amethyst mist lined the creek. The canyon cupped the twilight like a precious fluid. The evening was lovely. Life was perfect. At hazard—wasn't it always?—but perfect.

"You know, Spider Woman, she isn't really a mean old woman," Baptiste said. "I know one of the big stories about her, and as an outsider I can tell it even when it's not winter."

"Do it."

As Baptiste began to speak, Sam pictured the two-fingered spire back around the corner of the canyon, graceful, delicate, and beautiful. He wanted to hear something mythic about its occupant.

"An old woman told me this story at Laguna Pueblo. She had been stolen by the Navajos and got back to her own people. As she talked, she wove a 'slave blanket.'" He smiled at the irony.

"Spider Woman is a weaver, she said, and she taught weaving to the Dineh—it is one of the great gifts.

"Picture, though, the first weaving of all. At the beginning Spider Woman wove the world itself. She sat in her room and imagined a blue sky, and as soon as she saw it, sky existed.

"Next, the earth. She dreamed of a broad earth, huge in every direction, and, lo, there were many lands.

"Now Spider Woman realized that creating the world was a lot of work. Therefore she imagined three more spider grandmothers right in the room with her, and the moment she did, they were there.

"The four of them set to work weaving the world from the yarn of thought." Baptiste paused and then made a comment. "The way the old woman told the story, that phrase became a kind of chorus—'Spider Woman wove the world from the yarn of thought.'

"One grandmother made rock and sand and dirt to cover the surface of the earth. Another made the waters, those that cascade down from the sky, those that flow, and those that fill the lakes and oceans.

"Another grandmother set herself to filling the world with grasses, trees, and flowers—there were so many to be made. At the same time the fourth grandmother made animals—rabbits, bears, lizards, hawks, swallows, coyotes, and every creature that walks the earth, burrows under it, or flies above it.

"All these things the weavers made from the yarn of their imagination—they created the whole world.

"The old woman stopped and thought for a moment and then said to me, 'The Spider grandmothers created the sun and moon and all the stars in the sky. They created the Laguna, the Dineh, and all the other peoples. One day I will tell you these stories too.' "

The two men watched the last mint-colored light seep from the sky.

Sam gathered a few twigs and made a small fire. The desert evening was cool, and Coy stretched out close to the flames.

"You want to make a song?" said Baptiste.

Sam looked at him in wonder.

"We could make a song about Spider Woman creating the world."

Long into the night the two of them piped and sang and made up the words:

Spider Woman sits in her room
And pictures in her mind
Rocks and river and sky
        Grasses and trees and flowers
                Birds, turtles, and coyotes

As she pictures them
These things appear on the earth

Spider Woman weaves the world
From the yarn of thought

Now she pictures three more mother spiders
And together the four women weave
        The universe and all within it
                The four worlds below and
                        This world above

Four spider women weave all creatures
From the yarn of thought

As they weave all things
They bless them with names—
        Clouds and thunder and lightning
                Corn and squash and beans
                        Rabbits, bears, and dragonflies

Four spider women weave all creatures
From the yarn of thought

Together the four women spiders
They weave all things that are
Me and the words I tell you
You and the story you hear

Our universe is the web they weave
All that lives is the web they weave
Spider Woman weaves the world
From the yarn of thought

When he rolled into his blankets, Sam looked up at the ribbon of sky between the canyon walls. The sky, too, flowed—he knew that. The stars floated across the heavens. They did not wander—astronomers knew there were shapes in the paths they traveled.

But that part of the story was for another time.

He checked on Coy, at his feet. He looked over at Paladin, staked nearby. He replayed the story of Spider Woman in his mind, and as he fell asleep, he thought human beings were a little like her: they made music and poetry—clocks and kitchen utensils and maps and even businesses, hell, everything—on the loom of imagination.

Fifteen

"BEFORE I PUT out my questions," said Sam to Narbona, "I want to ask about this man. He seems . . ." Sam hesitated. Mentioning the rudeness of Nez Begay's stare would itself be rude.

Narbona laughed a little. "He is my grandson, Nez Begay. As a young man should be, he is ready to fight all the time, and he wants you to know it. Besides the reasons any Navajo has to hate the Spaniards," said Narbona, "he has something very special. Both of his daughters are now captives among them."

Sam and Baptiste looked at each other. Coy squealed and panted.

"My grandson went to the meeting at Turkey Spring hoping to retrieve his daughters. But the Spaniard Armijo, he had other ideas."

Now Narbona's voice had lost its edge of wry amusement. Armijo's stunt of showing up for an exchange with no captives at all—that was a cause for cold fury.

Sam stuck his neck out. "Nez Begay, my heart is good toward you. I am willing to help you."

Nez Begay said, "Maybe you would be wiser to be afraid."

They all sat and attended to those words for a moment.

"Like Nez Begay," Sam said to Narbona, "I went to the exchange, and came here, searching for two relatives, Lupe and Rosalita, my daughters and the sisters of my son Tomás. These women, they lived at Tosato."

Narbona said, "Nez Begay led the raid at Tosato, and he took them. I told him to take our young men there and make the Spaniards eat the poisoned fruit of their actions. We will do it again."

Nez Begay said, "And again and again."

After a silence Sam went on. "We do not expect to get our relatives back for nothing. We will pay for them."

Narbona studied Sam. "We do not have the women," he said. "Nez Begay traded them to the Utes."

Sam's heart sank. Ute country stretched all the way to the Great Salt Lake, and whoever had the girls had a big head start. Sam and Baptiste would have to go back to Santa Fé and get outfitted.

It struck him that he didn't know whether Narbona was telling the truth. "Which band of Utes?"

Narbona named the Utes near the mountains the Siskadee went around in a half-circle. Then he waited, thinking. "I would be glad to get money from you," he said. "I like gold coins, and have no reason not to sell captives. But I don't have these women."

Nez Begay said something harsh-sounding in Navajo.

Narbona ignored him.

They all waited.

"Is there anything else I can do for you?" Sam asked Narbona.

"Just carry my message to the Spaniards," said the old chief. "Maybe someone smarter than Armijo."

Sam nodded. He and Baptiste rose.

"You are welcome at my home," said Narbona.

Sam felt a gush of relief. He almost made the mistake of saying *thank you*. Instead he said, "And you at mine."

As they packed up to go, Sam said, "Did you catch what Nez Begay said that Narbona wouldn't let the translator say?"

"Yeah," said Baptiste. "He said he liked lying between your daughters' legs."

Sixteen

"I DON'T TRUST Nez Begay," said Baptiste.

Sam said, "Me neither."

"Narbona wants us to take his message back."

"Maybe Nez Begay figures our bodies would deliver it better."

So they traveled as far as they could that first day. It was a skill, traveling far without wearing a horse down to nothing. It required lightness and balance in the saddle and moving with the horse instead of against it. You also needed to pick the best route across a landscape continually gashed with patterns of erosion, like the shell of a walnut. The hardest part was concentrating all the time.

Sam was lucky to have Paladin. She was a natural athlete and had a big heart. But she was in foal, and soon Sam would not be able to push her.

They rode fast and didn't check their back trail—they had no idea whether Nez Begay was there.

They stopped for the night at a well-known camping spot, Sheep Springs, which they'd used on the way west. Travelers stopped here regularly, and a Navajo family lived in a hogan here during the heat of the summer and grazed their sheep. Sam and Baptiste drank, filled their flasks, staked the horses, laid out their bedrolls, and put their rifles next to the blankets. They built a nice fire out of sagebrush. Then they broke off more brush, piled it under the blankets, and slipped off to a boulder twenty paces away. A good place to watch.

"Coy will tell us if he comes," said Sam.

"Let's take him alive," said Baptiste.

"Right."

They would take turns on watch all night.

Neither one of them could sleep. They were too keyed up, wondering where Nez Begay might be, and when he would slip in.

Somewhere beyond midnight, according to the Big Dipper, Coy suddenly sat up, the hairs along his spine stiffened, and he growled low. Sam had taught him not to bark at times like this. He was pointing straight toward the fire. Since the wind was from behind them, Coy was hearing someone, not smelling them.

Sam's eyes searched the darkness, but in the half-moon he saw no figure.

Sam smiled at Baptiste. He was glad, actually—the waiting chewed on him. "You from the left, me from the right," he said in a quarter of a whisper, making arcing motions with his hands.

He put Coy on a lead and with a pistol, butcher knife, and tomahawk slipped into the darkness. This was sagebrush country. He would ease from bush to bush quietly. Action felt good.

Since Coy was pointing straight at the camp, Sam also moved fast. Nez Begay would discover their trick quickly.

There!

A man shape stood up on the edge of camp.

Baptiste shouted something in Navajo.

Sam dashed at Nez Begay.

The man shape turned and said, "Dad?"

* * *

SAM TURNED A knock-down charge into a hug.

"Tomás! What the hell are you doing here?"

"I've been following you."

Baptiste stepped into the firelight. "Tomás!"

Coy barked like the devil, off into the darkness.

"You've been following us?"

"The whole time?"

"Yeah. Listen, that Navajo, Nez Begay, he's somewhere around here. We better—"

Where Coy was pointing, on the outer edge of the firelight, Nez Begay rose and pointed his rifle at Sam and Tomás.

"You, Baptiste," he said, "over there with them."

Baptiste went.

"Now put down your weapons," he said, "or I shoot the arrogant boy who fought with me."

Coy sat and growled. He gave Sam an I-told-you-so look.

Sam stood back from Tomás and put his pistol on the ground.

"The knife and tomahawk too. All of your weapons, all of you."

They did.

"Put your hands on top of your heads."

They did.

Nez Begay stepped forward and felt their clothes for weapons, Baptiste first. He unbuckled Baptiste's shooting pouch and let it fall to the ground. "That's where you keep the little knife you cut rifle patches with," he said.

He slid Tomás's pouch off his shoulder and let it fall.

Sam started to unbuckle his pouch, but Nez Begay said, "Hands back on top of your head."

Sam obeyed, and now his hands grasped his hair ornament and his fingers began to twist.

"What do you want with us?"

If Nez Begay had wanted to kill them, he would have shot without warning.

"I want to find out how good you are at walking," said Nez Begay. "Walking all the way to Santa Fé. Naked. Without food or water." He chuckled. "My grandfather sends messages in what he says. I send them in what I do."

Baptiste said, "Why not just kill—"

In the instant Nez Begay looked at Baptiste, Sam struck.

The blade in the hair ornament sliced the Navajo's face open from the eyebrow across the bridge of his nose.

He whipped the muzzle of the rifle toward Sam and pulled the trigger.

Tomás rammed his head into Nez Begay's gut.

The rifle boomed, smoke erupted, and Sam was still alive.

He butted the tangle of Nez Begay and Tomás, and the three of them fell onto the fire.

From the bottom Nez Begay screamed, and they all rolled away.

SAM THOUGHT ABOUT the problem all night and half the day.

He stitched up the cut on Nez Begay's face. The burns on the Navajo's back weren't as bad as Sam feared. Baptiste killed a stray ram, and they slathered the wounds with fat. He also doctored the burns on Tomás's arm, and his own. They would ride tomorrow.

Sam showed Baptiste his hair weapon, and Nez Begay and Tomás watched. "It's something Hannibal had a blacksmith make," he explained. The ornament was four or five inches long and as thick as a finger, made of polished walnut. It was decorated with circles painted red, yellow, black, and white, the colors of the four directions. And in the middle of one of those circles it slid apart. Inside was a short blade, nastily sharp. Sam showed how he greased the joint of the two pieces of wood and stuck it back where it held his white hair out of his face.

"It works because enemies tell you to put your hands on your head," Sam said, "and because it looks innocent."

"The white man is cunning," said Nez Begay.

So you have a little humor. "It won't be cunning if too many people see mine, or get a blacksmith to make them one."

Sam thought about the problem more while they gorged themselves on mutton. Since the meat would spoil fast, they ate all they could.

"If we kill him," Sam said to Baptiste in English, "we make an enemy of Narbona."

"If we don't, Nez Begay will never stop coming after us."

"Right."

Sam gnawed meat off bones.

Sam handed Nez Begay a broiled rib. "You're coming with us," he said in Spanish.

An expression of loathing and fear flushed into Nez Begay's face. The stitched-up slash across his eyebrow slithered.

"Not as a prisoner," said Sam, "and you are not going to be a slave."

Everyone wondered what Sam was talking about.

"We are going to escort you into Santa Fé as a spokesman for your people. We will guarantee your safety. And we will demand that, when the captive exchange party goes out to meet with your people, you and your daughters will go with it."

Sam looked at three faces of disbelief, Nez Begay's, Baptiste's, and Tomás's. He grinned at them.

"Why?" said Nez Begay.

"Because it's right," said Sam.

Seventeen

IN SANTA FÉ things got done fast, but not as fast as Sam wanted. To get started for rendezvous—that was eating at him.

Sam, Baptiste, Tomás, Nez Begay, and two other well-armed trappers had an audience with the governor, with Armijo in silent attendance. Sam delivered Narbona's message word for word, and he saw approval in Nez Begay's eyes when he did so.

The governor ordered a man to take word to the Navajos that Narbona's grandson was being treated with honor, and that the exchange of captives would take place at the half-moon, as agreed, with Nez Begay and his daughters present.

The governor dismissed Sam, Nez Begay, and the men guarding him with official thanks. Sam didn't think he'd made any friends in the Palace of the Governors.

Outside Sam said to the Navajo warrior, "I have pledged my

honor to protect you. I want to act as a friend to the Navajo people. If you—"

Nez Begay stopped him with a hand. "I will do nothing foolish." He gave a little grin. "Sam Morgan," he said, "do you know you are a good man?" He gave a lopsided grin. From now on his scar would always make him look fearsome. "A rare thing among white people."

With the permission of Paloma's sister Rosa, Sam and friends took up residence at Rancho de Las Palomas. They used the *casitas primitivas*—Sam couldn't stand the thought of being in the big house with Paloma gone. It would stand empty, except for when Paloma's sister and her family came down from Santa Fé. Right now the rancho was the safest place for Nez Begay.

Sam got his outfit in order to go to rendezvous—horses and mules bought, hands signed on, last trade goods purchased. He and Sumner had maintained an arrangement for four years now—Sumner put up the money, Sam was the field leader, and they split the profits down the middle.

The whole arrangement made Sam smile to himself. In 1823 he came to the mountains as an illiterate backwoodsman, utterly green to the mountains. Now half the year he was a brigade leader and minor entrepreneur (he even knew how to spell it) and the other half lover to a rich Santa Fé woman. Also a father, twice. Plus, in his own way, a Crow named Joins with Buffalo, and a pipe carrier. One decade, a whole new man. The New World, as Hannibal liked to say.

Soon he would travel with the New Mexicans as far as the meeting for captive exchange, try to keep everyone levelheaded there, and make his way far north to the Siskadee, where the fur men held their annual get-together. For five years his life had revolved around two females—a long winter with Paloma and a brief summer rendezvous where he saw his daughter Esperanza. Now it turned on Esperanza and two other women, Lupe and Rosalita.

When he met with Sumner to go over the books for the trading expedition one last time, Sumner said, "Somep'n, it be missing." The black man's slave talk again.

Sam cocked an eye at his friend across the desk. Sometime in the last several years Sumner had acquired a small but beautiful home in the *viga y latilla* style found everywhere in Santa Fé.

"We need a fiesta. At the rancho. Your goodbye fiesta."

VIOLINS, MANDOLINS, AND guitars both large and small filled the evening air with music. The band wandered through the crowd, amusing some people, inspiring others to dance, and even bringing a tear here and there with a sentimental love song.

Sumner's idea for a fiesta had mushroomed. Paloma's sister, Rosa Luna Salazar de Otero, had not only welcomed the idea—she decided to make it a grand reception for the new ownership of Rancho de las Palomas and to invite the whole town.

Several hundred people made the short trip down the river road from Santa Fé, common people, artisans and craftsmen, merchants, and aristocrats of the five great families of Nuevo Mexico, Armijo, Chavez, Otero, Perea, and Yrizar.

Wine flowed abundantly. Doña Rosa was showing off her sister's vintages—wine later to be marketed throughout the province. Sam didn't care why the wine was flowing—he was just glad for the festive atmosphere.

Sheep, beeves, and pigs had been turning on spits over open fires all afternoon. "Everyone will eat, drink, and dance until they drop or go mad with passion," Doña Rosa told Sam. He liked her.

The mountain men had their roles to play—Sam and Sumner's little trading company had been announced as cohost of the party. It was named Rideo Trading, after the motto invented by Hannibal MacKye and adopted by Sam and Sumner—*rideo ergo sum*—I laugh, therefore I am.

"We will invent *divertissements,*" Baptiste said in a Frenchy accent.

Sumner's divertissement was to entertain people with card tricks and card games. First he made a good show by decking himself out as a dandy, a suit of lightweight wool in a daring plum color that flattered his black skin wonderfully, a white waistcoat with a golden watch fob, and an elegant, dove-gray beaver hat. He was outdonning the dons.

His card tricks were dazzling—Sumner would let a child pick a card from a deck, look at it, and put it back. Then the gambler would reach out and pluck the card out of the child's ear. He would give a man the four aces of a deck, let the fellow put them back at random, shuffle the cards once, and turn the four aces up on top.

The card game was even better. Sam and Tomás stood to watch for a moment. It was an old con, three-card monte. Sumner sat at a table with a sign laid on one corner—STEAL FROM THE RICH, GIVE TO THE POOR. Whenever a don passed, Sumner caught the fellow's attention and tried to seduce him.

Now Manuel Armijo himself drifted by, grinning and perhaps a little drunk. "El Gobernador, you, señor," Sumner cried, "may I interest you in a little game? It is child's play. In fact, watch—a child will win at it."

Then Sumner laid three cards in front of two kids who were standing there, gape-mouthed. One was a raven-haired girl of eight or nine, the other a redheaded boy of ten or twelve.

"Here you see the Gentleman, the Lady, and the Boy with a Hoop," Sumner proclaimed to the crowd. "Now watch carefully, my lad," he said, nodding at the redhead. The boy peered intently at the cards.

Sumner picked them up, held them where all could easily see the backs, and deliberately, one at a time, shuffled them. Then he laid them face down on the table.

"Now," said Sumner with elaborate formality—he did his show in the fanciest possible Spanish—"pick out the Boy with a Hoop."

The redhead shyly pointed to the card on the right end. Sumner turned it over and—*"Estupendo!"* he exclaimed. "This young man has won a peso."

He handed the boy a coin. "And the lady wins too," he announced, giving another to the girl. The kids beamed.

Sumner addressed Armijo. "Don Manuel, surely you can win at a game conquered even by children?"

"Your sign alarms me," said Don Manuel.

"I'm sure you are a generous man. If you lose, you will make a small donation to someone less blessed than yourself."

Armijo stepped forward, intrigued.

"Bet whatever you like, Don Manuel."

Armijo set out a ten-peso piece.

Sumner went through the same rigmarole with the cards. He shuffled the three of them so slowly that anyone would be sure which was which.

Armijo pointed—and chose wrong.

"The Lady. I venture a guess that such a choice is characteristic of you, Gobernador."

Armijo laughed, and the crowd joined in.

Sumner quickly distributed the pesos to several kids in peasant clothes. They got excited.

"This is an easy game, Don Manuel, and money comes to you as sunshine falls on the grasses of the field. Another game—a hundred pesos this time."

Armijo plunked down the stacks of coins.

Sam and Tomás grinned at each other. A hundred pesos was about three weeks' wages for a laborer.

Once more the rigmarole with the cards, once more the easy patter by Sumner, once more the fatal moment of choice—and Armijo picked the Lady again.

Sumner declared, "Don Manuel, it is clear that romance is in the air for you tonight."

He scooped up the pesos and gave a stack each to two different men, field hands from their dress.

"A thousand pesos, Gobernador? You are a great man in Nuevo Mexico . . ."

But Armijo laughed, waved Sumner off, and walked on.

"The Ocampos are here from Albuquerque," Baptiste said softly to Sam.

They found Nez Begay studying the musicians. He was an intimidating sight, face scarred, his long hair tied back in a chongo, his chest bare, muscular legs left bare by his breechcloth. He seemed puzzled by the music. Twice he had refused wine. Sam had kept two trappers with him all evening, just in case. His comment then was, "You say I'm a guest, but I feel like a prisoner."

"We have a surprise for you," Sam told him.

Nez Begay nodded, his massive face showing nothing.

"Come."

They went to the courtyard of the main house. It tugged at Sam's memories, but it was the best place for this meeting, quiet and walled off, with a well at the center and flowers around the borders.

Sam opened the gate and led the way. Señor and Señora Ocampo and their family stood nervously by the well. Sam had never met them, but Baptiste introduced him and Nez Begay. No one shook hands. It didn't seem right. Señor Ocampo gave a tight half-bow, and he and his wife and two teenage sons walked away.

Left behind were two Navajo girls, perhaps seven and ten.

Nez Begay and the girls looked at each other in amazement. Suddenly his eyes erupted with feeling, almost with violence.

Nez Begay turned stiffly back to Sam and struggled to make his face blank.

Sam said to Baptiste, "Let's go."

Beyond the gate Sam and Baptiste climbed the wall and sat on it with their backs to the Begay family and their rifles across their laps. As Sam looked around—there could always be trouble—he heard low murmurings and exclamations. A quick glance back showed the father on his knees, the daughters in his arms.

THE FIESTA WAS winding down. It had been a big event, but Sam's responsibilities were over. Two trappers guarded the *casa primitiva* where Nez Begay and his daughters spent the night.

Sam got an entire bottle of wine and sat down in the courtyard with Baptiste and Tomás.

"Do you think the girls were too young to be . . . ?" he asked Baptiste.

"Yes," said his friend.

Beyond the courtyard a few people still milled around. Laughs pierced the darkness. The torches Doña Rosa had set out made the leaves of the cottonwoods glow. The violins, guitars, and mandolins spoke of love.

"Ah, romance," said Baptiste.

Sam was sure some people were finding romance behind buildings or in the willows. He wished he felt like romance himself. "Why aren't you chasing the girls?" he asked his son.

"My motto with women is '*veni, vidi, vici,*'" said Tomás, meaning "I came, I saw, I conquered." "But sometimes I like to sit around with the old men."

He got a grin from Baptiste and a jaundiced eye from Sam.

Sam took a slow sip of his wine and looked over the rim of his cup at Baptiste. Maybe he was a little tipsy. "You know," he said slowly, "it's time, past time. We are riding together. You're an odd duck. I want to know your story."

"Me too," said Tomás.

"Fill your glasses full," said Baptiste. "This is going to take a while."

Baptiste had been born high on the Missouri River and carried in a cradleboard to the Pacific Ocean and back. "She is a Shoshone," he said, "my father a French Canadian. She and her friend were abducted, and he bought them to be his wives."

At home four languages were spoken, French, Shoshone, Mandan, and English. "Languages have always come easily to me.

"When my mother brought me to St. Louis to get an education, at the invitation of General Clark, that was the end of my life as an Indian."

They sipped and pondered that for a moment.

"When I was eighteen and working at a post up on the Kansa River, I met a man. He is an actual prince, Prince Paul, from Württemberg, in Germany. A good man, young, loves the wilderness, like me, loves hunting. He invited me to come home with him and live in his castle.

"A real castle."

Baptiste went on, "So I learned German. We went on hunting trips. We traveled to Spain and North Africa. I had the time of a young man's life and at last came back to America."

Then he gave a philosophical shrug. "So who am I? A Shoshone, a French Canadian, an American? A musician, a trapper? A red man, a white man? Maybe I am so many things I have become nothing at all." Something in his voice was forlorn.

Sam wondered whether Baptiste was too far into his cups.

Tomás now spoke in an orotund voice. *"Nunc est bibendum."*

Sam and Baptiste hooted. "Latin?" said Baptiste, spilling wine on himself. "What does it mean?"

Sam said, "'Now it's time to drink.' It's the only phrase he knows. Well, besides *'veni, vidi, vici.'* Hannibal MacKye taught it to him."

"Not correct," said Tomás. "I know one more."

"What is it?" said Baptiste.

"Suppedisne."

"What does it mean?"

"Did you fart quietly?"

Eighteen

Sam and Tomás slept late, rose blearily, got a stack of warm tortillas wrapped in paper, and started on horseback for the rancho of Don Manuel Armijo. Their minds weren't on the don's hospitality, or any kind of business—this was strictly Lupe and Rosalita, Joaquin and the infant Francesca.

As they rode, Sam remembered that May of five years ago, when life tossed Tomás and Lupe to Rancho de las Palomas on the same day, both slaves, the day Sam, Sumner, and Paloma bought them and set them free.

In the spring of 1828 the teenage boy had been wild with troubles. Aside from the shock of seeing his village attacked, his parents killed, his sister raped and then hanged, he was staring straight into a future as a slave.

Freeing him didn't calm the angry waters. The next day Tomás went berserk and tried to kill the don who bought his sister. Soon he also had to sidestep the police, with Sam's help.

After his assault on the don, Tomás had to skip town ahead of the law. Since Tomás still needed a family, he and Sam made one, jury-rigged, but a family.

At Armijo's rancho Paladin balked for a moment at the front gate, like she didn't want to go in. Sam didn't blame her. This was where Tomás and his sister Maria were sold at auction. Sam clucked and they trotted to the *jacales*.

When they found Joaquin, he was better. Instead of sucking on her father's nipple, Francesca was in her grandmother's arms. And Joaquin no longer looked blank and dead. His hair was wild and his face wilder—it was like each wiry strand of hair was throwing lightning bolts.

Sam and Tomás swung out of their saddles and tied the horses. Sam walked over and looked at the baby. She had a swatch of very black hair and eyes on the alert.

Sam turned to Joaquin, then stepped back—Joaquin was almost in his face. "We're leaving tomorrow morning."

"Now that there is no hope of finding Lupe," answered Joaquin.

"We're not talking about that now," said Sam.

"You are not. It does not bother you that some Indian has her every day, maybe several Indians have her every day."

Sam didn't rise to this bait.

"Why are you so sure this Navajo," Joaquin plunged on, "this kidnapper and murderer, why do you think he tells the truth?"

"I know him," said Sam.

Joaquin sneered. "Who would want to look into the heart of a murderer?"

Sam didn't answer. Joaquin was drunk enough to bounce off all the walls.

"What will happen after you have wasted time with this exchange of prisoners?"

Sam wanted to slug the jerk.

Tomás butted in. "I go after me sister, the one who is also your wife. Maybe if you sober up, I will bring her to you."

Sam let them glare at each other for a long moment. Then he said, "I have given my word to find Lupe and Rosalita and bring them back." He stepped toward Joaquin and grabbed him by the shirt. "And you, *mi amigo*, are going to ride with us and help out."

SAM WENT FOR a walk at first light. He loved the early morning this time of year, as the days got longer and longer and the sun rose farther and farther to the north. His dad had told him that the Welsh back in the old country celebrated the longest day of the year—stayed up all night and drank and partied and made whoopee in the bushes. He wished he would be at rendezvous by June 21, so he could party all night with the other mountain men on the solstice, but he wouldn't—way too much to get done.

Man and coyote padded all the way around the two camps, Mexican and Navajo, and headed for Turkey Spring, just below the ocher rocks. Coy stepped up to the trickle and lapped.

Sam knelt by the water, scooped some up with his hands, washed his face, and ran his fingers through his white hair. Then he put his face in the stream and looked at the bottom. Flecks in the sand glinted back at him blurrily. He opened his lips and sucked the cool water in. Then he raised his head out of the water and shook his head.

Coy shook himself, as though he'd gotten wet too.

A fellow had to come up here to get a drink of really clean water. Hosteen Tso had brought his outfit in early and taken the good camping spot near the head of the spring, forcing the New Mexican party to camp a little below. And drink water the Navajos and their horses and dogs had already drunk from, and stepped in, and probably worse.

Yesterday's meeting, though, had gone very well. Sam had insisted that the New Mexicans bring some hostages other than Nez

Begay's daughters. Armijo grudgingly brought along one old woman. At least the the weavings of her remaining years, Sam thought, would not be slave blankets.

By luck Hosteen Tso also brought three captives, all children from the raid at Tosato. They couldn't have learned to be Navajos in so short a time, and their fathers and grandparents would be glad to get them back. Maybe these two peoples could begin to trust each other a little, and cooperate. But Sam knew the New Mexicans would keep pushing into Navajo country, and the Navajos would resist, and more men would be killed and more women and children stolen.

Oddest of all oddities: the fiercest, most stubborn Navajo was Narbona, who was born Mexican. It all made Sam's head spin.

Yesterday afternoon Armijo and his functionaries sat with Tso and his warriors and threw pledges around like dust in the wind. Sam had kept Joaquin and his tornado feelings away from the palaver, and the other most volatile man, Nez Begay, was not angry these days.

Now Sam said to Coy, "Why did I bring Joaquin?"

He answered for the coyote, "Because you're crazy."

"Do I like Joaquin?" he asked Coy. "Or am I punishing him?"

"You're just crazy."

"Yeah, well, you know what Hannibal says."

Lunacy was a favorite topic with Hannibal MacKye. He had a saying for it: "If you can't hear the music, you think the people dancing are lunatics."

As far as Sam was concerned, that explained his entire life.

Sam took another drink of the sweet spring water. He was happy—he had accomplished something. This morning they would exchange captives and ride away, the Mexicans to the east, the Navajos to the west.

What was on Sam's mind was his own small outfit, headed north to look for Lupe and Rosalita. Joaquin would bring all his drunken bluster along.

The Utes would merely think Sam was crazy. Morality? We paid a fair price for these slave women.

Sam would buy them back if he could. If he was lucky, it wouldn't cost him a year's profits. The Utes would throw this idea back in his face: You do the same thing to our women and children. "Morality," some warrior would say in disgust.

Sam took a deep breath in and out. He wondered if this quest to find Lupe and Rosalita was hopeless. Maybe so. He wondered if Joaquin would grow up through all this. *Could* you grow up in middle age?

Sam had other worries. How would he stay clear of Tomás's teenage moods?

Sam sighed. He had been in the mountains for ten years. He'd learned some things. Part of what he'd learned was not to worry about the future until it tried to trample you. Then a few moves were in order.

His task was to find the women. Everything beyond that was up to the gods.

Rideo ergo sum—I laugh therefore I am. That was Hannibal MacKye's motto, and Sam's.

ALL THREE OUTFITS were ready to break camp and go. It was best for all to leave at once. Each would check its back trail. They had found agreement here, and a sense of good will. All had better sense than to trust that completely.

Sam put his moccasin in the stirrup and swung up onto Paladin. Tomás reined up beside him. Baptiste would ride at the rear of the pack mules and spare horses, Joaquin and the hired men alongside.

Tomás grinned at his father. "Moving always makes me feel better," he said. "Just moving."

Sam looked down the line and started to cluck to Paladin. Just then Nez Begay and his daughters came galloping up. They bore down on the trapper's party fiercely and stopped in a spray of sand. Nez Begay teasing.

He looked directly into Sam's eyes. This time it was a compliment, a sign that Sam was not a stranger, to be avoided for fear of contamination.

"I have a small gift for you," he said. "The man you are looking for is Walkara."

"Walkara," Sam repeated, uncertain.

"A new leader among the Utes. I traded your daughters to him. He does a big business in slaves."

"Walkara."

"Now, foolish white man," Nez Begay said with a sly smile, "one thing more. You remember what I told you about saying *thank you* only when you mean . . ."

"I do," said Sam.

Nez Begay nodded slightly at his daughters, who were grinning. "Thank you," he said.

"Thank you," said the older daughter.

"Thank you," said the younger.

The three Navajos spurred their horses and were gone, fast.

Nineteen

WALKARA.

This name was new to Sam, and he had dealt with Utes for years. However, it was on the tongue of every Ute he met as he worked his way north. Walkara is the leader of the Noochew people (as they called themselves). Walkara is a great horse thief. Walkara trades many, many slaves. Walkara is a friend to the beaver men. Walkara—you must speak with him.

So Sam rode north along the mountains and then up the Siskadee, leading a pack train, plus Tomás, Baptiste, Joaquin, and four hired men. He had fine, hot June days. He was on the way to the Ute village and also on the way to rendezvous, far upstream from here, where Horse Creek came into this same river. Just below the Uinta Mountains, in a good country, well watered, grassy, full of beaver, he came to the village of Walkara.

The chief didn't let Sam's outfit walk right into camp. At least a dozen warriors rode out to meet the strangers. Sam had seldom seen such a display of Mexican silver—silver ornamented the bridles, the stirrups, the saddles, everything. As they approached, Sam said to Baptiste, "Where are these people getting this stuff?"

"Trading slaves," said Baptiste.

Sam addressed the lead rider. "My name is White Hair. We come in friendship to see Walkara," he said in signs. He didn't speak Ute.

The rider introduced himself and three others. "We are Walkara's brothers," they said.

The warriors studied Sam curiously. He knew they were noticing the Crow beadwork on his moccasins and breechcloth, against the cloth of his Mexican shirt and beaver hat. But Utes knew beaver men took on Indian ways.

Some warriors spoke to each other quietly. Sam wondered if trouble was afoot.

"That's Shoshone," Baptiste said. "They're making little jokes about how funny we look."

Sam shot Baptiste a look. "How does a Ute come to have Shoshone warriors under his command?" The two tribes were traditional enemies.

"Walkara must be one hell of a Ute," said Baptiste.

A few minutes later they were seated in council, and Walkara showed that he was in fact a hell of a Ute. *"Bienvenue,"* he said in French. *"Bienvenido,"* in Spanish. "Welcome to my camp," in English. He grinned at his own expertise in languages.

"Nah haintseh, kimma," Baptiste said to him, offering a welcome in Shoshone.

Walkara laughed out loud. *"Kimma,"* he said. Welcome. *"Nah haintseh, tsaan puisunknna en."* Which meant "Glad to see you."

"This is a regular language convention."

"Babel," said Baptiste.

"Enchanté," Walkara said, and roared with laughter at himself. "My name is Yellow Chief." His face was painted with yellow markings. "In the Noochew language Walkara means 'yellow.' White people call me Walker."

"I am White Hair," said Sam, "this is Baptiste, and this is Tomás."

Walkara was tall and handsome, eagle-beaked, and bore an amazing aura of fierceness. Though he appeared to be only in his mid-twenties, he carried himself with an expectation that anyone would do whatever he said—anyone, including whatever peons of beaver men sat with him now.

Sam asked Tomás to put gifts in front of Walkara, tobacco, beads, and knives. Sam usually took the youth into council, as a way of teaching him.

Walkara tossed his head as though the gifts were trivial, and these guests invited by his dispensation alone. He would sneer at anything, Sam judged, including however many guns you had, and however many men—he would scoff at anyone's strength but his own. If you were before him, you breathed by his gracious consent.

Sam began with casual inquiries in Spanish, which sounded like the best of the chief's languages other than Ute. He asked how the weather had been. He inquired about the spring hunt, knowing that Utes often rode east to the buffalo country. He asked whether Walkara had any beaver skins or buffalo hides to trade.

"Perhaps," answered Walkara, which meant yes. He said it in a tone that indicated he didn't want to spend time talking about such petty matters.

"Tomorrow morning?"

A shrug that meant yes. Then, "You are going to the beaver man rendezvous?"

"Yes."

"After we find me sisters," put in Tomás. Sam flicked a glance at him: let me do the talking.

"It is a long way." The rendezvous was at Horse Creek, fifteen or twenty sleeps above there. "The route you travel is dangerous," said Walkara.

Only because of the Utes. This man crowded you at every moment.

They talked of this and that. Always Walkara's eyes gleamed, and he acted like a man playing a high-stakes card game and winning.

Not knowing what else to do, Sam just laid the words out. "We seek two women taken by Nez Begay at Tosato."

"The white man dances through many words and finally speaks what is on his mind. I am more direct. I gave Nez Begay horses in exchange for five slaves, three women and two children. I have many horses."

It was a point of pride with the Ute people to keep far more horses than they could ever ride or use in any way.

Sam gave the be-quiet at Tomás again. The youth's face gave him away.

Then Sam looked at Walkara and saw knowledge in his eyes and a smile on his lips.

"These two women, they are my son's sisters," Sam said. No point in being coy now. The price had already gone up.

"What are their names?"

"Lupe and Rosalita."

Something passed across Walkara's face, but Sam couldn't read it.

"I will tell you where these women are. Not merely that. I will escort you to them."

Tomás nearly jumped.

"Yes?" Sam was on the lookout for a trick.

"Escort you directly to them," repeated Walkara. He drew a slow smile.

"We accept with thanks," Tomás blurted out.

Walkara looked at the young man with sly indulgence. "Lupe and Rosalita, I traded them to my friend Pegleg Smith. He and my brother left here traveling to the very rendezvous where you wish to go, so he can trade them again."

"Pegleg!" cried Tomás, looking hard at his father. "That son of a bitch!"

Sam stopped him with a shake of the head. Both of them remembered the fight that crazy son of a gun had with Tomás, and the proslave talk that provoked it.

"Pegleg Smith is my brother friend," Walkara said. His face maintained geniality.

"How long ago did they leave?"

"One moon," said Walkara.

Sam looked sideways at his son, wondering if Tomás realized this timing wasn't right. "Pegleg usually makes it to rendezvous," he said.

They looked at each other, Sam, Walkara, and Tomás.

"I escort you directly to them," said Walkara again.

Lots of questions, thought Sam. "Sometimes," he said, "you get lucky."

THAT EVENING SAM, Tomás, and Baptiste were guests at Walkara's lodge for a good supper. The young chief already had two wives, and plenty of fresh meat. He was cordial, and talked expansively about his ambition to improve his people's lot through trade with everyone—the Mexicanos, the beaver men, the Comanches, even the Shoshones.

Sam raised an eyebrow at him.

"I don't make enemy with Shoshone," said Walkara. "Trade, I trade, all peoples trade, we all happy."

Sam just looked at him.

"You, you bring me the slave blankets from Santa Fé and Taos, also anything silver. I like silver. In return you get beaver hides, buffalo hides, plenty. You white men like the hides."

"Maybe so," said Sam.

Tomás gave him the evil eye.

Walkara, though, seemed not to notice. "I even think of the Californios," he told them. "You beaver men, you travel to California."

Sam nodded.

"You yourself, you been to California?"

"Yes." He said no more. He wondered if this man, suddenly affable, intended to trade slaves from the Pacific to the Gulf of Mexico.

"You and I go to California," said Walkara. "My friend Pegleg, he says California has many, many horses."

Sam could almost feel the heat radiating from Tomás. He and his son were both thinking, *horses and slaves*.

"We have plenty of time to talk business at rendezvous," said Sam.

THEY SLID ALONG the trail in the last of the light, considering. Sam told Tomás and Baptiste, "There's things he's not saying."

"What do we care?" said Tomás. "He is helping us find me sisters."

"All right. I need to ride on ahead and see Esperanza. You two bring Walkara along."

"And keep an eye on him," said Tomás.

Sam shrugged and then addressed his son. "I need something. I can't ride Paladin. It's too near her time, and I'm going to push hard. I'll leave her with you."

"And we'll have a new foal when we get there," said the young man. "But what will you ride?"

"Alice, and lead the mule."

Alice was a two-year-old Appaloosa from Paladin, barely trained. Sam had been leading her as a packhorse.

"Dad, that's no good. I have a better idea."

Sam looked into his son's smile. The youth was fond of Alice. He had named her, and intended to spend the days at rendezvous making her into a good saddle horse.

"Take Vici. Vici's got lots of bottom. You couldn't do better. Use Alice for a second mount."

Tomás was proud of his horse, justifiably so.

"You sure?"

"Damn sure."

"Good. Thanks."

They stretched out on their bedrolls.

The next morning, when the beaver men were ready to ride, the column of Utes paraded up, Walkara at their head.

Sam reined Vici over to him, and Tomás brought Paladin alongside. Walkara eyed the medicine hat mare and gelding with the appreciation of a connoisseur of horseflesh. Baptiste sat his black stallion.

"Baptiste and Tomás will ride with you to rendezvous. I'm going ahead and tell everyone you are coming and choose a good place to camp."

"White Hair, why do you not ride with us?" said Walkara.

Sam said, "It is a matter of the heart."

Walkara cupped his breechcloth. "I think it is a matter of the man berries."

Sam nodded. It was good to know the Yellow Chief could be wrong. He touched his heels to Vici and was off.

Twenty

TRAVELING ALONE IN Indian country—a thought to make your skin pucker. Yes, the Utes were reasonably friendly to the beaver men. So were the Shoshones, whose territory bordered the Utes' on the north. But any fur trapper made a tempting target. Besides having two fine horses, Sam was carrying weapons, and he had good tools of mountain survival in his belt and pouches. By Indian standards he was a rich man, and an easy target for a single, silent arrow.

So Sam rode all night and part of each morning and forted up to sleep during the heat of the day. He alternated riding one mount and leading the other, to keep from wearing either horse out. He avoided skylining himself. He used brush or timber as cover when he could. He kept his eyes roaming always, and felt like one of the buzzards that floated overhead. Sam wasn't looking for prey but predators.

He didn't hunt. He carried a dozen pounds of jerked meat, enough to get him through a journey he hoped to cut in half, to eight or nine days. He didn't build fires. And he kept his mind on his business.

He had one respite every day. He found some brush to hide in, staked his horses, noted the routes of escape, and stretched out to sleep. Before he drifted off, he thought of the heart reason he was hurrying to rendezvous—Esperanza. During the short nights of late June, riding under a waxing moon, he had the same thought over and over: *I'm going to see Esperanza, and my brother-in-law Flat Dog, and Julia.*

It was a story he didn't tell, because the pain was too raw. In 1823 he came to the mountains, joined the Crow people, and made best friends with two young Crow men, Blue Medicine Horse and Flat Dog. The next year he married their sister Meadowlark.

He had to fight another suitor for Meadowlark, Red Roan, the son of the chief, who was also courting her. Foolishly, Sam led Blue Medicine Horse into battle and got him killed. Then the family opposed Sam's courtship fiercely. Yet Meadowlark chose Sam.

The newlyweds got away from the Crows and went to California with Jedediah Smith's brigade—Sam wanted to be in the first outfit to cross the continent to the Golden Clime, and Meadowlark wanted to see the big-water-everywhere. There she bore a child, and in giving Sam Esperanza, she died.

Sam brought the infant back to the Crows, where she belonged. He entrusted her to his closest family, Flat Dog and Julia, to raise, and to her grandparents to watch over.

When challenged, he killed Red Roan.

Now he was unwelcome in the village where his daughter lived. So he saw her once each summer, at rendezvous. Flat Dog and Julia made the journey to do a little trading, and let father and daughter get to know each other.

Already Sam was late to rendezvous. Flat Dog would be waiting and wondering whether Sam had gone under. He would be patient. But every day late was one day Sam didn't get to see Esperanza.

He pushed the two horses, and he pushed himself.

* * *

SAM POINTED NORTH along the Siskadee. When it started its big turn around the Uinta Mountains, flowing in the shape of a sharply curved scimitar, he cut straight across, through the pines and aspens, enjoying alpine air and relief from heat. Coy was visibly perkier in high country, and Vici had bounce in her step.

When he came out of the mountains, he rode down a little creek through a narrow canyon and ran smack into a camp of Blackfeet.

Rotten luck—they saw him when he saw them. The young men hollered like hell and ran for their horses.

Sam dropped the lead on Alice and put his spurs to Vici. Straight up the mountainside he clambered. Vici sprayed dirt from his hoofs, dodged trees, and clattered across occasional rocks. Up and up and up Sam urged him, spurring and slapping his hindquarters with his hat. For long minutes at top energy Vici gave Sam all his powerful body had to give.

Sam's mind searched for his best chance. He thought it was to get to a divide where more than two canyons dropped away, and maybe fool his pursuers.

He reached a ridge and saw that some of the warriors, starting just a quarter mile lower down, had crossed this spur at a low spot and were pushing their horses up the canyon.

He stopped Vici—the horse was heaving for breath and couldn't do this any longer.

Sam was out of choices. He jumped to the ground, slipped off Vici's bridle and reins, slapped his ass, and sprinted up the hill. Coy squealed once, looked back at Vici, and trotted along with Sam.

From behind came whoops of triumph. That meant some Blackfeet had found the abandoned Alice. After a while he would hear a second round of cries, and that would be a painful moment. Tomás's horse gone.

He ran upward.

And ran.

He stopped and chuffed like a steamboat. Coy panted.

Sam ran.

Finally, he saw a breath of a chance. A red outcropping was split by a vertical crevice. Brush sprouted from the bottom like a beard from a billy goat's chin. The surface between here and there was sandstone. He dashed for the cleft.

He picked up Coy, scrambled up the rock, and dropped behind the brush without disturbing it. He turned sideways and slithered through a narrow place. Coy padded through easily. Beyond that the crack opened out to several feet. Sam checked it farther in and above—in both places it narrowed to finger width.

He looked around. There was debris on the floor, leaves, small limbs, pinecones, and rocks, some of them as big as his head. He started piling up the debris in a way that might look haphazard.

Coy sat and looked at him peculiarly.

Whoops and shouts of delight down the mountain. They had found Vici. Captured Vici.

Sam picked up the single big stone left, hefted it high, and slammed it down on his wall.

SAM SAT. AND sat. And sat.

Coy curled up and napped.

Sam thought, and thought, and thought.

He took an occasional sip from his flask. He poured water into his hat and let Coy lap it up. He listened to the shouts and the war cries. The young warriors invoked their medicine, their invulnerability to projectiles of stone, steel, and lead. They sang songs to make their medicine stronger. Some, he knew, would paint their faces and their horses.

Sam couldn't be skeptical about other people's medicine. He carried the sacred pipe himself. During a sun dance he had seen beyond, and knew that power lived there. But he didn't know exactly what worked and what didn't. He didn't know whether medicine could make a man impervious to arrow, knife, tomahawk, or lead blown out of a barrel. He didn't believe, but he didn't disbelieve.

Part of him thought that medicine was thinking with your heart as well as your head. Using your vision, not just your eyesight.

He knew that smoking the pipe brought him calm and clarity.

Pipe? Damn, I lost my pipe. It was in its bag in his possible sack rolled up in his bedroll on Vici's back.

In the shadows of this cleft he felt a chill.

Calm and clear, he told himself, and he breathed.

Think.

Blackfeet were hostile Indians, always ready to fight everyone, red man or white. They made no alliances, observed no truces, granted no mercy. This band must have been heading south for a visit with the Arapahos, far from their own country, or maybe returning back north. Sam just blundered right into them. Like all Blackfeet they would be bloodthirsty, which was all he needed to know.

He was scared, and his heart hurt. He felt like he'd run away and left his entire life.

I lost my pipe.

I lost Vici.

I still have Coy.

He took inventory of what else he had.

Right in his hands he held a good fifty-caliber rifle—the Celt, his legacy from his father. In his belt a pistol of the same caliber, a tomahawk, a butcher knife, and a throwing knife. Over his shoulder Vici's bridle, reins, and lead—he couldn't get to rendezvous without a horse. In powder horns, two kinds of gunpowder. In his shooting pouch, a bar of lead, a tool to make it into balls, a cloth, a patch knife, and other handy items. Dangling from his neck, his field glass. In the *gage d'amour* that also hung from his neck, flint and steel. The gage d'amour that was the first thing Meadowlark ever gave him.

He had two other weapons, the hair ornament, a gift of Hannibal MacKye, and his belt buckle. The buckle popped out, revealing a wicked-looking blade—Gideon Poorboy had forged it for Sam.

He had his beaver hat, moccasins, leggings, breechcloth, and a cloth shirt. These were not to be thought of lightly, especially the moccasins and hat. He wondered whether the moccasins would take him all the way to rendezvous.

If he ever got out of this crevice.

And he had Coy. Also not to be thought of lightly.

He heard a rat-a-tat-tat of hoofbeats. They roared by.

The riders would be back, with a tracker, going slowly.

No tracks led to this crevice—he had walked up on stone.

Probably they wouldn't inspect this hole in the rocks.

All right, inventory, what did I lose? Not only Vici but his saddle. Alice. A water keg. Bedroll. And in the bedroll, spare clothes, extra moccasins, and a volume of poems by Byron. That book had cost more than a horse.

Options? It was foolish, but he was stuck in a crack in a rock wall with no one to talk to but his rattling mind. He needed to make his mind clear and simple. Usually, he would smoke the pipe to get there. Now he couldn't.

He felt a spurt of anger, bile in his gullet.

Put anger away. Clear and simple.

I can go back over the mountain and wait for my friends to come up.

He played with that in his head.

Or I can steal Vici back and go on to rendezvous.

He didn't have to play with that. He had to go see Esperanza, so he had to steal a horse. Why not Vici?

I want my pipe.

No way to know in such a large camp who had it. No way to find out. Some things you had to put out of your mind.

Vici would be in the horse herd. He began to imagine just how he would steal one of scores of horses. Maybe he could get away undetected leading just a single mount. Maybe he needed to kill a sentry. Maybe . . .

He heard walking horses. Voices. A horse stopped in place, tapping its hoofs and blubbering. The tracker was here. Maybe these warriors would steal his life.

The party moved on.

Sam went back to imagining, and maybe sometimes he dozed. When he woke up, the world was dark.

Twenty-one

By the full moon he inspected the horse herd. It was a huge throng of horses, guarded by young men stationed at several key points. Sam had to circle the herd and get various angles to study it out. He slipped carefully from ridge to creek to hillock, looking. A medicine hat pony would be very distinctive—a white animal with black markings on the head and chest. The white back and rump should gleam in the moonlight.

Sam stole from place to place around the herd all night, careful not to come near any sentries. He glassed the herd from every angle, and he didn't see Vici.

Before dawn he walked downstream, the opposite direction of where the warriors searched for him yesterday. He and Coy bunked among thick willows, and napped in that cover all day.

He slipped back onto the ridge above the herd in the twilight this time, and saw Vici right off. Saw something, in fact, that seared him.

Vici was limping, couldn't bear weight on his left forefoot. Alice grazed nearby.

He sat leaning against a tree and watched Vici and scratched Coy's head. How in hell had this happened? Clearly some warrior had claimed Vici and ridden him and . . . They hadn't come back to camp last night, maybe had bivouacked out somewhere, looking for Sam. Riding your quarry's mount to hunt him down—that must have appealed to him. *Did you abuse my horse, you bastard?*

He thought of what the injury might be, probably a stone or stone bruise in the frog, and that mattered. He thought of how he could get Alice out. He'd have to leave Vici. No way he could get to rendezvous on a lame horse.

AN HOUR BEFORE first light he was in place. Maybe he had it figured out. At least he was going to give it a shot. His one hope was knowing the country. That was worth something. Just upstream was Flaming Gorge, boated by General Ashley when he explored it in 1825—a huge, deep canyon flanked by steep, red walls. Almost impenetrable.

Right now Sam's obstacle was a sentry. The man stood beside a lodgepole pine at the far downstream end of the herd. In the light of the half-moon Sam had watched him with the naked eye and glassed him. Though the fellow never moved, he was clearly awake. A good sentry was dangerous.

Sam and Coy eased through the trees. Sam didn't worry about Coy making noise. If the sentry heard the coyote, he'd think nothing of a song dog moving around at night.

Sam slipped from tree to tree. Maybe the sentry would look back, but the dark trunks and absolute stillness were his protection.

A good sentry didn't lean against a tree because he might fall asleep. Unluckily for him, that meant his back showed.

Sam padded closer and closer. He kept himself calm, which was simple: You accepted in advance that whatever happens, happens.

Putting your feet down quietly, avoiding limbs—all that was easy if you were calm.

Gradually, he crept to within a dozen paces. He stopped. He listened to the night and heard nothing. He watched the still figure and saw nothing unusual.

He drew his big knife, cocked it, and with the confidence of a decade's practice, hurled it.

The sentry's knees buckled. Only a small sound exploded from his lips—*hnnh!* He crumpled to the ground.

Sam ran forward and jerked his knife out of the back. He caught a brief glimpse of the man's face—*I don't have to like necessity*.

He darted into the herd, not running but moving fast. Not much time to get going. Down in the herd he couldn't see well and nearly got disoriented. But he had Vici's spot triangulated, as Jedediah Smith had taught him, and he moved with confidence. The animals stirred, uneasy about a man among them at night.

Sam saw Vici, put his arms around his neck, and breathed easier. He looped the lead onto him. He knelt and lifted his front left leg. He felt a stone in the frog—that explained the limp. Gingerly, he drew it out. Big stone, bad bruise.

He put the leg down tentatively. Sam stood up and patted him. "Sorry, boy," he whispered, "I can't take you along." Which stung.

Now came the tricky part. He walked gently toward Alice, touched her muzzle, looped the lead over her neck. In a flash the bridle was on and the bit in her mouth.

Sam vaulted onto her, raised the Celt into the air, and pulled the trigger. Ka-BOOM!

Now he wanted a riot. "Hi-iy-iy!" he yelled. He ran Alice at nearby horses, he cut back and forth, he bumped shoulders and hindquarters. He raised his pistol and fired again—BOOM!

Alice almost jerked Sam off, not following a cut, but he stayed on her back.

"Hi-iy-iy!" he shouted. He maneuvered to drive some mounts downstream. Sure enough, a bunch took off. "Hi-iy-iy!"

He looked all around. Light was rising back into the world. The sentries probably could see him. Certainly they could see two score of their horses, hightailing it.

"Let's go," shouted Sam. "Hell's a-poppin'!"

He touched his spurs to Alice, and Coy yipped.

"Hallelujah!"

Twenty-two

THE FORTY OR fifty galloping horses cut a trail like the path left by a tornado. But one rider sliding away from the tornado on a stone surface left no trace at all.

That would not be enough, Sam knew. Within an hour the herd would stop running, and the Blackfeet would find it. Soon they would figure out that the thief had not gone beyond that point, but had slipped off onto a side route. Sam needed that head start. He could also do something they wouldn't expect, maybe wouldn't believe. He could descend into Flaming Gorge.

From there he would go the only way possible—across the river. Through Flaming Gorge the river was huge rapids. In June, in the spring flood, only a madman would try to swim it. Or a man who was truly desperate.

When he got to the river, he looked along his back trail and studied the canyon rim and the gullies that led down. He saw no one. It made no difference. To go back up to that rim would be suicide.

He looked at the river. He rode up the river and looked, he rode down the river and looked. The only route was straight ahead, and it was worse than he'd imagined. The waves were enormous, and the rocks were worse. Boulders the size of freight wagons blocked the current. If you got washed up against one . . . And the back side of the big boulders might be more dangerous—the water sucking back up against the rock would pin you there.

The only route was across.

He hunted for a decent ford until he saw the Blackfeet coming fast down a gully.

Out of choices. He kicked Alice downstream and looked again at the least awful of the routes. It looked . . .

Out of choices.

He wondered if Alice would plunge into that water.

He turned and looked back. The Blackfeet had come out of the gully and were galloping on the slanted ground a couple of hundred yards upstream.

Time.

"Let's go, boy," he told Coy.

He kicked Alice, and she charged into the boiling waters.

SAM LIVED A lifetime per minute.

In the first seconds he was amazed at the raw power of the current. He got woozy from the enormous, ice-cold waves battering them. He jammed his attention on the first of the king-sized boulders. He turned Alice downstream to drift below it, and make sure they didn't cut too close behind.

A wave knocked him straight off the horse.

He held on to the reins, got hold of Alice's mane, and heaved himself back up.

By the time he accomplished that, they were thirty or forty paces downstream of where he meant to be. They were rushing up on a huge cottonwood caught on some rocks, with its root ball pointing straight at him.

Madly, he reined Alice back where they came from, then straight downriver. They had no chance to cross above the stranded cottonwood.

The river swept them into the dead, downstream branches. Sam hoped he would just scrape through branches and lose some hide. A big branch knocked him off Alice again, this time straight backward. He lost the reins.

Sam went down. A hoof clipped his forearm. The river pummeled him, churned him, threw him around. He couldn't see. He couldn't breathe.

He banged a knee hard on a boulder and beached like a fish.

Alice was to his left, headed back for the side she came from.

Approaching the bank, the Blackfeet whooped.

Sam dived for Alice, missed, and grabbed her tail. He muscled himself back onto his filly's back, seized the reins, and turned her across the river.

For a couple of minutes they fought obstacles that were merely harrowing. They swam above a boulder the size of a toolshed, drifted below the next one, and swam above several that were only the size of grizzly bears. The waters splashed crazily over them, caught the light, and pitched foam high into the air.

Across and down went Sam and Alice, across and down, picking their way. Alice was wild with fear and exertion. Her mouth frothed and her eyes rolled.

Suddenly, she was on her feet. She clambered across fist-sized stones and soon was out of the water to her hocks—standing in the middle of the river.

Sam turned and looked at the Blackfeet. They launched a bird flight of arrows.

He whacked Alice on the rear, and she plunged back into the current. *You are one plucky horse,* thought Sam.

He saw some arrows streak past. Others plopped into the water nearby. He whaled Alice with his hand.

Quickly, they came up on a boulder with its peak rising out of the water, and angling back like a mountain.

Sam hadn't seen it in time. Straight into the boulder they went.

Sam got tossed downriver.

Alice flipped over the boulder, legs waving in the air.

Sam was swept downstream. He saw another boulder coming, slanting away from him, and rammed himself onto it hard.

Where's Alice?

His eyes scoured the river. Nothing. Over the tumult of the rapid Sam launched his piercing whistle. Nothing.

Suddenly he saw her, far downstream, floating on her side. He whistled as loud as he could. As Alice floated away, she tried to lift her head, and then let it fall back into the water.

A few moments later she floated into a big fir tree that was grounded in the channel. She disappeared under the branches. The tree would pin her to the bottom, and the current would hold her down forever.

No chance.

Sam looked toward the bank and made his choice. He dived into the freezing water and kicked like hell.

Ten paces short of the bank, he swam into an eddy and bobbed gently upstream in the current. Sam reveled in the calm.

He remembered how to breathe. He inspected his knee and his forearm—nothing worse than scrapes and bruises. He turned and looked across the river and upstream at the Blackfeet. He grinned. He climbed up onto a boulder, turned his back to them, dropped his breechcloth, and mooned them.

When he looked at them again, they seemed to be shouting and shaking their fists.

From among them a cloud of white smoke arose, and Sam knew one of them had fired a musket. He knew it wouldn't be accurate at this distance, over a hundred paces.

He waved.

He thought of firing back—amazingly, the Celt was still locked in his hand—but his gunpowder was certainly soaked.

He started checking to see what he might have lost in the river, aside from Alice. The inventory seemed all right. He felt astonished that he'd survived. No body parts were torn off, no essential survival gear missing. Even his field glass was safe inside his shirt.

Then he realized what was gone.

Coy.

Gone.

Twenty-three

Sam walked up and down the bank, from bush to bush, calling out, "Coy! Coy! C'mon, pup! Coy."

Occasionally he launched an earsplitting whistle, but he didn't have any hope for Alice.

He walked for more than a mile downstream, then walked upstream to the point opposite where he'd jumped in. Then he walked a little farther, turned around, and walked the entire mile downstream again. He called to Coy. He whistled again.

By this time night was full on.

He lay down and slept. Coy would probably come back during the night. If Coy was alive, he would find Sam, that was for sure.

That night he dreamed, over and over, of how he met Coy. He'd been walking down the Platte River toward Fort Atkinson, though he didn't know it was the Platte, or where the fort was. He was alone, on foot, and almost out of balls to use for hunting. He was half starving. And he still had five hundred miles to go.

Just to bring things to a fine head, a prairie fire got started. Sleeping in a grove, Sam smelled the smoke, got up, and spied the fire to the northwest—moving straight at him.

He took measure of things. He was too far from the river to run to it, though he could hear animals trying exactly that. Their shapes flitted through the darkness, black ghosts.

The creek. He stepped to the creek and lay down in it. Not deep enough—it left half his body exposed. He tramped around in the dark water, but none of it was more than a few inches deep.

He was about to decide to die bravely when he heard a mewling. He looked toward the carcass of the buffalo cow he'd shot that day. He'd gutted her out, and would butcher her in the morning.

Just then the fire hit the creek a hundred yards up, and the crowns of the cottonwoods lit like torches.

The mewling again. A coyote pup was sniffing and scratching at the slit in the cow's belly.

Sam got the idea. He ran to the cow, picked up the pup, lay down, and wormed his way backward into the buffalo.

Dark. Quiet. Safe? Or would he roast alive?

The trees around him exploded in flames—he could hear the roar, and the popping of branches.

Suddenly his knees burned like the devil.

He rolled over.

In an instant his ass was getting cooked. The pup pissed on him.

He rolled back over and screamed—his knees were frying.

Soon it was over.

He stayed inside the buffalo until morning. Then he and the pup squirmed out and looked at an ashen world.

Among the dead, Sam was sure, was the pup's mother.

He'd gained a companion.

Later, when he told the story, Sam also gained a name, Joins with Buffalo.

But the companion felt more important.

Now, when he woke up this morning, no Coy.

He walked the bank again. By mid-morning he decided to put an end to this self-torture. Under a cover of thin, cobblestone clouds he started out of the gorge.

No Coy, no Alice, no pipe, no hope.

Twenty-four

HE WALKED NORTH and thought about Coy. Drowned? Head bashed in? Leg broken? Why hadn't he heard the pup complaining? Funny to think of him as a pup, since they'd been together ten years, but he was a small coyote.

Sam tramped along. Rendezvous was eleven or twelve sleeps to the north for a full party with pack animals, maybe half that many for a well-mounted man alone and in a hurry. He didn't know how many sleeps for a man afoot.

He hoofed it. Black's Fork came in too full to cross safely. He walked up it for a full day, found a ford, crossed a divide, and got back to the Siskadee.

For two more days he walked under a blazing sun, the next day under halfhearted rain clouds—they dropped sleek lines of dark moisture, but the rain dried up halfway to earth.

He was hungry, but he didn't care. The noise of shooting would be dangerous, and besides, Coy was dead. Sam ate roots, not bothering with a fire. He consumed rose hips until he was weary of them. When he found cattails, he pulled them and ate the soft bottom parts.

Coy, Coy, Coy. Occasionally, he thought of Paladin—he would get his horse back at rendezvous.

He would have to tell his son that Vici was gone, and Alice was dead. Both of Tomás's horses.

Every step, almost, Sam thought of his pup. Then, gradually, his mind turned from what was behind to what was ahead. Esperanza. Flat Dog. Julia. Esperanza.

After a week he stumbled onto the carcass of a buffalo. The wolves or coyotes or ravens had been at it, or all three, and there were only tidbits left. He scraped off the tidbits, built a squaw fire, and broiled them. Muttering a hope that they wouldn't make him sick, he ate the pieces half-burned.

He stayed at the carcass the rest of the day, trying to fill his belly with snippets. That afternoon he also sliced up his hat and snipped some thongs off his leggings. He studied his tattered moccasins with a frown and laboriously tied the strips of felt around them. A poor improvisation, but better than walking barefoot.

He looked at the remnants of the soles of his moccasins. He'd heard men tell of eating their mocs, but what did they eat? Those thin, hard, dry, wretched fragments? No point—nothing there. Maybe they meant they ate the tops. Sam needed the tops.

He put one foot in front of the other and trod north. Every day, ahead and to the right, the Wind River Mountains got closer. Esperanza's village wintered in a warm valley near the head of Wind River. *I am walking to you.*

He saw the Big Sandy come down from South Pass, high on the south end of the Wind River range. He pushed north.

New Fork flowed in across the river. Most times he could have hoofed it to rendezvous in a single day from here, but he was near the end of his string—limping, half barefoot, half naked, scratched, bruised, and gaunt from not eating.

He staggered forward all that day. He would cache tonight, get another chill sleep, and stride into rendezvous tomorrow, erect and proud.

He limped to within a mile of Horse Creek—the camps would be around the mouth—and found a bed of grasses for the night. He was hungry as hell, but he'd eat tomorrow. He was beat up, but he'd feel good tomorrow. Tonight he'd wash in the river, especially to get the blood off the places where he was scratched, and in the morning he would walk in.

He heard hoof clops.

He reached for the Celt and crawled toward a cottonwood trunk.

A pony's head appeared over the bushes, and above its head, the face of a child.

She looked at the scrawny, bedraggled white man. She made a face.

"*Papá?*" said Esperanza.

Twenty-five

SAM'S DAUGHTER SLID down from her pony. "Papá? " She stepped gingerly toward him.

Sam held out his arms to her.

She didn't come into them. She was always a little standoffish. The six-year-old wasn't sure of Sam's place in her life. She solved part of the problem by calling Flat Dog "father" in the Crow language and Sam "father" in Spanish.

"Bang, you're dead," said Flat Dog in English.

Sam grinned at his brother-friend.

"They said you—" said Esperanza in Spanish. Her English was iffy, and her voice now quavered.

Sam felt good to hear the quaver. He stepped forward and swept his daughter off her feet. He held her and gave her a kiss on the cheek, just like a dad.

She wiped it off.

Flat Dog dismounted and offered Sam his hand—the Crow liked that white-man custom.

Sam shook it warmly. "Dead?"

"Tomás came in two days ago, said you should have been here already."

"Something came up," said Sam.

"Not your hair, I see," said Flat Dog.

"Damn near." Sam set Esperanza on her pony.

"Where's Coy?"

"Dead."

Sam saw sadness flush into Flat Dog's eyes. Then he said, "You look like you need something to eat."

"Let's go."

JULIA FED HIM, fed him, and fed him some more. The mountain way was to eat all you could when you got the chance. Some men could eat ten pounds, it was said, at a sitting.

Sam realized he must have been wandering around the desert longer than he realized, and in worse shape. People looked at him like he was a ghost—even Esperanza was leery of him. Now she sat nearby playing with some painted cornstalk dolls packed up from Santa Fé. From time to time she looked half secretly at her papá. Occasionally, she would offer a doll to her cousin Azul, six months younger, and the boy would stab the doll with his toy arrow.

The sun was down behind the western mountains, and twilight took its leisure in the valley of the Siskadee. The light itself seemed blue-gray. The creek curled dark into the river. Cottonwood leaves stirred in a lazy downstream breeze. The desert evening was cooling off. At dark everything would breathe easier.

Sam sat in front of Flat Dog and Julia's tipi—he was no longer a tipi-dweller himself, but theirs felt good to him. While he was here, he would live with them like a brother. That was half comfortable for Esperanza. Flat Dog's younger brother, the one living brother, was one of the ones she called *masaka,* father in the Crow language, so in a way she was already used to having two dads.

Julia handed Sam a cradleboard—no, a baby in a cradleboard. "A boy," she said.

The baby was sucking his thumb in his sleep. The cradleboard made Sam's mind run to Esperanza when she was a month or so old.

"Two months," she said, "Rojo."

"Rojo? First blue, now red? You going for a flag?"

She laughed, took the cradleboard, and hung it from a limb. "While you're here, I'm going to practice my English," she said in English.

Julia was the best woman Sam knew. He and Flat Dog met her at Los Angeles pueblo, and Flat Dog was smitten instantly. The seventeen-year-old Señorita Julia Rubio had tawny hair, golden skin, and green eyes, altogether a mad attraction to Flat Dog. When they looked at each other, even that first time, lightning jumped between clouds.

She was the daughter of a rich don proud of his Californio heritage. Flat Dog's rancho was his tipi.

In a whirlwind Julia eloped with Flat Dog, married him at Mission San Gabriel, and took up the rough trapper life with him. When her father had her abducted and brought home, she cooperated with Sam and Flat Dog in her own rescue and fled with them down the Los Angeles River in a wild flood. While she bore Flat Dog's son in a rainstorm on the bank of the river, Sam and Flat Dog shot it out with her father.

To cap it all, she rode more than a thousand miles with her husband, joined his family in their village of buffalo hide lodges, adopted his sister's daughter, and settled in to become a Crow.

These memories made Sam a little dizzy.

Tomás and Baptiste came trotting up. Sam jumped to his feet and hugged Tomás. His son was only half-comfortable with that. "I'm eighteen," he said the last time Sam hugged him. Both children standoffish, for different reasons.

"What happened?" said Tomás. They all sat down.

Sam looked into his son's eyes. "Vici is stolen. Alice is dead."

Tomás's eyes flamed.

"Let it come out in the whole story before you . . ." Sam waited, and Tomás nodded.

Flat Dog, Julia, Esperanza, Azul, everyone came close to hear the tale.

Sam recounted how he blundered down the creek and onto the Blackfeet, ran away uphill on Vici, had to abandon him and Alice, and hid in a cleft. "I lost my pipe," he said.

Flat Dog nodded. He knew Sam would carry the pipe in a bag behind his saddle, and he knew how serious this loss was.

Sam told briefly of Vici being injured and how he ran part of the herd off and so stole Alice back. He saw that Tomás's eyes got shadowy when he heard about Vici and Alice.

Sam forced himself on. He told in detail of his flight into Flaming Gorge and of the river. "It was damned scary to go into that water. Alice was plucky."

Now Sam used his hands to show how he and Alice swam downstream of a certain boulder, swam hard to cross the current above the next one, and so on. Both of the times he was knocked off Alice got told with high drama, and how he grabbed the mare's tail and clambered back on—amazing in a raging river, everyone agreed. Sam put juice into the story, for Esperanza's sake.

But he couldn't stall forever. He had to tell how he and Alice fetched up on the big rock, she tumbled on over, and floated into the dead fir that sucked her under and held her.

He held Tomás's eyes and took the anger. Then he let himself look at Esperanza. His daughter looked at Sam gape-mouthed, which was an improvement on Tomás.

"*Querida,*" he told her, "a man can't lift a horse pinned by a dead tree with his hands." He didn't need to mention the current too.

Sam watched his daughter as he told the rest of the story. Her skin was a light honey color, her eyes hazel, and her hair a kind of rust brown, one of the colors of lichen growing on rock. He thought she was beautiful, and he saw Meadowlark everywhere in her face and graceful body.

He told how he hunted and hunted for Coy on the bank. Looking directly at his daughter, he spoke of his pain when he realized his companion of ten years was dead, and of leaving without his friend.

He made short shrift of the struggle of walking all the way to rendezvous. He told about finding the buffalo carcass and scavenging a little meat. He saw Esperanza looking at his ribs, which stuck out like rafters. *Oh, well,* he thought, *not always a hero.*

Not to Tomás either. The young man stood up with sulk in his shoulders and walked away. In a couple of minutes he came back leading Paladin. "Here's your horse," he said. "She threw a nice filly. I took care of both of them."

"Tomás, I'm sorry. Vici and Alice . . ." The youth's only horses. "Vici was a great one."

Tomás handed Paladin's reins to Sam and walked away. "Tomás." The youth turned back. "I want you to have Kallie."

Sam's son threw him an icy glare and walked off.

Kallie was a three-year-old mare out of Paladin. Sam had in mind to use her as a trail horse, saving Paladin for buffalo running and trick riding. She wasn't as developed as Vici, but few horses were. Vici was also out of Paladin—he looked just like her—and Tomás had put several years into training her as a buffalo horse and a circus trickster. It would take a lot of time to make Kallie as good as Vici.

Sam rubbed Paladin's ears the way she liked. Then he checked out the new filly. She was pretty, the third of Paladin's offspring with markings just like her mother.

He asked Baptiste, "Where's Joaquin?"

"Staggering around drunk," Baptiste said. "You want to walk, see people?" Friends not seen since last rendezvous. Trading stories, getting the news, finding out who'd gone under and who'd brought off a miraculous escape. Camaraderie warmed by firelight and lubricated with whiskey.

"Tomorrow," said Sam. "I need some rest."

Baptiste nodded, patted Sam on the shoulder, and walked into the evening.

The vagrant got up, said good night to Esperanza, who barely noticed, and led Paladin to the creek. He watched her slurp up the clear, cold liquid, and thought how good she'd been to him for ten years, how hurt he'd be if he lost her. Like Tomás was.

When he'd staked her again by the tipi, he ducked inside. Whoops! He had to stick his head back out and ask to borrow blankets. He stretched out in the tipi. Sleep might not come soon—mountains to the west meant a long twilight—but the blankets felt good. It was strange lying down without Coy at his feet. It would be strange for a long time.

He came awake when Julia put Esperanza and Azul down in the blankets across the fire pit from him. He barely opened his eyes. In the shadows Esperanza lay down, sat up, looked at the man who claimed to be her father, made a face, and flumped her head down.

SAM WOKE IN the predawn light, as was his way. When he looked around, he saw his semiannual packet laid near his head, a letter from Grumble. He picked it up and checked on Esperanza, sleeping contentedly. He wished he could check on her every morning of her life. Then he slipped outside, pulled Paladin's stake, and led the mare down to water. It felt odd for Coy not to walk with them for this morning ritual.

When he'd restaked the mare, he walked over to the tent where his trade goods would be offered during the day. No one was stirring this early. He ducked under the flap, got the lap desk where the records were kept, and took pen and paper. Then he walked down by the creek to read.

Twice a year he heard from Grumble, in December when he got to Rancho de las Palomas, and in July when he got to rendezvous.

Now he would have to send Grumble an address other than the rancho. He didn't know what it would be. Maybe the Young and

Wolfskill store in Taos, for he wouldn't winter in Santa Fé again. He didn't know where he would go from rendezvous. He needed to find Lupe and Rosalita. He needed to get a new pipe, and that would be tricky.

Grumble was the second-oldest friend of Sam's new life, the life he chose in the West.

The first was Hannibal MacKye. When Sam's eighteen-year-old heart was broken by a girl, he ran into the night and to Hannibal's fire. There he got the piece of advice that changed his world: "Everything worthwhile is crazy," Hannibal told him, "and everyone on the planet who's not following his wild-hair, middle-of-the-night notions should lay down his burden, right now, in the middle of the row he's hoeing, and follow the direction his wild hair points."

Sam carried a written-out copy of those words for years, until it fell apart at the creases—carried it even before he learned to read.

The second friend was Grumble. A day or two later the middle-aged con man with the face of a cherub saved Sam from the Pittsburgh police. When they ran and hid, they ended up in the hold of a keelboat that carried them all the way to the Mississippi River, the border of the West. Along the way Grumble taught Sam to be a very junior con artist, and the two of them made a third fast friend, the madam Abby.

Now Abby and Grumble ran a house of music, dancing, dubious games of chance, and ladies of no reputation in Monterey, the capital of California. And Grumble wrote to Sam faithfully twice each year, sending his packets by sailing ship all the way around Cape Horn:

December 26, 1832
at Monterey, a small place of great pretensions

My dear young friend,

This is Boxing Day, the feast of Saint Stephen, the first Christian martyr. When I was a boy in the bishop's house—

An orphan, Grumble had been raised by the bishop of Baltimore—

this was the day when the bishop opened the poor boxes and gave money to the poor. As a clever gesture in his honor (which the good father would be ashamed of), I have always made it a day to give special attention to taking money from those who have too much. In every city of Christendom known to me, and even in this strange if entrancing place, the dens of iniquity are full of sinners the day after Christmas, and their pockets full of money. Since I know you would want it, I will put a tithe of the take into the poor box tomorrow, I promise.

Not that I need to perform any sleight of hand to get pesos. The citizens of this place give them to Abby and me gladly in exchange for our iniquitous services, as do the sailors who frequent the port. In its way this is a cosmopolitan small town, for ships from every port of the world call here continually. And you know that I must have my little amusements.

Grumble was a gambler and con artist of exceptional talent, and Sumner's teacher. Sam knew that these little card games would only whet his appetite. He liked the big cons, such as performing a miracle healing before a crowd and getting a hundred people to pay him to lay hands on them, or staging an elaborate ruse with a helper on a steamboat, getting off, and repeating the con on a different pigeon on the return trip.

Abby has built a fine adobe house in the hills above town, where she lives like a grand lady. As you will suppose, she also carries on in the tradition of the great courtesans. The object of her heart is usually the richest man in the region or the commandante of the presidio. (How does she direct her affections so cleverly?)

My abode is the garret of our cantina. Living in a rabbit hole suits me.

Your friend Gideon Poorboy prospers to a remarkable degree.

Gideon. Which made Sam think of the silversmith's wedding present to him and . . . Paloma, making her way to the shrine of the Virgin of Guadalupe.

Gideon rode peg-legged with Sam to California, and there apprenticed himself to a goldsmith and silversmith who made liturgical objects for the missions.

The señoras have put him in vogue, and he is forever fashioning the gaudy jeweled rings, brooches, and hair ornaments they adore. Now a young woman of good family has claimed him for her own. Instead of losing his pesos to me (I am incorrigible), he rocks and coos an infant son.

California and Californios, I confess, interest me more and more. Their costumes are colorful, their streets drenched in enchantment, and their manner of life languid and sensual. I had not imagined that Catholics could be so blithely unaffected by the stern doctrines of the church.

Monterey Bay, of course, is mesmerizing.

Sam thought it was the most enchanting place he'd ever seen. For him it was also danger and death.

More Americans come to California each year. The Mexicans know that the nation to the east, with its hunger for land, must eventually seize this western coast. Many would prefer American governance to their current subjugation to the whims of Mexico City. Life is easy here—any man can be a prosperous farmer, artisan, tradesman. And California does not have the American madness about color of skin. The races mix comfortably here, and that must increase: More people of different nationalities come with each ship, and more children of mixed blood are born daily. The engine of miscegenation is at work, and will overpower all.

Sam was damn well in favor of that, for the sake of his children.

I confess that I write these semiannual letters in order to get back your news. Please write immediately and start your letter on its long journey by mule pack, riverboat, and sail-powered venturer of the high seas. We long for word of you.

In fact, why don't you just come to see us? It won't cost you either dollars or pesos. You and I could take a ship to San Francisco, or Los Angeles, or San Diego, and filch a year or two of your meager earnings from the officers. Or if you have lost the taste for genuine fun, you could always steal a thousand or two horses from the missions. In any case, COME.

I predict that you will end up living in this clime. A young man with a mixed-blood child would do well to think of California.

Abby sends her love and I my avuncular affections,
Grumble

Sam had to write back immediately. He was late to rendezvous, and the pack train might pull out for the States any day. He dipped his pen and put it to paper—"Dear Grumble and Abby—" He remembered with gratitude that the men who taught him to read and write English in the winter of 1827–28 were Grumble and Hannibal.

This return letter would not be easy. He had to tell Grumble about Paloma's illness and journey of death. But he could also report good news about Esperanza, and Tomás.

As he began to write, he wiggled his right foot, and suddenly realized that Coy wasn't next to it, curled up.

Another loss to confess.

He listened to the bubble-gurgle of the creek and wrote.

Twenty-six

"LUPE AND ROSALITA aren't here," said Tomás.

Baptiste added, "Pegleg isn't here."

"What?" This was a slap in the face. As Julia handed Sam his cup, he sloshed hot coffee onto his hand.

"Nobody's seen them," said Tomás.

"Walkara says they're on their way," said Baptiste.

"But he's a slaver and a liar."

Sam thought.

"We figured you didn't need to hear this yesterday," said Tomás.

Sam smiled inwardly. For Tomás, holding back must have been a struggle.

"So what do you think?"

"We go make the *diablo* tell us," said Tomás.

* * *

Walkara's first words were, "They'll be here."

Sam shook his head. "It's late. We were all late, and they are—"

"My friends, you must be patient."

The so-called friends of the Ute chief waited irritably for an explanation.

"Pegleg," said Walkara, "he is like me. He wants to make a life trading. He wanted to go to rendezvous, to see what an . . . opportunity it might be. He will come."

"A whole month he hasn't showed up," said Sam.

Walkara shrugged. "Pegleg naturally wants much, much to trade. Perhaps he visited the Shoshones to give them our fine horses for their hides. Perhaps he rode across the mountains to the east to see the Arapaho, who would be glad to exchange the furs of animals for horseflesh as good as the Ute people own."

Tomás gave Walkara a disgusted eye, and Sam went along with that.

The chief grinned at them and spread his hands. He was enjoying this. "My friends, let us suppose even further. Maybe Pegleg rode east to find the Comanches. The Comanches like to buy women, and your sisters are fine ones."

"You son of a bitch."

"The Comanches also like to sell women and children. Maybe Pegleg went looking for a bargain. I know he liked your sisters, but a man gets tired of any woman."

Sam seized Tomás by the arm. He was surprised he didn't have to catch the youth in mid-charge.

"Well," said Sam, "Walkara. You think maybe Pegleg went to Taos?"

Tomás's head jerked sideways at his father. This would really get his goat.

Walkara shook his head no. "The great trade fair in Taos takes place in the autumn," he said.

The chief and the beaver men stared at each other. Then the trappers stalked off.

"You are always welcome at my lodge," called Walkara. "The coffee is always hot for you."

When they were well out of hearing, Sam said, "What do you think?"

"The ass wanted to come and be introduced at rendezvous by someone well known, and he used us," said Tomás.

"Yeah," said Sam.

"But any of it might be true," said Baptiste.

"Yeah."

They trod along in disgruntlement.

"Here's something else," offered Sam. "Pegleg ran into the same Blackfeet village I did and got captured." He didn't have to add, *The men are dead and the women are captives.*

Each man padded along on this thought for a while.

"What do we do?" asked Tomás.

"Wait," said Baptiste.

More steps.

"Yes," said Sam, "wait. Maybe they'll show up."

"Waiting makes my belly boil," said Tomás.

"SOUNDS TO ME like one horse is pulling you east and one pulling you west," said Flat Dog.

"Eat," said Julia. She put a bowl into Sam's hand. The pot was already hanging over the fire, filled with the same meat and roots and onions he'd gobbled up last night.

"East and west?" said Tomás.

Julia gave him food in place of an answer, and handed the same to Baptiste.

"One is, he needs to find your sisters," said Flat Dog. He said nothing about the other.

Tomás gave his father a querying look.

"We'll talk about it later. Where's Joaquin?"

"Wherever he fell down drunk."

"Chasing poontang," added Baptiste.

"You know," said Tomás, "that son of a bitch Walkara pushed us like hell getting here. Now he goes around like a king. If he gets his way, he'll be the Emperor of the Southwest."

"I said eat." She put a second bowl into Sam's hand. "You're gaunt."

Sam ate three full bowls.

"You walk around rendezvous," said Baptiste. "Tomás and I will start the trading. We'll sell out today. Good prices. Money is flowing like whiskey."

Sam cocked an eye at his friend. Baptiste grinned. "You'll see why."

Sam wandered through the Rocky Mountain Fur camp. Sam and Flat Dog had worked as trappers for this outfit for most of a decade. Until recently it was the only sizable company in the mountains. Now they had competition from the American Fur Company. Draconian competition, Grumble would have called it.

Sam had gone to the first rendezvous in 1825 and every one since. This one, he soon found out, was the most peculiar.

Sam meandered among the tipis, tents, and brush huts dotting the bottomland along the creek. Men were either sleeping off their drunks or rousing themselves to morning coffee. Tonight would approach riot, but now all were stuporous. Four dozen or so employees of Rocky Mountain Fur, those who brought the pack train, were organized into messes. Here groggy men had fires going, perking the coffee and reheating whatever they had for dinner. Sleeping figures were scattered everywhere in blankets, the chance of rain in mid-July being next to nothing. Last night's women were gone back to their own camps, mostly the Shoshone circle. Through the trees Sam could see their lodges, tipi poles like spears against the sky.

Three big camps elbowed each other along the river, above and below where the creek came in—Rocky Mountain Fur, American Fur, and the Shoshones. Maybe three hundred trappers altogether had arrived, some with wives and children. Some weren't white men but Delawares, Iroquois, and French Canadians, yet they were thought of as "us." The Indians were a big lot of Shoshones, plus some Crows, Flatheads, Nez Perces, and others. Somewhere up and down the creek they all herded horses and mules along the creek or river, and kept an eye on them. Rendezvous was a gigantic truce, but it was also a show-off and a king-sized competition. Some of the Indians thought stealing horses was fine sport.

"You risked your life foolishly," said a voice. The accent reminded Sam of Grumble's when he was doing his fake Englishman.

"Do that near every day," said a soft Virginia tongue. "Hey, Ol' Sam," Joe Meek went on, "set with us."

Joe and a stranger sat before a low fire and big coffeepot. Sam joined them.

"The captain here is trying to reform my ways. My drinking habits, I mean."

"I say," said the stranger, "William Drummond Stewart here, captain, Fifteenth King's Hussars."

Sam shook the outthrust hand and said his own name, which seemed bare naked next to Stewart's. But at least a plain American knew better than to stand between Joe Meek and whiskey at rendezvous.

Sam liked Meek a lot. He was a Virginian with sweet, slow speech and an easy manner that tricked you, because he was the devil's own fool. Joe Meek would do anything—ride straight at Indians and dare them to shoot him, or leap off a galloping horse's back, grab a tree limb, and do a flip over the limb and back to the ground—Sam had seen Joe do more wild stunts than any man in the mountains, and have more fun doing them.

"You hear about the crazy wolf?" asked Joe.

Sam shook his head.

"Rabid, definitely," said Stewart.

Sam had trouble keeping a smile off his face. These Brits' accent always tickled him.

"Coupla nights ago, mebbe three, a white wolf come into camp. Drooling it was, real gaunt, it comes right here and bites three men. So Cap'n Stewart here, he rides on into camp that same night and finds me passed out right next to the path with the wolf's tracks.

I might have had a few too many, or maybe a whole lot too many. It was a long winter."

"So I have asked my friend Joe here, 'Why must you get so drunk? Or if you do, then put yourself somewhere safe. Had that wolf noticed you—it must have passed directly by your prostrate form—it could easily have mauled you as well as others.' "

Joe grinned and shrugged.

"Those bites are usually fatal."

"Well, Cap'n, I allow as how that wolf might have killed me. Blackfeet couldn't do it, nor starving till I ate my moccasins—them things didn't do it—but that wolf, he might have got the job done.

"On the other hand—I'm showing I can learn to talk the way you do—have you considered this? I was so full of whiskey, my blood so brim full with the juice of fire, I might have cured the wolf!"

Stewart snorted and shook his head. Then he turned a proper smile to Sam. "Morgan, where are you in from?" That lingo showed that the Brit was picking up a normal way of talking, not like however he conversed over tea in some castle. The man's swaddling clothes were probably silk.

They told their stories. Then Sam wandered on and soon found Tom Fitzpatrick and his boy Friday preparing the day's trading.

"Mornin', White Hair."

Sam liked to tease Fitz about his hair. A year ago, on the way to rendezvous, Fitz endured an adventure like the one that Sam just went through, and arrived in worse shape—was found unconscious on the riverbank, in fact. That harrowing episode turned his hair from red to white overnight.

"Mornin' back to you. Glad to see your white hair. Heard you'd joined the immortals."

"They let me pass by," said Sam. "This time."

Fitz turned back to setting items out, a cornucopia of the products of industrial enterprise, hauled to the far Rocky Mountains.

"Sublette and Campbell brought a hundred twenty mules this year, loaded with two hundred fifty to three hundred pounds apiece," Fitz said. "Wonder if there's anything left in St. Louis."

"Manufactured goods," said Sam with a hint of irony in his voice. He'd always been uneasy about factories.

"Indians have their medicine," said Fitz, "we have ours."

They were the oldest of mountain friends. When they were taking the furs down the Platte River the spring of '24, each of them got separated from the main outfit and ended up walking the same seven hundred miles to Fort Atkinson to get saved, neither knowing about the other.

"So you and me, we've run the gauntlet again," Fitz said.

"Seems crazy," said Sam.

"Mountain luck."

Men who risked their lives together, got attacked by the same enemy, nearly lost their lives to the same winter winds and the same starving times—only those men were welded together like Sam and Fitz.

"Things are getting damned hard," said Fitz. He was one of the owners of Rocky Mountain Fur, and the brains of the operation.

"Baptiste and Tomás said goods are selling highest ever."

"Shinin' times," said Fitz ironically. "We've marked them up several hundred percent. But there's a rub, lad. Hell, enough rubs to take a man's hide off. I've paid as much as nine dollars a pound for beaver."

The usual price was four dollars.

Sam grinned. "Sort of balances out."

"Balances to losses," said Fitz. "It's the damned monopoly." He meant American Fur. "They aim to hound us into the grave." Last year American Fur Company had followed Rocky Mountain Fur all over the trapping country, obliging Rocky Mountain Fur to teach them every creek and beaver dam.

"Their new devilment," Fitz went on, "is to pay high for beaver and give unbelievable wages. They've got John Jacob Astor's cash to spend forever; we don't. Sad lot the fur men will be, when it's only Astor calling the tune."

"And here I thought the mountain life was supposed to be fun," said Sam.

"Way things are going, more fun for the trappers than the owners. Well, top trappers like you."

Sam looked at him.

"I need you, Sam. I want to hire you before they do. I can offer a year's contract at a hundred twenty-five dollars a month."

"What?"

"You heard me."

Fifteen hundred dollars a year. Sam had signed on a decade ago for fifteen dollars a month.

"The best men can get that. I'll hire your boy, too. Tell Baptiste I can pay him until my brains run out my nose."

Sam had to chuckle. "The privileges of owning your own business," he said.

Fitzpatrick shrugged. "Are you in?"

"I'll talk it over with Tomás and Baptiste," Sam said. "We've got something going."

"Just don't go to work for Astor," said Fitz.

"No."

Sam stood up to wander on.

"You know Beckwourth did it, just that?"

Sam turned back to Fitz. "He wouldn't."

"He's with the Crows up on the Big Horn, cajoling them to take their trade to American Fur."

Beckwourth, the mulatto, had also stood shoulder to shoulder with Sam and Fitz and Gideon Poorboy in the early days.

"I guess a man's got to look out for himself," said Sam.

"Some do only that," Fitz said in a sour tone.

"Where's Milton?" Meaning one of Fitz's partners in Rocky Mountain Fur.

"Tent right over there. Campbell's talking to him, no doubt scragging at him for money. Bill's on the upper Missouri building trading posts." Though Milton and Bill Sublette were brothers, they were owners of different outfits: Rocky Mountain Fur, which hunted, and Sublette and Campbell, which freighted the hides to St. Louis.

"Posts?" A new way of doing business.

"That's the word. You going to see them, I'll stroll along. Bow and scrape and play the peasant."

"They're our friends."

"Milton is my friend. Campbell is a bloody Scot."

"He's Irish."

Fitz gave Sam an odd look. "His family comes from Ulster. Campbell is a Scottish name, and he's a Prot." Sam looked so puzzled that Fitz added, "Protestant. No Irishman."

Fitz extended a ruined hand, and Sam helped him up. "All this and a jug will get a man drunk." The hand got crippled when a gun blew up.

"What has it come to, when a friend and a Prot own an Irishman's arse?"

ROBERT CAMPBELL, MILTON Sublette, and Milton's wife Mountain Lamb, as it happened, were playing host to Walkara. The big chief sat cross-legged in front of the low fire, stirring heaping spoonfuls of sugar into his black brew. Though all the men should have been preoccupied with sneaking glances at Mountain Lamb, considered the most beautiful woman in the mountains, the smell of the scene was greed. When Sam sat down, he felt like he was sitting with vultures hovering close to get the most meat off a corpse.

"Greetings, my friend Sam," said Walkara in English, like nothing had happened between them. "I present to these men to bring trade to me like rendezvous."

"We trade with this man," said Sublette, nodding at Fitz. "Him only. Monopoly."

"Mo-no-po-ly?"

"He's the only one we sell to."

"And he sells to all the trappers."

"That's the way the world works," said Fitz.

"Monopoly," repeated Walkara. Sam could see him figuring it out. We share the carcass and keep you away.

Walkara shrugged. "Then I trade in Taos."

"I'll buy your furs," said Fitz.

Walkara shook his head. He didn't know the words, but he understood the difference between wholesale and retail. "Taos." Now he looked craftily at Sublette. "Maybe I trade you slaves."

"Slaves?"

Walkara nodded. "Navajo, maybe Apache, maybe Mexican slaves. Women, good-looking women, and children."

Sam glared at Walkara, and the chief threw back a lecherous smile.

"We ain't in that business," said Milton.

Walkara laughed. He seemed to think everything in life was a joke, maybe a wicked joke. He shrugged and said, "Business is business." He got up and gave a big grin. "We all of us do business someday. We all get rich together." He walked off.

Mountain Lamb brought the coffeepot. Sam, Fitz, Milton, and Campbell eyed each other over their cups. For Sam the fair-haired Irishman—well, the Scot Prot—always seemed hard to get next to.

Sam didn't know Milton as well as he knew his brother Bill. In Sam's first year in the mountains he, Bill, and Jim Clyman had got caught out overnight and damn near froze to death. In the morning Clyman saved them by finding a live coal the size of a kernel of corn in the previous night's fire.

Now Campbell told Fitz, "I was asking Milton if you have funds to pay your notes."

Fitz threw Sam a sardonic glance. "Don't know how many packs we'll get." Or what he'd have to pay for them in trade goods.

"We are your freighters with pleasure," said Campbell, "but your bankers only with reluctance."

Sam knew that Sublette and Campbell charged fifty cents a pound for freighting the year's furs from rendezvous to St. Louis.

As Campbell pressed Fitz and Milton about the debt, Sam got up and left. He hunted beaver when he liked and where he pleased and did a little trading on the side. A businessman had worries—a free trapper didn't. Except for those horses pulling him east and west.

Twenty-seven

DUSK. HIGH MOUNTAINS to the west, their summit ridges sharp and dark against a sky fading away from bright blue. Higher mountains to the east, realms of eternal cold. Cool air washing down the alpine slopes into the valley of the Siskadee. Sam sat with his feet in the river, and even in midsummer the cold water brought to him the first hint of the coming of autumn, and beyond that, winter.

The air was changing color, sliding from the gold of twilight to the blue-gray of evening. An hour ago he watched the yellow sunlight flickering on aspen leaves—now the light was silver, and soon the leaves would hang dark and still. He thought how the aspens in a few weeks would turn golden, or even flame-colored, and how the dwarf oak, higher up, would go from green to scarlet. Autumn in high places.

Paladin flabbered her lips in the edge of the river. Sam looked at her affectionately, and thought of the companion who wasn't here,

Coy. He wondered about Lupe and Rosalita, torn away from their worlds. He pondered Tomás and his relentless anger.

He shook his head to chase away the mood. He lifted his kaleidoscope to his right eye. Some of his personal belongings had been packed up on the mules and didn't end up on the bottom of the river. He was glad about the kaleidoscope. Looking at it was a trip into a special world.

He turned the cylinder, entranced. Now, in the twilight, the pictures seemed different, less dazzling and more velvety. He could look into the kaleidoscope for a long time.

He chuckled to himself. The meaning of life, the old Mexican told Hannibal. Odd, the interior of the kaleidoscope did feel like a church. *But damned if I find any meaning.*

Now the light in the valley took on a lavender sheen. The pine forest on the mountainsides threw deeper shadows. Not even the moon or stars were out yet, in a sky crumbling from blue to black. An inner door opened to emptiness and solitude.

SUDDENLY SAM MADE a conscious decision—not now. Rendezvous was his big annual party. Instead of feeling melancholy, he needed to wrap the camaraderie of the summer get-together around himself like a warm cloak. He put on his moccasins, led Paladin to the tipi of Flat Dog and Julia, and sat a few minutes with Julia and Esperanza. His daughter scratched in the dust with a stick and then put big pony beads into the little rut. Sam saw that she was making a face in the dirt and wondered whose it was. Probably Old Woman's Grandchild or other Crow heroes from the mists of time, ones she'd heard stories about.

"I'm going to the dance," he said.

Julia gave him a big smile. "Bring my husband home before he gets into trouble."

By chance Flat Dog was the first person Sam recognized at the big circle. They smiled at each other. Flat Dog was as good a man as he knew, solid, dependable, lots of times funny, always a fellow to ride the river with. They'd trekked from the eastern edge of the Rocky Mountains to the Pacific Ocean and back together, and from Flathead Lake in the far north to Mexico's Gila River. Now the two of them started wandering around the circle, looking at all the beaver men and Indians dressed up for the dance.

Everyone was decked out handsomely, the Shoshone men especially fine. They wore their buffalo robes, painted with colorful depictions of battles they'd fought and other great events of their lives. Their leggings showed thongs of beaded buckskin so long they trailed the ground a foot behind. In their right hands they bore fans made from the entire wings of golden eagles. In the crooks of their left arms they carried muskets in sleeves of blanket, fringed. Their hair, glossy black, fell to their shoulders. Their faces were painted according to the medicine they had seen on their quests for visions.

Smiling, Sam thought to himself that they were really military officers in dress uniforms at a fancy ball.

All the Indian women were splendid. They wore elk hide dresses tanned café au lait. The capes of the dresses were ornamented with the white tails of the ermine, and the bodices showed off beadwork in bright colors and elaborate geometric shapes. From the fringes at the hems of the dresses dangled bells, which made music when they walked. When they danced—soon now—the bells would make a great, jingling rhythm, one song of many feet.

Sam looked at the young Shoshone near him. Her face was rouged brightly with vermilion, and the center part in her hair inked scarlet. Her dress was sheepskin, tanned white. Her hair was rubbed glossy with a blend of oils and herbs she probably made herself, and brushed with many, many strokes by her sisters.

Sam and Flat Dog wandered on and came to a hand game. In the center of the circle of players Tomás was dancing and singing and deftly manipulating the fox bone that was the talisman of the game. Apparently he was on a roll—he had won a pile of beads, a blanket, and several knives. Now he laid down a string of Russian blues, faceted beads that were much prized, in front of a young, beautiful Shoshone woman. The woman's luck had been running bad, because she sat half naked, covered only by a trapper's cloth shirt. The men in the circle, Joaquin among them, watched avidly.

The woman slipped out of the shirt and put it next to the Russian blues. Tomás pointed at the beaded belt, the last hint of clothing she wore. She took it off and laid it next to the shirt. She was mesmerized. Sam wondered whether she was transported by alcohol or entirely by the gambling itself.

Now Tomás went back into his act. He sang, he chanted, he danced, he made wild rhythms with his voice—all this to fog the mind of the woman. At the same time he played with the carved bone. He held it out for the woman to see. He hid it in one fist. He brought his hands together, opened them in a clasp, and closed them back into a fist—the bone might have changed hands, or it might not. Over and over he did this, laughing at the Shoshone and looking at her with wild eyes.

Finally, he threw his fists apart. The silence felt like an exclamation. He looked his challenge at the naked woman—make your choice.

She thrust out an arm, indicating that her bet was that the bone was in the dancer's right hand.

Tomás opened the hand. Empty. Joaquin cheered.

Tomás picked up the beads, shirt, and belt, and set them with his own belongings. Then he lifted the loop of beads with a finger, held them out to the woman, said a few words, and beckoned with a hand.

The woman got up, her bare skin aglow with the light of the nearby campfire.

Tomás handed the fox bone to another gambler, threw Sam a sardonic glance, and led the naked woman out into the darkness, one arm around her waist.

Joaquin's eyes followed the two of them avidly, and Sam knew where this evening would end for him as well. Sam was all mixed up. He wished Tomás didn't do things like this, and wished he himself felt like doing them.

Half an hour later Sam saw the same Shoshone woman, again

sitting in the circle, again gambling, dressed in nothing but the Russian blues around her neck.

AS THE STARS began to gleam, the music rose—fiddling. That meant feet would also rise and fall, and spirits would rise. Good times on the strut. Sam walked to the tent where his outfit's belongings were pegged down for the night, slipped in, got his tin whistle, and followed his ears to the jig.

It was Fiddlin' Red—Sam loved the man's playing. Red had such a patriarchal beard that he used it as a pad for the fiddle, both above and beneath. He knew how to moderate a couple of jigs with a ballad and set feet twinkling again with a reel. When Red played, people danced.

Sam sat on a boulder to listen and watch.

A voice in his ear: "And why, do you suppose, does God leave the likes of us above the ground?"

Sam turned his head right into the grinning-fool face of Robert Evans. The old friends grabbed each other by the shoulders.

"I came out with Fontenelle," said Evans, meaning the caravan captain for American Fur. "I yearned for a taste of mountain water again."

"Long time," said Sam.

Both of them knew how long, and didn't want to talk about it. Sam last saw Evans when the Irishman left the rendezvous of 1830 with Jedediah Smith to go back to the States. Evans and Diah had decided, for different reasons, that the settlements were the place for them. Evans had in mind "a bit of an easier life," he said, "with no Blackfeet in sight."

Jedediah's reason was more complicated. One black midnight—talking at Sam on a roll, like he was drunk, which Diah never was—Diah turned the conversation to confession. He acknowledged to Sam that he was a sinner. "If I don't turn myself over to the care of a Christian church," he said, "I will lose my soul."

The darkness in his eyes hinted that he'd already lost it.

"Diah, I can't help wondering what grievous sin you've committed."

It was said lightly, but Sam could see it struck a nerve. He waited to hear, keeping a smile off his face. Of all the men in the mountains, only Diah never drank, never brawled, never chased women, and always sought peace rather than war with the Indians. While the other men caroused, Diah read his Bible, wrote in his journal, and drew his maps of the West. The man was righteous. As far as Sam was concerned, that was one of his shortcomings.

"There are sins of the heart, Sam." Diah stared into the forest. "Sometimes I fear I'm giving my heart, where Jesus Christ should reign—maybe I'm giving dominion over my soul to other powers." Diah paused long before he added, "The wilderness, it has a hold on me." He smiled to himself and made a play on words. Pronouncing the word to rhyme with *child,* he said, "Let's call it wi-i-i-ldnerness."

Sam heard the haunting in his voice and said nothing, not a word. Nothing anyone could say.

Captain Smith led the annual caravan back from the wi-i-i-lderness to St. Louis, bought a fine house, welcomed his brothers to join him there, and settled down to the life of a respectable man. Diah's profits from fur trading were enough to keep him comfortable for life.

But he got restless. After arriving in St. Louis in October, he was already headed west again in April. Trading, this time, not trapping—bound for Santa Fé. Then, if he felt like it, he told his partners Bill Sublette and David Jackson, he might take a trading caravan on to Chihuahua, or even Mexico City.

It seemed that civilization wasn't enough for Jedediah. Maybe his soul was safer in church, but he had itchy feet, or a roving mind, or a wayward heart.

Tom Fitzpatrick brought back the word to the fur men in the mountains. Diah's outfit had tried the Cimarron Cutoff, a dry crossing. When they began to get desperate for water, Diah rode out ahead, alone as always, to find a water hole.

They never saw him again, nor heard from him.

Several weeks later his guns showed up in Santa Fé. Some Mexicans had traded for them from the Comanches. And the Comanches told the story of how their young men chanced on a lone white rider at a water hole, drinking, and surrounded him, and . . .

No one ever found his body. His bones bleached in the sun, and his flesh dried in the winds. Maybe a lone coyote sang a song for him. Sam hoped so. That's what a song dog was for.

Now, in the darkness of another rendezvous, stirred by the fiddling, alive with comradeship, Sam and Evans spoke not a word of yesterdays. Sam thought, *The devil take the past.*

"Let's make some music with Red," said Evans.

Evans himself had given Sam the tin whistle and taught him to lift his spirits with it.

They sat at Red's feet and tootled along. When he bowed out a sad song, they played a high, floating obbligato in harmony. When he switched to a quick tempo, Evans played the melody and Sam sang, or vice versa. They had a fine time through many tunes, and Sam was about to turn in when Evans said, "'Tis our duty to play the captain's song."

He stood up. "Mountaineers and friends," called Evans, "we propose to sing a song to a great leader who has crossed the divide. Here is 'The Never-ending Song of Jedediah Smith.'"

The trappers cheered. They knew the song well, and they liked the way it bounced along—nothing maudlin about this one. Some of them had even helped write it. The members of Diah's first California brigade made up the verses as they wandered through the desert toward the western shore, not knowing where the devil they were going or how to stumble their way back. Just writing a song lifted their spirits.

Sam, Evans, and Red launched in vigorously.

We set out from Salt Lake, not knowing the track
Whites, Spanyards and Injuns, and even a black
Our captain was Diah, a man of great vision
Our dream Californy, and beaver our mission

(chorus)
Captain Smith was a rollickin' man
A wanderin' man was he
He led us 'cross the desert sands
And on to the sweet blue sea

The song told of their first trip to Californy, when they wandered, starved, and thirsted until "we got to drink mud," and even ate fleas.

It spoke of California, a life of pure ease. Only one problem—they couldn't get home.

It recounted the journey of just three men over the snowbound Sierra and the parched desert. One of them collapsed. They covered him with sand, and that evening Diah carried water back to him, "good as his word. Die? That's absurd."

It told the story of their triumphant return to rendezvous, and the huzzahs for Captain Smith, who brought them through.

Then came the stanzas Sam and Evans penned later, when Diah's never-ending song found an end.

On the Santa Fé Trail, it was four years after
The men came to trouble, they couldn't find water
Jed Smith rode ahead to find the Cimarron
He found the Comanch, their eyes hard like stone

Not a living man knows where his bones are a-bleaching
His flesh, it is dust that drifts in the haze
The life that he lived is all that needs preaching
The coyotes on the night wind are singing his praise

Sam let his throat close. He put down his whistle. They sang the entire song once at the rendezvous of '32 and now at this one—he supposed they would sing it as long as there were rendezvous. It felt good that something would last, for a while.

But now he felt a yearning. He put down his whistle, stood up, caught all his breath, and exploded forth a volcano of coyote yawps. Completely mad they were, these bestial yowls. He entered into a coyote, felt its heart, let its blood become his blood. He looked out at the world through coyote eyes and HO-O-O-O-WLED.

Evans joined him, sounding just as wild.

As one the trappers jumped in. They crooned, they roared, they bayed, they bawled.

From inside the coyote mind, with coyote voice, Sam cried louder and louder.

Other voices fell away, but he didn't notice.

People murmured. They tapped each other on the shoulder and pointed, and one by one they all stopped.

Robert Evans halted and gazed intently at Sam.

When Sam didn't notice, but just howled louder and stronger, Evans grasped Sam's arm. Softly, he said, "Look before you."

Sam shook his head, trying to come back from another realm, to return to being ordinary Sam Morgan, here in this place, now in this time.

"Be quiet and look before you," repeated Evans.

It was listening that told the story. When Sam fell silent, one voice still cried out. In that voice, as in the voices of song dogs everywhere, was all the longing in the world, and all the knowing of loneliness.

Sitting on his haunches, his face lifted to the night sky, crooning for everything that is soul-felt, crouched Coy.

Stunned, Sam walked forward, fell onto his knees, and hugged his friend.

Coy licked his face.

Twenty-eight

COY HAD A broken leg, the right front.

Sam roused Esperanza the next morning, thinking she'd like to help take care of it. Mountain medicine, hook by crook. Azul followed her out of the tipi.

Coy hopped around behind Sam three-legged. "Look," Sam told the kids, "he's skinny, way skinny. When your mom gets meat out, you can feed him by hand. A lot. Not just today but tomorrow and every day."

Sam squatted and patted the ground. Coy came to him and sat. Sam held the coyote with one hand and felt the bone with the other.

Someone said, "Let me do that."

Sam started. The speaker was with Joaquin. Both of them looked like they'd boozed all night and forgotten to sleep

"This is my friend Peanut Head," said Joaquin. Peanut Head was a burly youth with a head the shape and color of a peanut. His scalp was discolored and slick as a shelled nut, as though disease had made it barren. His face was equally hairless. His chin and forehead seemed to jut out, leaving his face receded.

"You look like the man in the moon," said Esperanza.

"Shush," Sam told his daughter.

Peanut Head smiled and made a silly face at her.

"I've been around farmyard animals all my life," he said. He stooped and felt the leg in a tender way. "Leave it be. I'll come back in a few minutes."

He set off, and Joaquin sprawled on the ground. The kids petted Coy and cooed soothing words to him.

Before long Peanut Head was back with a strip of green deer hide and what looked like a broken wiping stick from a pistol. Sam held Coy, Esperanza stroked his head and scratched his ears, and Azul smoothed his tail. Peanut Head cut thongs off his own leggings, laid the rod along the lower leg, fitted the deerhide tight around leg and rod, and wrapped the thongs tight and tied them. It was done quickly and well. Coy squealed, but he didn't try to get away.

"When the hide dries," Peanut Head said, "it will hold."

"Hold," said Joaquin blearily.

"Does that hurt?" asked Esperanza.

"Yes," said Sam, "it probably hurts a lot."

Sam let Coy up, and he hopped around on three legs, just as he'd done before.

"If the bone knits," Peanut Head said, "he'll eventually put weight on it."

"Weight on it," echoed Joaquin.

Sam picked up the coyote and held him in his lap. Coy snuggled in.

Flat Dog and Julia came out of the tipi, Julia carrying Rojo on his cradleboard. She hung the baby from a limb. Sam introduced Peanut Head to them. He spoke politely, and bore himself with a gravity beyond his years.

"Imagine," Sam said to Esperanza, "what this little fellow has been through. Alice and I nearly got washed away by that river. Coy must have hit something hard with that leg, probably a boulder. Somehow he swam through the rapids and got to shore."

Azul made a roar like rapids and mimicked big waves with his hands. The kids had crossed swift rivers with their entire village when traveling.

Flat Dog joined in. "Coy must have laid on that shore for a long time—he was worn out by the river, for sure."

"I was exhausted," said Sam. "Coy, he must have been out cold on that bank. Otherwise he would have heard me calling. I walked up and down looking for him twice."

"You went off and left him?" asked Esperanza.

"Yes," said Sam. "I thought he was dead. That hurt a lot."

Esperanza looked at Sam with widened eyes. She reached for Flat Dog's hand and said, "Papá."

That bothered Sam.

Julia poured a round of morning coffee, including Joaquin and Peanut Head. Then she cut up Jerusalem artichokes, wild onions, diced elk meat, put those in the kettle with water, and hung the kettle from the tripod over the fire. Breakfast.

"Sooner or later," Sam went on, "Coy began to walk. Three-legged."

Joaquin hopped around the fire on hand and knees, one hand in the air. He looked comical, and the kids laughed.

"How did he find us?" asked Azul. He was practical-minded.

"He probably found the place I slept by smell. Then he followed my scent all the way here."

Joaquin mimicked sniffing the ground and following a trail. The kids pointed and giggled.

"It was ten sleeps from there to here," Flat Dog said, "a lo-o-ong way, and it took Coy more sleeps."

Esperanza's eyes rounded and got big.

"Following my odor all the way. Coyotes have really good noses," he told his daughter. "You and I couldn't do that."

"Milagro," said Esperanza.

"Yes," said Sam. "In English *milagro* means 'miracle.'"

She looked at him strangely.

He went on in English, knowing it was good for her. "Now you want to work with the horses?"

THEY'D STARTED WHEN Esperanza was four. She showed good balance on her pony, and Sam thought learning some tricks would be fun. Now they spent half a day running through the routines, Flat Dog practicing on his specialty and Sam drilling Esperanza and Azul on their ponies. Esperanza's was named Vermilion. Tomás watched sullenly. The mount he'd trained was gone for good.

Baptiste brought his harmonica, because Esperanza's pony was used to working to music.

Joaquin and Peanut Head hung around and applauded the kids a lot.

"Sam," Esperanza said when they were finished, "can we do it? Can we parade?" As an afterthought she added, "Papá?" She remembered to call him that when she really wanted something.

Sam thought. "All right," he said, "let's try it." Things might go awry, but only the few Crow families would see.

First Sam took the two kids and walked through the Rocky Mountain Fur camp so they could see some of the fun. Some men were running foot races, two-on-two competitions, challenge the winner. They watched Jim Bridger win two straight races.

Sam raised a hand to him, and Jim said, "'Lo, Sam, good to see ye above the ground." In 1823 Jim had been a man in disgrace. Left to bury Hugh Glass, he abandoned the wounded old man and then told everyone Glass died, as he was supposed to. The story fell apart when Glass showed up in a fury. Bridger had since proven himself over and over. That was why he was a respected brigade leader and one of the owners of Rocky Mountain Fur.

Other men wrestled, which Sam hurried the children past, because it could get rough. Everything but eye-gouging was allowed.

Several men were competing as rifle marksmen. They fixed a

playing card to a cottonwood and shot at fifty paces. When they all hit the card, Old Bill Williams proposed that they shoot at the horseshoe nail that pinned the card to the tree. The first shooter hit the nail. Sam, Esperanza, and Azul walked on.

They found other men vying to show who could jump the farthest. When Joe Meek's turn came, he ran fast toward the starting mark, did a cartwheel, bounded on two feet into the air, and did a complete flip before landing upright. Though he didn't go the farthest, the competitors gave him the prize by acclamation.

Esperanza said, "I want to do that."

"Me," said Azul. "Me."

Maybe we could go on tour with a family of acrobats and trick riders, Sam thought. But he didn't mean it.

When the sun angled down and people gravitated back toward their own lodges, Sam, Flat Dog, Tomás, Baptiste, Joaquin, and Peanut Head gathered willow branches and built a ring fourteen paces across in the middle of the Crow circle. Then Sam alerted the people while the riders brought their mounts.

Sam strode to the center of ring. "Everybody watch!" he barked like a circus ringmaster. "Here come the medicine riders!"

He made arm motions, and Baptiste blew some entry music. All three horses entered the ring parallel. Both kids came without saddle or bridle, but Flat Dog had full equipment plus bows and arrows.

Sam waved his arms in a certain pattern, and the horses shifted from a walk to a canter around the ring. Another wave and they reversed direction. A third motion and they ran to the center and loped in a tight circle. Sam's arms and Baptiste's tunes worked together.

Crow men were gathering fast, and the women trilled. Joaquin and Peanut Head cheered loudly. Sam could see Esperanza getting excited about her stunt.

Now, responding to Sam's signals, the ponies raised their forelegs, pivoted for a half-turn, and came back to earth. They demivaulted first to the left and then to the right. The Crows, true horsemen, watched in amazement.

Now came Esperanza's solo turn. With her pony loping around the outside, she stood up on his back. She waved happily to the audience. Then, to a big crescendo from Baptiste, she bounded off, landed on her feet, bumped down to her knees, and leaped back up.

The trills and shouts were loud for the six-year-old. Joaquin and Peanut Head made the most noise. Esperanza bowed to the audience as Sam had taught her, and the Crows laughed.

Tomás clapped his hands, but Sam could see his heart wasn't in it. In a couple of years Kallie might do tricks, but Vici could have done them now.

Azul's turn. As his horse walked, the little boy scooted onto its rump and did a backward somersault onto the ground. He hit too far back on his bottom and bumped his head hard. He tuned up to cry, but the cheers of the audience changed his mind, and he grinned.

Now Flat Dog performed the grand finale. He galloped sunwise around the ring, slid under his mount's belly, both hands free, and shot arrows fast at the audience—actually well high, but it made the effect.

The kids jumped back onto their ponies. All three mounts came to the center of the ring and, ducking their heads between their hoofs, bowed to the audience.

Esperanza leapt off the pony into Sam's arms.

Twenty-nine

"WHAT ARE YOU going to do about your pipe?" said Flat Dog.

He and Sam were bringing the horses back from the creek. Most animals were turned out with the herd. Specially trained horses, though, buffalo runners, warhorses, or show animals like these—such mounts were watered on a lead and then kept staked by the tipis of their owners, under close watch.

Sam let his breath out. "I'm stumped." The pipe was the other horse pulling on him.

Brother-friends don't have to say much. Sam and Flat Dog staked the horses in silence.

The first problem was, there could be no hope of getting the pipe back from the Blackfeet. The only solution was to get a new pipe. Which Sam could do, *if* . . .

There was a right way to go about such things. First, Sam would have to go to the medicine man who gave him his original pipe and report it stolen. A ceremony would then be performed to take away that pipe's power, so it could not be misused.

Then, if Sam had carried the pipe honorably, he could ask for another. In asking, gifts of tobacco, red cloth, and a blanket were customary, and after the ceremony you gave a feast for the medicine man.

But Sam was cut off from all that. Bell Rock, who made his first pipe, carving the bowl from red stone and the stem from wood, lived in the village of Rides Twice. Sam had killed Rides Twice's son.

They now sat on the ground near the fire pit, which was dead ashes on a hot July afternoon.

Julia came out of the tipi—the children were evidently napping—and started cutting deerhide with scissors, a sign of her Californio upbringing.

"You and I go to Bell Rock together," said Flat Dog.

Sam looked up sharply.

Julia stopped in her work. She was making a pair of moccasins for Sam. She'd already made one, and would make several. Crows were famous for their excellent moccasins. "It's too dangerous," she said.

"There's a way if we're careful," said Flat Dog.

He laid out his plan.

Sam looked inside himself and decided maybe he could hope. He needed a pipe. He felt stripped naked without it.

"Too dangerous," repeated Julia. Normally, a Crow wife wouldn't speak up to her husband and brother-in-law so bluntly. But Julia's veins flowed with the blood of a powerful family.

"You might get around Rides Twice that way," she said. "A leader would not go into another chief's camp and attack a guest. But you cannot get around Owl Woman and Yellow Horn. Yellow Horn will come for you. Or worse, he'll send a young relative after you."

SAM WISHED HE didn't remember Owl Woman, and wished he didn't respect her. She was a village grandmother who had the ability to see beyond, and that made her influential. What she saw in one vision was that white people were death to the Crow nation.

A decade ago she spoke against Sam to other villagers. Finally, through Bell Rock, he asked her to explain why she didn't want him in the camp.

Her explanation was eerily powerful. She spoke of a vision, or dream. In it she was alone and lost in the Yellowstone country. Her husband, children, friends, the entire village, all the Crow people, she couldn't find anyone.

She wandered and came near a place she knew, a lake which emptied at one end into the big-water-everywhere to the east and at the other end into the big-water-everywhere to the west. Sam knew such a lake.

Now she began to hear the people—they were crying and moaning, but she couldn't find them. She walked on toward the lake.

Riders began to pass her, white people on horses. They didn't look at her because they had no faces. Their visages were blank, and turned toward a horizon far, far away, beyond where the sun sets. Silent, faceless, they rode past her.

Then Owl Woman came to the lake and saw. "On the pond were lily pads. Except that the lily pads were faces, the faces of the Absaroka people under a film of water. The faces were dead, the people were dead. In rows, many, many of them, they lay dead. Their countenances were ghastly white, their eyes frozen open, their lips vermilion.

"I stood by the side of the pond and looked at the faces of all my people, dead. The white people marched by on their horses, never noticing. Forever they went on, forever and forever. And the people's death went on forever."

Sam would never forget her voice as she said these words, and the power of her vision. She told him then that the only way for the people to live was to avoid the white people altogether. Though she knew most Crows welcomed the fur trappers and were friends to them, she thought that was a terrible mistake.

Sam told her that night how wrong she was. White people, he

said, would never come to this country. It was not the kind of place they liked—they wanted flat country they could plow and plant. They wanted big, thick rivers that could turn their mill wheels and make steam for their factories. The Rocky Mountains were too dry, too steep, too cold—white people would never want such a place.

He would tell her the same now.

But she was set against him, and had set her husband against him, and he might not get the chance.

THAT EVENING JOE Meek sat down with them to supper. It was a mob—the four of the Flat Dog family, Sam and Esperanza, Tomás, Baptiste, Joaquin, and Peanut Head. Julia fed the lot of them.

Tomás seemed to be attaching himself to Peanut Head and avoiding Joaquin, which struck Sam as a good idea. Peanut Head was Tomás's age, and usually sober.

Meek was an old friend and in good form, boosted by the kettle of whiskey he shared with everyone. Joaquin swigged enthusiastically. Joe had a good time telling grizzly bear stories. Seemed like Joe had a good time doing most anything.

In his soft Virginia speech he started with a story about the time he heard—and then saw—two of the silvertips nosing into camp early one morning. Joe jumped right up and climbed the nearest tree to get away from the bears. His partner Clement, though, was too lazy to get out of his bedroll. "Them b'ars," said Joe, "got real curious about whatever smells were coming from them buffalo robes. They nuzzled the robes and made grunting sounds and nuzzled some more.

"'They're discussing the most tasty parts of you,' I shouted down to Clement." The way he pronounced it made the French name sound like "Claymore."

"'Now boys, that man is plump, just the way a ba'r likes 'em. Otherwise he'd be perched up here with me. Plump is good, a hungry b'ar can't beat that. No, no, stay away from them feet, them are bony. And don't bother with the head neither—it's hard, and he ain't got no brains, or he wouldn't be laying there playing possum. I'd go for the ass. He's got a big ass, plenty of fat, you ain't never seen nothing like it. No, stay away from them ribs, there's no meat on 'em, and he ain't got no heart. If he had heart instead of being a Frenchy coward, he'd be up here safe with me.'

"After a while the bears got bored and wandered off."

"Joe," said Esperanza, "you see in your life many grizzly bears?"

"Young lady, I have seen more griz than there's needles on a pine tree. And I have shot more than you have hairs in your head."

Esperanza rubbed her hair briskly with both hands and shook her head.

"Listen up. You kids know how to tell a grizzly bear from a black bear?"

They both said no, and their eyes got big.

"So here it is. The bear comes, you scratch up a tree fast as you can go, and now what? Here's how you tell. If the bear climbs the tree and eats you, it was a black bear. If it BE-A-A-AR-HUGS the tree, pulls it out of the ground by its roots, and slams it down and eats you, it was a grizzly."

Everybody laughed, but the kids looked nervous.

"Let me tell you," said Joe, "about Daniel and the lion's den. You know that Bible story?"

They didn't, so Joe gave them a quick fill-in.

"So here we go. One spring up near the Yallerstone me and Clement and Hawkins and Doughty, we seen a griz and set out to chase it, spring being a hungry season after winter. That b'ar, she skedaddles right into a cave.

"Hmm. We thought on the cave and thought on our bellies, and we was more hungry than scared. So three of us decided to go in and roust the b'ar, while Doughty went up above the cave to shoot her as she came out.

"We creeps inside real easy like, and by the half-light we sees the b'ar. And the other b'ar. And the other b'ar. The first one is on its feet, the others layin' down.

"We looks at each other real skeery like. At a time like this your hind feet, they get to wantin' to go pitter-patter right on out'n there. But I has a better idea. It's spring, and I says to myself, they are just waking up from their long winter's nap, and maybe . . .

"I slips forward toward the sow on her feet, and I pokes her with the muzzle of my rifle.

"She acts kinda peeved, but she backs away.

"I goes after and pokes her harder.

"She snarls, but she pads back toward the entrance.

"That Clement and Hawkins, believe me, they is flat-FLAT against the wall, prayin', 'Don't mess with me, don't mess with me.'

"I gives one more poke and thar she goes outside, lickety-split.

"BOOM! And we knows Doughty has shot her.

"Now everyone gets into the act. We runs at one of them other b'ars and prods 'im with our rifles, and he stirs a little bit and finally gets to his feet, I mean paws, and out he goes.

"BOOM! We're doing good, and now we're grinning at each other like mad fools.

"We attacks the last b'ar, a sow, like we was swordsmen and our rifles the sharpest sabers. This b'ar she musta believed we was exactly that, because she hops right up and follers her cave mates out the door.

"BOOM!

"The three of us go runnin' out, and I'll be damned if Doughty hasn't shot all three of them. And he is standing above the cave laughin' like a hyena, slapping his knees and staggerin' around.

"'Daniel?!' says I. 'Daniel?! We know now—why, he war a humbug. It was spring and them lions was half-asleep. Half-asleep!'

"'Daniel?! We done out-Danieled him. We counted coup on 'em, damned if we didn't—we counted coup on 'em!'"

And Joe cut loose a war whoop to end all war whoops.

"Sam," said Esperanza, "you made the tree leaves shake."

Thirty

"WALKARA," SAID SAM, "where are they?"

"Join me," said the chief, sitting by his fire and enjoying his morning cup.

"No, thanks." Sam, Tomás, and Baptiste stayed on their feet. "Where are they? The truth."

Walkara watched the steam rise off his brew. Finally, he said, "Truth? Very well. I don't know. All I know is, they headed east."

"You told us rendezvous."

Walkara shrugged. "I made that up." Then he gave them a big grin.

"What does east mean?" snapped Tomás, throwing the words at Walkara's happy face.

"I told you before. Arapahos, Cheyennes, Comanches. For trading slaves. Especially Comanches, good slave trade. Your sisters, they are probably Comanches now."

* * *

THEY STOMPED BACK toward Flat Dog and Julia's lodge. Now the horses were pulling Sam east and west *hard*.

"Let's start for Comanche country," said Tomás. "Now."

Fortunately for Sam, Baptiste spoke up. "That was more than a month ago. They're finished and gone on by now."

"Probably back at Walkara's camp," said Sam.

"Seems to me like Joaquin has given up on his wife," said Baptiste.

"I don't give a damn," said Tomás. "I no give up. Let's go somewhere."

They came up to the lodge, and there sat Joaquin and Peanut Head in front of the fire.

"You've said hardly a word about Lupe since we got to rendezvous," Tomás said to Joaquin.

The man was always drunk, always hail-fellow-well-met, always chasing women, always ready for coffee and breakfast from someone else's pot.

"Lupe, she is *mi esposa,* she lives in the center of my heart," said Joaquin.

"You don't act like it," said Tomás.

Joaquin shrugged. "I am a man. I have the urges of every man. You are the same. But Lupe, she is queen of *mi corazón.*"

"So you want to find her," said Sam.

"*Claro.*" Sure.

"I'm going after them," said Tomás. "Both me sisters. Wherever they are."

"I say the same," said Joaquin. He started to add something, but lowered his head. Then he looked at them with damp eyes and said, "Lupe, she is carrying my child. My son."

Sam and Tomás looked at each other across the fire.

Sam said, "We've got an obstacle. Actually, two obstacles."

Tomás rolled his eyes. "You, not we."

"In the first place, we don't know where Pegleg is."

"So we look for him," said Tomás.

"It would be like looking for a piece of dust in a whirlwind."

"Mi corazón," said Joaquin.

Now it was Sam who wanted to roll his eyes. Instead he said, "Pegleg will go to Taos for the winter."

"My sisters," Tomás said, "are being sold from man to man."

Sam had nothing to say to that.

"I don't see how you fortheget that," said Tomás, "even for one second."

"I don't," said Sam. "The first lead I have is in Taos."

"Taos in the winter," said Joaquin.

"Second problem. I need a pipe," said Sam.

"Oh, for God's sake," said Tomás. He said that even in front of Flat Dog. Tomás thought civilization had passed Indian ways by. He'd told Sam the pipe was a ridiculous superstition, and didn't give a damn about Sam's actual experiences with it.

Sam, however, didn't say anything when Tomás went to mass with Paloma in Santa Fé, or about the rosary he wore around his neck, with a small representation of the Virgin of Guadalupe dangling from the bottom.

"So what's your idea?" Tomás asked Sam. It sounded like he wanted to add, "O great leader."

"Go to Crow country with Fitzpatrick. Get a pipe. Do a hunt. Find Pegleg in Taos next winter."

"Pegleg, he probably goes to Taos in the winter," mumbled Joaquin.

"So maybe I will find me sisters by meself."

"You're too young for that," Sam said fast.

"*Verdad?* I am eighteen. How old were you when you came to the mountains?" Tomás rushed on. "Eighteen. How old were you when you walked seven hundred miles alone"—his words underlined the oft-spoken words with sarcasm—"to get to Fort Atkinson?" Now he stood up and leaned directly into Sam's face. "How old were you when you killed a white man for the first time? Twenty-one, and he was a 'giant.'" Tomás's voice grew soft and singsong. "Excuse me again, how old am I?"

Peanut Head's eyes burned at this talk, and Sam wondered why.

He deliberately turned his back on Tomás. "You have no idea what you're getting into."

"Like you had no," said Tomás.

Sam turned back to his son. "What if Comanches own these women?"

"A man does not add up the risks," said Tomás, "when it is slavery."

Sam looked into his son's eyes, thinking, *You expect the world to be a fairer place than it is.*

"Yes," said Joaquin, "we are men." He thumped his chest. *"Coraje."*

Sam stared at him. *Between the empty-head and the hothead . . .*

"So what exactly is your plan?" said Tomás.

"Right now," said Sam, "I'm going to take Paladin to water." He stood and strode off.

"I'LL WALK WITH you," said Peanut Head.

Coy trailed along, three-legged.

"Damn," said Sam loud and hard, paying no attention to Peanut Head.

Peanut Head said, "I think his leg is coming along all right."

Sam counted his angers. *Gideon Poorboy lost his leg. Blue Medicine lost his life. So did Third Wing. Meadowlark died. Paloma died. I seldom see Esperanza.*

He let Paladin walk into the creek. Vexation worked at him like a toothpick. He met Peanut Head's eyes, saw the flame again, and wondered what it meant.

"Sam, Tomás said you killed a giant white man. How did that happen?"

"I've killed more men than I wanted to."

"Tell me about that one."

Irritation chinked at Sam. "His name was Micajah. He wasn't a bad man, I don't think."

"You killed a good man?"

"It was righteous."

"How could that be?"

Sam looked into Peanut Head's eyes but saw nothing.

"Way righteous."

Paladin came out of the water and stood beside Sam.

"I hear you keep hidden weapons."

Sam turned to the newcomer. He was careful not to lift a hand to his hair, or to his belt buckle. "Maybe more than one."

"Where?"

Sam eyed him. "I'm not inclined to say."

Peanut Head shrugged and smiled. "Any tips you can give me, I'd be glad to have."

Sam studied Peanut Head's face. He seemed a modest youth, more brawn than brains. "That's all yesterday's troubles now." He stood. "I have plenty of today's."

FITZPATRICK WAS WAITING for Sam at the lodge. "I need ye to lead a brigade for me."

Sam glanced at Tomás, who sat head down. "Can't help you. I'm going to Crow country like you, but to get a pipe."

Tomás's eyes flashed fire at Sam.

Fitz said, "You know us and American Fur Company have divided the country for the coming year?"

"No." This was big news. Could the two cooperate?

"They're mostly west of the mountains, we're mostly east. They'll trap the Salt Lake country, the Teton country, the Flathead country, and all that around the Snake River and the Salmon. We'll trap the Siskadee here, the Big Horn, the Yellowstone, and the Three Forks as well."

"Good idea." Sam looked at Tomás edgily. The Crows Sam needed to see would be on the Big Horn.

"How about you?" Fitz said to Tomás. "I'll give you fifty dollars a month."

Tomás shook his head. "Me sisters are missing."

Fitz turned back to Sam. "I need one thing from you sure and true. Next summer you sell me your fur."

"That's a bargain." He thought. "You think you and American Fur Company can share the mountains?"

Fitz shook his head. "The bastards are gonna trample us into the ground with their money." He grinned wryly. "You think I can really afford to pay partisans fifteen hundred dollars for a year's work?"

Sam saw it. One good decade, and now the beaver-trapping world was slip-sliding away.

Suddenly, Fitz called out, "Hey, Bill, come sit."

Old Bill Williams walked rickety their way. The man was all bones sticking out, knees, elbows, and nose. He looked disreputable, his buckskins black with grease, his hat with a hole big enough that his red hair stuck out. You could even see that it was turning gray. But he was whipcord strong, and his bright blue eyes spoke of a lively intelligence.

Old Bill kept his own counsel and had a reputation. It was said that it wasn't smart to ride in front of Bill Williams in starvin' times.

"Hydee, Sam," said Bill, "I don't recollect ever'body's name."

"Tomás," said Tomás curtly. Sam suspected that Bill always forgot the name as a way of teasing. "This is me friend Peanut Head."

Bill reached for the kettle with the whiskey, swigged, and scratched Coy's ears. Sam wouldn't let Coy be around Old Bill in starvin' times either.

"I need you," Fitz told Bill. He made the same offer he'd made to Sam and ran through the reasons.

Bill sat, thought, and chewed his wad. "Don't allow as I could." Bill always seemed to trap alone, or slip away from any companions he had. Now he spat out a brown glob. "I'm glad to have this little set-down with 'ee, though. Got something to communicate."

He reached for the kettle and swigged again. "This here, you might say I done had a vision."

Sam smiled and deliberately didn't look at Tomás. Bill had come

West as a preacher to the Osage. The Indians, though, had been the ones who did the converting. Bill carried a pipe now and made medicine with it. He prayed to the four winds. And it seemed like he'd gone even further and made up his own way of seeing the world from lots of things he'd heard, a sort of patchwork quilt of wisdoms.

"I seen how I'm gonna come back," said Bill. "Yessirree, I did. I'm comin' as a elk, a bull elk.

"Now, ever since I've knowed that, it has worried me some. One of you boys—my friends—is liable to make meat of me."

He stared at them wild-eyed.

"So I've figgered out a way around that. Listen here. If'n I see you, I'll give you a signal that it's me."

He fixed Tomás with his eyes. "You mindin' what I say, boy?"

Tomás gave him a flat look.

After a moment Bill gave up on the indignation. "See here, it's a simple signal. You know how elk look at things off to one side, not ahead?"

He gave Tomás another look, suspicious about the youth.

"Well, whatever side you're on, I'll wave that antler in a little circle." He fixed each of them with his eyes. "Like this." He wobbled his head round and round.

"You payin' attention? You hear what I'm saying? Like this." He wobbled his head again.

"Got it, Bill," said Sam. Bill stood up, in a hurry to spread the word.

"Don't you be burnin' powder in my direction, you hear? Just recollect what I told you."

"Not for anything would I blow a hole in your elkdom, Bill."

Thirty-one

"STUPID OLD FART," said Tomás. He wobbled his imaginary antlers.

Flat Dog walked up with a bundle of sticks, sat beside them around the fire pit, and started straightening arrow shafts.

Sam locked eyes with his son. "I'm going to Crow country."

"Pegleg is south," Tomás said with an edge. "Me sisters are south."

Sam pursed his mouth. "The pipe comes first."

Tomás threw off an exasperated sigh. He turned to Peanut Head. "First he throws away Christianity for this primitive religion." To Tomás Christianity and Catholicism were the same. "In Santa Fé we have a most beautiful place of worship, the Church of the Virgin of Guadalupe. When Paloma and I go to mass, to hear the great words, my father sits outside and puffs on his pipe."

He smirked at Sam. "What is it, you see the future in the smoke?" He made a wavy, rising motion with one hand.

"You're stepping into the shit," said Sam.

"He takes a secret religious name, Joins with Buffalo."

Now Sam was truly offended.

Tomás plunged on. "He goes backward from man to beast. What you think of that?"

Peanut Head kept his face rigid.

"He makes medicine." Tomás gave a mocking laugh. "He does a dance where you go without food and water until you see, how do you say, hallucinations."

"Tomás," said Sam, "you're offending your uncle."

"Flat Dog is not me uncle," said Tomás. "He is not your brother." He jumped up. "And the way you act, you are not me father."

Sam stood up, put his face straight in Tomás's, and grabbed the boy's shoulders. "You sit down and act right," he said, growling.

Tomás swung. The fist caught Sam right on the bridge of his nose. Blood flooded out.

The two men glared at each other, stupefied.

Tomás uttered a strangled cry and ran off.

"Goddamn it!" yelled Sam, and used his sleeve to stanch the blood.

Thirty-two

JULIA HANDED SAM a wet, cold cloth for his nose.

He put it on and said nasally, "What got into him?"

Nobody answered for a while. Then Flat Dog said, "Everything, I expect."

Sam would have snorted, but he didn't want to blow blood on himself.

"Maybe now is the time for the beads," said Julia. Her kind eyes flicked to Esperanza.

Sam thought and nodded. One-handed, he drew a rolled piece of hide from his shooting pouch and squatted down by his daughter. Her eyes were on the bloody compress on his nose. Sam unrolled the hide—it was a beaded featherburst in gay colors.

"Papá!" she squealed. She loved pretty beadwork and quillwork.

"What do you say?" asked Flat Dog in English.

"*Gracias*," she said.

Flat Dog gave her a look.

"Thank you," she said the second time.

"You're welcome," said Sam, sounding like he had a bad cold. "Here's what you do with these." The beadwork was on a disc of sheepskin tanned white. "You sew it to your dress, right in the middle, like this."

"I'll do it for you tonight," said Julia. She took one wet cloth away from Sam's nose and gave him another one. The nose was swollen into a pear shape.

"I want beads," said Azul.

"And I brought you some," said Sam. He handed the boy two strips of beadwork, blue and white pony beads to ornament his shoulders. Flat Dog and Julia would know that Azul's ornamentation, with beads the size of the boy's finger joints, was quickly done, while the tiny beads in Esperanza's featherburst took dozens of hours.

"Keep it going," Julia said softly to Sam.

"I have something else for both of you, too."

He brought out the multicolored yarn. He had gotten it in Santa Fé, several feet of it. He and Paloma had played with it until they figured out what the best lengths were, and he cut it and tied several pieces into circles the right size.

"One piece for you"—he handed it to Esperanza—"and one piece for Azul." He handed the rest of the ball to Julia, who looked dubiously at the pear in the middle of his face.

"Papá!" Esperanza squealed. Last year he'd given her some emerald ribbon to tie up her rust-colored hair and flatter her hazel eyes, and she loved it. Every day she made a bow in her hair, partly to show she knew how to tie the knot.

Azul looked at the string like it was a mess a dog made.

"These are for playing a game," Sam said. "It's called cat's cradle. I used to play it with my mom and my sisters."

He wondered if his mother was still alive. He'd had no contact with his family since he knocked his older brother Owen cold nine years ago.

"So. Your mom knows this game, and she and I will show you how to play."

Julia was ready. She and Sam squatted opposite each other, and she began with the yarn around her hands, thumbs outside. Then a loop around each hand. "Now watch," she said. She used the middle finger of each hand to reach across, catch the loop from the other hand, and make a pretty series of diamond shapes and triangles, all in different colors. "This," she said, "is what we call a cat's cradle."

"Let me, let me!" cried Esperanza.

Azul bunched up his string and squinched it between his nose and upper lip, like a mustache.

"Wait," said Julia. "Now this is where it gets good. Tricky but good."

Sam put down the compress—at least his nose wasn't leaking red any longer. He reached out and pinched some of the *X*s made by the taut yarn. Then he pulled his hands far apart, stretching the yarn, made a scooping motion, and—lo and behold—the entire cat's cradle was on his hands.

"Estupendo!" cried Esperanza. "Let me, let me!"

"Just a minute," said Sam.

Azul watched in puzzlement.

Sam held his hands out to Julia, she pinched some strings and made some motions, and—a brand-new shape was in her hands. "This pattern is called candles," she said, and held out her hands to Sam.

Quickly, they went through the manger pattern, the diamonds, and a couple of more.

Esperanza fell silent. She was awestruck.

"All right, now," Sam told her, "you try it with me."

They worked on it together. Julia and Azul did too, but Azul didn't put his mind much on it.

Quickly, Sam had a cat's cradle small enough for Esperanza's hands. It took three tries for her to switch it from his fingers to hers. "Hot damn," she said in English.

All the grown-ups laughed.

Esperanza ran around the fire, holding her cat's cradle to the sky.

Sam looked at Flat Dog. His eyes were direct, warm, and open to Sam. They didn't spend as much time together as they wanted, but Sam felt their bond now.

The sun was well down behind the western mountains, and the sky was the color of mother-of-pearl. Sam breathed the mountain air in and out through his mouth. He watched his daughter run in mad circles. Finally, she stopped and faced him.

"All right," he said, "do you want to try doing the manger pattern now?"

"Yes!" said the little girl.

Much later, when the children were tucked in, Flat Dog said, "How's your nose?"

Sam said, "It hurts to be a dad."

SAM HELD THE kaleidoscope against the reddening dawn and turned it. He loved looking at the designs, and could do it for hours. For fun Sam start-stopped several turns fast. Then he rotated the instrument slowly and steadily, hands like a machine. He savored the shifting patterns. Since they reminded him of stained-glass windows in a church, they brought Paloma to his mind.

He reached over and rubbed Coy's ears. He wondered where she was now. If things went according to plan, she and Hannibal got to Chihuahua City in early June and stayed there a while. Another month to Durango, plus stops there and in Zacatecas to trade at the mines. Maybe they would be leaving about now for Mexico City, another month and a half away. He pictured her kneeling in front of the Virgin of Guadalupe.

He wondered how ill she might be. He wondered whether she thought of him.

He hung his head for a long moment. Then he chided himself, lifted the kaleidoscope and kited off again into its world.

* * *

Flat Dog came out of the tipi. "No sign of Tomás?"

"Nothing." Sam slipped forward onto his knees, poured Flat Dog a cup of coffee, and put more wood on the fire.

Two days and they hadn't seen or heard from him.

"He's run away from home," said Sam.

"Like father, like son."

Sam gave a rueful smile. He'd run away from home on Christmas Day, 1822, right after his girl announced her engagement to his older brother Owen. "Probably he signed on with someone."

"We'll find out who he went with."

"Yeah."

"Maybe he'll get that big money we're missing out on," said Flat Dog with a grin.

"Yeah."

Sam looked around at the camps, where men were stirring. Today most trappers would pack up and move out. Robert Campbell would take the Rocky Mountain Fur pack train across South Pass to the Big Horn River, down it to the Yellowstone in bull boats, on down the Yellowstone to Fort Union, and then on the Missouri River to St. Louis by steamboat. The brigade leaders of both big companies would point their outfits toward their designated hunting grounds. The many Indians were heading back to their villages.

Sam's friends Fitzpatrick, Bridger, and the other partners would spend a year paying ruinous wages to beaver men. American Fur would do the same. They would make big hunts and maybe no profit. Sam couldn't guess what it would all come to.

This was one year Sam might have gone back to work for Rocky Mountain Fur. But he couldn't. Fitz's offer was stunning, and Paloma wasn't waiting for him in Santa Fé. *I have to get a pipe.*

Esperanza and Azul tumbled out of the tipi. Julia would be nursing the baby inside. "Hola, Papá."

Sam picked her up and gave her a hug. "I've got something to show you." He put the kaleidoscope to her eye.

"Oooh, pretty."

He rotated it.

Esperanza squealed.

He turned it again.

Another squeal. She grabbed it and made the turns. Choruses of excitement. Coy yipped and jumped up and down, excited in his coyote way.

"Mí, mí," said Azul, reaching for the kaleidoscope.

Sam took it and held it against Azul's eye. "Estupendo!"

Esperanza seized it back and looked. "Papá, I want it. Can I have it, can I? For my own?"

"This one is mine. I'll get you one."

"I want it," said Azul.

Sam put the boy on his lap and watched Esperanza playing with the kaleidoscope. "I want it," he said again. At least Esperanza wouldn't decide to use it as a hammer.

Sam breathed in and out. He was headed for Crow country, going with his daughter back to her people. Half of him was glad. Half of him thought he'd get his hide shot full of holes. He and Flat Dog had a plan, and his experience told him that plans make a lot of sense until you meet your foe.

I want a pipe.

They would make a big party going to Crow country, Campbell's party and Fitzpatrick's united. Stewart, the British captain, said he would tail along with Fitzpatrick. Altogether it made a fine escort for Sam, Flat Dog, and the other Crows going home.

On the Big Horn the Crows would veer away from the trappers. They would rejoin their tribe for the great autumn buffalo hunt, all the villages together. After this huge event, the village of Rides Twice, with Flat Dog and his family, would drag their travois a dozen or so sleeps back to the high mountain valley where they wintered. The people had made this summer-winter pattern since before the memories of the grandfathers of the oldest men, the Crow way of living. Esperanza walked that same road.

She saw a mountain jay light on a limb. Quickly, she put the kaleidoscope down in the dust, walked over to the jay, and chirped at it. She didn't yet distinguish between one bird song and another. Sam rescued the kaleidoscope.

He knew intimately the places the village lived. During his first mountain winter with them in the high valley of the Wind River, he met Meadowlark. At their autumn camp he held his sun dance and saw beyond. Where they circled their lodges for summer camp, he brought Esperanza back to the tribe and, challenged, he fought and killed the chief's son, Red Roan.

These places were in his bones. These people were his adopted people. He was a member of a warrior society, the Kit Foxes.

But this village was the one place he could not go.

When Esperanza, the family, and the rest of Rides Twice's people left for their winter camp, Sam would probably have his pipe. But he wouldn't have Esperanza or Tomás. And he might be dead.

Thirty-three

AN OUTFIT OF Crows on the trail: eight or ten Crow families rode along the Little Big Horn River, the women sitting on their high-backed saddles, children bareback on their ponies, other ponies dragging the travois that bore the lodge covers, blankets, robes, and the rest of the families' belongings.

Flanking the women and children were the warriors, the big-bellied grandfathers, the watchful fathers, the active young men. They were alert, for they were the guardians.

Among them were Sam Morgan and the young Peanut Head. Sam didn't know why the devil Peanut Head didn't take Fitz-patrick's high wages, as others did. And Tomás did, Sam supposed. He didn't even know what brigade his son went with. Every partisan said, "Not me."

Peanut Head had told Sam, "I want to spend some time in a real Indian village and go on a real Indian buffalo hunt."

"You're acting like a pork-eater," said Flat Dog mockingly. "Go for the money."

"What's a pork-eater?" said Peanut Head, proving he was one.

"The Frenchies started it," said Sam. "Way I heard it, they had canoemen that took the supplies out to the forts every spring, and then paddled back to Montreal. Along the way they fed these paddlers gruel with some pork in it. The actual traders, the ones who stayed out in Indian country, took to calling them pork-eaters, because they didn't live off the land."

Peanut Head nodded. Sam wondered if he could even tell the difference between poor bull and fat cow.

"I wish Baptiste had come with us," said Peanut Head.

"He's taking the money," said Flat Dog, chuckling. Actually, in the chaos of departure, they didn't know who Baptiste went with either.

Right now Sam sat on Paladin next to Flat Dog and his paint. Sometimes Sam watched his daughter instead of the countryside. She had the superb balance that comes readily only to those who ride from the time they can toddle.

Coy trotted alongside Sam, his tongue dangling. The August afternoon was hot. Dogs looped their tails down and hung their heads. The sun pounded the energy out of man and woman, child and beast.

But the travelers were eager. Tomorrow they would join a village of their people where two creeks flowed into the river from opposite sides, a place the Crows called Lodge Grass. It would be good to see relatives and catch up on the news—this group had been gone from home for three moons. Their ponies' hoofs tapped out, "Tomorrow, tomorrow, tomorrow."

A few days ago these Crows left behind an outfit of trappers higher into the mountains. Now the fur men poked along in the same afternoon heat and on the same trail.

Here where the Little Big Horn River was still girlish, lean Tom Fitzpatrick of the ruined hand rode out in front of his men. High in the Big Horn Mountains they had stopped to do business, men riding up the river's tributaries in pairs, setting their traps and bait sticks in the shallow water as the sun rose, retrieving drowned rodents as it set. The women of the outfit scraped the fat off the hides, stretched them on willow hoops, and lashed them into packs for the mules. That gave an initial education in the routine of a beaver outfit to the new hands, who included Captain Stewart, the veteran of Waterloo.

Then Fitz had brought his men out of the mountains to seek the Crow camp at Lodge Grass and trade.

He was all eyes and ears, and he spoke to no one as he led the way. He watched the river for anything that might be a sign of danger. Was a duck scared up? Perhaps by an enemy. Did the berry bushes thrash about? Did they even stir? Maybe a grizzly feeding. Did antelope suddenly run off? Something jumped them up. Was there movement on any sage-topped hillock or ridge? Not every Indian in Crow country was a Crow.

Yes, this river, and the Big Horn Mountains and Pryor Mountains behind them and to their left, were presumably safe, its inhabitants friends. Yes, this party was big enough to fight off most enemies. And a man who took that for granted was looking to have coyotes sing over his bones.

Behind Fitz traipsed the women and children of four of the trappers. A Shoshone wife carried an infant in the cradleboard on her back. A Ute woman kept her eye on a boy and a girl of four and six. A middle-aged Cree, mate to her French-Canadian husband for two decades, thought forward to the winter, when she would not have to travel. The fourth woman was the beautiful young Shoshone who had traded away both her clothing and her virtue at rendezvous. Now she was a new bride, belonging to a young Virginian who was shy, slow of speech, and wearing a dazed smile of satisfaction.

With him at the rear were the other mountain men, a ruffian crew if ever there was one. Captain Stewart rode off to one side, avoiding the dust of the outfit. Stewart was mounted handsomely and carried a Manton rifle that was the envy of even the best hunter in the Rocky Mountains. He was remembering Europe, cities, music, the theatre—things as alien to the Rocky Mountains as elephants.

About thirty other trappers trekked along with Stewart, French Canadians, Delawares, Mexicans, one free man of color, and white American backwoodsmen from the States.

Ironically, the ones with the strongest claim to civilization, aside from Stewart, were the Mexicans. Taos and Santa Fé had great churches, commerce, and priests who taught people to read and appreciate some of the finer things of life.

The backwoods of America featured no such amenities. There men grew up wild and fed themselves with the rifle as often as the plow. As mountain men, they grew even wilder. Soon the first missionaries would come to the West, take one look at the beaver hunters, and move on quickly to preaching Christ to the Indians. The mountain men, they would tell their mission board back in the States, were beyond redemption—more savage even than the savages.

Where a nameless creek flowed into the Little Big Horn, Fitz lifted a hand and without a word called a halt to the day's travel. Here the four women put up their travel tipis. The men rope-corralled the horses and laid out their bedrolls. They fed on elk meat, freshly shot in these mountains. And their dreams were of the Crow women in the camp at Lodge Grass, for Crow women had a lust for beaver men unmatched in the mountains.

Thirty-four

SAM SHOVED HIS wiping stick into the hard dirt. Too hard. He stared at the end of the ramrod and at the ground.

"Go ahead," called Flat Dog, chuckling, "break it."

Even the pork-eater Peanut Head laughed, knowing that Sam wouldn't be able to ram his lead balls into the Celt after that. "You'll be waltzing around these mountains naked," he said foolishly.

Bell Rock grinned at the newcomer. The medicine man was built like a frog and had a deep, basso voice. He, Flat Dog, and Peanut Head were sitting under a cedar tree on a rocky outcropping thirty steps away from Sam, out of the brutal sun.

After a moment's consideration Sam whacked out a hole with his tomahawk, set the stick in it, and piled the dirt around the base. It stood.

Now he tied his bandanna onto the stick and looked back at the two Crows and the pork-eater. They were where Sam wanted to be. He hurried back into the shade.

Behind and below them the ponies were tied to cedar limbs, nibbling on what little grass there was. Coy and several Crow mutts lay on a ledge above them, tongues out, looking down at their human beings.

"Those dogs are wondering what on earth we're up to," said Sam. He lay down on his belly between Flat Dog and Bell Rock, the Celt roughly pointed toward the bandanna flag.

"I'm thinking of taking a nap myself," said Bell Rock in his big Moses voice.

"Listen," said Sam, "this works." He'd told his friends those antelope a quarter of a mile off would get curious about the flapping bandanna and come to check it out.

"Lazy man's way to hunt," said Flat Dog.

Everyone smiled.

"Just the way I like it," said Sam.

They stopped talking and eyeballed the cluster of pronghorns. Sam glassed the animals. "Can't tell," he said, "there might be a buck among them." Both sexes bore horns.

"Male or female, fresh meat," said Flat Dog.

They had gotten lucky finding Bell Rock. This was the medicine man who originally made a pipe for Sam and dedicated it in a ceremony. Some palavering would have to go on to get him to dedicate a new one. Bell Rock would have to know Sam was a true pipe carrier.

This was part of Flat Dog's risky plan—that Bell Rock and family would visit his parents' village at this time before the big autumn buffalo hunt, and Sam could find him there, away from Rides Twice's camp.

Now one antelope was facing straight toward them. Maybe he saw the flag. Maybe in a few minutes he would come close to inspect it. Maybe two or three of the antelope would.

Then the Celt and the other three rifles would rumble. Sam wondered whether Peanut Head was a good shot.

He smiled to himself. He wouldn't be able to reload—his wiping stick was the bait.

Soon five antelope were a hundred steps closer. The sun reflected off the rolling plain with its late-summer grasses, brilliant gold in the afternoon. The glare made Sam's eyes want to close.

Coy growled. Sam could tell his coyote's growl from the dogs'. He jerked his head around and saw something above the rocks, just below Coy and the dogs—a tawny half-circle against the sky.

Suddenly, it moved sinuously, like a whip.

"Mountain lion!" Sam hollered.

All hell broke loose. Coy and the dogs set off an avalanche of barking. The cat roared. Paladin and the other ponies leapt backward and ripped their reins off the cedar limbs. The ponies sprinted off.

Four prone men jumped up and spun to try for a clean shot.

Paladin ran hard straight at the mountain lion, screaming.

Sam fired the Celt and missed.

The cat sprang at Paladin's neck.

She dodged—the cat raked a claw along her flank and tumbled to the ground.

Sam ran forward, getting his pistol out.

When Sam was just two steps in front of him, Peanut Head shot. Sam went down.

At the same instant Paladin wheeled and stomped the cat with her hoofs. Like a flash the mare pounced and got the lion's tail in her teeth. She planted her hoofs and swung the cat. Round and round the feline spun, spouting out caterwauls of anger. On each loop the lion's head bounced off the rock.

Sam crawled away. On one turn the cat's head whacked him in the ass.

For four full revolutions Paladin whirled the snarling creature, and after the last head bump, she flung the beast out across the earth, tumbling.

Sam stood up and reached toward Flat Dog, laughing. Bell Rock was holding the muzzle of Peanut Head's rifle down, not that it mattered now.

The lion stirred feebly to get onto its feet, but Paladin was far too quick. She pounded the cat with her front hoofs over and over. She turned the creature into a tattered rag.

Then she got down on her knees, not caring that the lion looked very dead, and bit the animal hard a dozen times.

Bell Rock checked Sam's head. "Your hair is scorched," he said.

"Too close!" Sam said in Peanut Head's face, but he couldn't help laughing. "Too damn close!"

Paladin stood up and observed her handiwork. She gave the lion her full attention, ready for the slightest motion.

A stray breeze made the cat's whiskers flicker.

The mare rose up on her hind legs and slammed her front hoofs into the cat's head one more time.

Bell Rock cheered.

"Some job of hunting we did," said Sam. He was loosey-goosey on his feet. "Too close!" he told Peanut Head again.

Flat Dog whistled. Coy came trotting back, followed by the dogs.

"We sure saved the dogs, didn't we?" said Sam.

"You sure there's not a hole in your head?" said Flat Dog.

"No, but it powdered my hair," said Sam, still fingering his locks and laughing. Deliberately, he took control of himself and walked to Paladin. He took her reins, a cedary branch still tangled in them.

"Peanut Head," said Flat Dog, "you're dangerous."

"Not as dangerous as this horse!" said Sam.

Bell Rock grinned at the medicine hat mare. He had made Sam a gift of her years ago, and helped train her. "Don't know as I'd want to ride an animal as can do that," he said.

Both Crows eyed Peanut Head sidelong. He just stood there looking sheepish.

Paladin turned her eyes into Sam's. She shivered her skin all over, as if to say, "What are you staring at?"

Thirty-five

WHILE SAM, FLAT DOG, and Bell Rock were out hunting, Tom Fitzpatrick brought his brigade to the forks of the creeks at the place called Lodge Grass. While he set up his camp, an old friend rode in with greetings, Jim Beckwourth. This husky mulatto and Fitz went back to the earliest days of the Ashley-Henry men, the great days of exploration of the mountains, making friends with tribes, and figuring out the entire business. They had ridden hundreds of hard miles together, and saved each other's ass more than once.

Fitz was glad big Jim happened to be there. Tomorrow Fitz would ride into the village to pay his respects to the chief of the village, Plays with His Face. Beckwourth would help things go easier. The brigade leader and Plays with His Face would express their happiness at seeing each other again. They would smoke the sacred pipe. Fitzpatrick would make the villagers some gifts, tobacco, and lots of the foofaraw that so much pleased the women, bells, ribbons, vermilion, and many beads, especially those the color of a robin's egg, called Crow blue. Then they would trade news: perhaps the Crows had attempted a peace treaty with the Blackfeet (though it would mean nothing). Young Crow warriors had made a splendid horse raid against the Headcutters (Sioux). And on and on.

Normally, Fitzpatrick would tell Plays with His Face something else important, that he and the other leaders of the Rocky Mountain Fur Company were the true friends of the Crow people, and not those other white men, the ones who stamped AMF on their furs. Fitzpatrick and his fellow chiefs would give the Crows the best deals on merchandise, and act the part of friends in every way. But since Jim had mentioned that he was now working for AFC, Fitz wouldn't speak these words right in front of his old friend. Both he and Beckwourth had lived among the Crows from the early days, and it wouldn't do for them to quarrel now.

All this would open the door to the trading that would occupy the rest of tomorrow and more. The Crows would want to exchange the fine work their women did—excellent moccasins, beautifully tanned buffalo robes, and the prized pelts known as Crow beaver—for blankets, knives, awls, pots, wool strouding, a few guns, a little whiskey . . .

Departing the next morning, Fitz put the camp in charge of the officer who had distinguished himself against Napoleon at Waterloo. "If Crows come to camp," Fitz told Stewart, "treat them as welcome guests."

The Crows came to camp, and how—four or fivescore of them, all full of cheer. They told stories of the last year's heroics, or fun, or silliness, to their comrades the beaver men. They laughed, they slapped backs, they did what old friends do when they meet after long absence.

While the young Crow men socialized, an older man named Bugling Elk regaled the British gentleman with stories in good, broken English. These tales were lollapaloozas. When his little niece got lost, he had been told by a bird exactly where she was, and saved her life. When the people were hungry, he had put his head to the ground and detected a herd of buffalo two sleeps away. And he fought with Head Cutters who outnumbered him five to one, whipped them soundly, and came home with four scalps.

Stewart must have enjoyed this storytelling. He did, however, follow procedure. He kept several men on guard. Bugling Elk even teased him about it—why do you act this way among friends? A routine precaution, explained Stewart.

Suddenly, rifles, pistols, war clubs, tomahawks, bows and arrows, filled every red hand. Every guard had a knife at his neck and was obliged to surrender his flintlock. Bugling Elk's smile, still in Stewart's face, took on a demonic edge.

And the pillage began. All guns were seized. Everything packed on the horses' backs, all the wonderful manufactured goods, all the tobacco and whiskey, all the beauty-making items the Crow women loved—everything was claimed. Bugling Elk himself stripped Captain Stewart of his watch.

Then the horses. The Crows loved horses, and were the master horse thieves of the mountains. Besides, they needed these animals to haul off their booty. Yes, we want the traps too, all of them, and the kegs of powder. Yes, the furs too.

With a last laugh of derision they were gone. "John Bull," Bugling Elk called back to Stewart, "he done be John Poor Bull."

Late that afternoon Tom Fitzpatrick rode in to find his camp picked clean. Stewart pulled a hangdog face. "Not your fault," rasped Fitz. "They would have fooled me too, would have fooled any of us."

He turned straight around and rode back to the village, marched into the council lodge, and demanded the return of his outfit.

Plays with His Face shrugged. "Young men will be wild," he said. "Who can control them?"

Fitz looked at Plays with His Face, and his mind spun furiously. Why was the chief so nonchalant? Where was Sam Morgan, who was a Crow himself and might be able to set things straight?

Fitz suddenly added it up. "Where's Jim Beckwourth?" he asked the chief abruptly.

"Gone hunting."

Now it all made nasty sense. American Fur. Big Jim here in Crow country, which was supposed to belong to Fitz this year. No doubt he'd promised them the sky in return for their trade. He had told them they didn't need to be nice to the other outfit of trappers, not any longer. Probably he'd fought with them against their persistent enemies, the Blackfeet and the Sioux. No doubt they'd admired his warrior swagger. And no doubt, Fitz told himself, Beckwourth was the villain in the case.

Now, negotiating, he kept a polite face. Anger would backfire. A show of rage would likely get his entire brigade wiped out, for he was vastly outnumbered. He talked quietly. He pointed out that his men could not survive unless they got the horses, rifles, and powder back. He also wanted the traps. Crow men didn't much care to trap anyway, Fitz added.

After an hour or two he had a few horses, a few guns, a little powder, and a few traps. He stood up, knowing that was all he would get. He held his fury sufficiently in check to say a half-polite goodbye, and hightailed it out of there.

He also hightailed out of the entire country. The Crows couldn't be trusted any longer. Fitz rode toward Jim Bridger's brigade, so that humiliation, even disaster, wouldn't mean death.

But Jim Beckwourth had better watch out. In Fitz's eyes he was a damned traitor.

Thirty-six

SAM, FLAT DOG, Bell Rock, and Peanut Head—all outsiders in this village—rode into an exuberant celebration. For the Crows most manufactured goods were the stuff of fantasy. Maybe the power of the sacred pipe, the vision quest, the sun dance, and the sweat lodge were real as rocks and trees, but blankets, iron pots, powder and lead, and especially guns were gaudy prizes barely to be imagined. The Crows wondered, and sometimes asked the beaver men, what medicine brought such miracles, what gods had power to grant such marvels. They had been amazed, from the beginning, that the trappers would trade these glories for something as commonplace as the skin of a dead beaver. They had whispered among themselves that these beaver hunters were really dumb.

A young man walked by flipping a steel butcher knife into the air and catching it by the handle. He beamed at his new toy.

"What's going on here?" Sam asked him.

"We showed the white man he is not so smart," said the Crow.

Sam stiffened at the term. "What white man?"

"Broken Hand," said the Crow.

Sam looked at Flat Dog, Bell Rock, and Peanut Head. So Fitz had come here and gotten robbed—by Crows!

Coy made a whining yowl.

As the four men watched, Crow men, women, and children tried out every part of their windfall. It was enormous—they had taken an entire year's worth of trade goods, an amount that would have been traded perhaps to a dozen villages. Women spread out entire bolts of wool and cotton cloth, then wrapped themselves in it and whirled around, giggling. Men played with locks of rifles they would never have been able to afford. Boys threw steel tomahawks at trees, practicing. Girls ran around tinkling bells with both hands.

The riders walked their horses a little farther and saw several men pass jugs filled with whiskey. Fitz had carried several kegs of pure alcohol. "Bad news," said Sam.

Immediately, he dismounted and went to them. "I'll show you how to make it good," he said.

Coy trotted up to a man who was already half-drunk, the liquid from the jug running down his forearm. The coyote licked a little of it off. Instantly he gave Sam a sour look and wiped his tongue on his furry foreleg.

The drinkers were sitting in a circle in front of a lodge, queer expressions on their faces. *Pure alcohol will do that.* Sam looked over his shoulder at his friends, still mounted. "You best find out what's happened," he said.

They rode off, Flat Dog leading Paladin.

Sam turned to the drinking companions. "There's a trick to making firewater," he said with a big smile. He sent one of them for a keg of creek water and got another to bring a twist of tobacco—the camp had a windfall of tobacco now.

The drinkers stared at him foolishly, their minds already woozy.

What is a booze-out this big going to do to these people?

In a few minutes he had one keg of whiskey mixed half and half with water and seasoned with tobacco. "We should put in some black pepper and a couple of red chiles," he said, "but we don't have any."

His companions passed the new jug and slurred out words of approval. Sam suggested in his fluent Crow that the whole camp share this keg and put the rest away for later.

"No," said one.

"Too much fun," said another.

"Too much of it will kill you," Sam said flatly.

"Shut up, white man," said a drinker, his cup heading for his lips.

"This man is my brother-friend," said Flat Dog, coming up behind. "He is a Kit Fox, a carrier of the pipe, and a sun dancer." He looked hard at the drinkers. Probably some of them were also members of the Kit Fox society. "Listen to him," Flat Dog said. "Too much whiskey will kill you."

Most of the drinkers shrugged. Two filled their tin cups and walked away.

Sam slipped off with Flat Dog. "How the hell did this happen?"

"You better hear it from Beckwourth," said Flat Dog.

Sam put an edge into it. "Beckwourth?"

"YOU SON OF a bitch," said Sam.

"Now ain't that a way to talk to a comrade," said Beckwourth. His story was quick in the telling. He'd encouraged the Crows to trade with the trust instead of Rocky Mountain Fur. "Ain't no dishonor in that. I am loyal to the man that pays me."

"So they robbed Fitz."

"They pushed things a little further than I said. You know they is the best horse thieves in the mountains."

"You put them up to it."

Beckwourth hesitated. "Sam, this child is gonna give you the benefit of the doubt. Considering."

Considering, Beckwourth was saying, that the two of them had spent a winter together in Rides Twice's village. Considering that they'd shared a lot of campfires and a lot of meat, that they'd fought their way together through hard times and laughed their way through shining times.

"You son of a bitch," repeated Sam.

Coy uttered a low ruff.

"Your emotions always did ride faster than your brain," said Jim.

"I thought we were on the same side."

"The white side?" asked the black man.

"You know better than to talk like that."

"Like I said, I'm for the man that pays me." He put on a clever little smile. "Did you know they paid me to build a fort down at the mouth of the Big Horn?"

Sam flashed hot. "The Big Horn? Just now at rendezvous they divided the hunting grounds fair and square for this year. Fitz got Crow country."

Jim spread his big hands. "I just do what I'm told. Me and Tulloch built that fort last coupla months. It's doing fine. Now I'm ambling around among my Crow friends"—he made a sinuous movement with one hand—"reminding them where they can go to trade. Earning my wages."

Sam forced himself to calm down. "Did Fitz leave here stripped?"

"He was here talking with the chief, like usual. Then he come back all righteous indignation. After he calmed down, Plays with His Face give him back horses, guns, powder, lead, traps—some of each one."

Sam looked at Flat Dog and took thought. "I guess," he said, "we don't have to go after him and rescue his ass."

"Mister Fitzpatrick is as good as mountain men get, good as you and me, Sam. He be fine."

Sam looked around the camp. "I don't know how fine things are here. There's a blow-out—"

An awful, strangled cry shut them both up.

SAM, FLAT DOG, and Beckwourth ran toward the sound. It was gone before they got there.

Coy whined.

One middle-aged Crow stood over another. He held a knife out at a fierce horizontal, hand and sleeve dripping with blood. The other man's chest was a puddle of red.

Sam looked the attacker in the face. He seemed struck dumb by what he had done. Sam chopped his uplifted wrist hard with the edge of one hand, and the man dropped the knife. He fell to a knee, holding his wrist and moaning.

Flat Dog said, "He smells like a whiskey barrel."

A young woman ran up screaming. She threw herself on the bloody man and wailed.

The attacker rose and stumbled off.

An elderly woman scurried up and knelt in the dust, silent tears streaming down her cheeks.

"Who is this man?" Sam asked her.

"Yellow Horse. My brother, her husband." She held the bloody man's hand, stroked his hair back off his forehead, looked into his eyes.

Yellow Horse tried to say something to her, but it drowned in his throat. Sam knew he wouldn't speak again.

The young woman sent up a shriek that frightened birds out of the trees.

"Why?" said Sam. Crow people didn't kill each other, just didn't.

"This young woman," said the elderly woman, "she was married to the man who did this. Half a moon ago she left him and went to my brother's lodge."

"So this is jealousy?" said Sam. That seemed odd, because Crow marriages seemed to shift at will.

"No," said the woman, "it is your whiskey."

FLAT DOG AND Sam found Plays with His Face right quick. He was half-drunk.

"Kit Foxes!" cried Flat Dog. "Kit Foxes!"

Bell Rock stepped up alongside and sang: *"Iaxuxkekatū'e,*

bacbi'awak, cē'wak." Bell Rock's voice was passion, and Sam joined him partway through. The words meant, "You dear Foxes, I declare, I want to die."

Three men made their way through the crowd to them.

"We are Kit Foxes, the three of us, the three of you," Flat Dog told the newcomers. "One of the duties of Kit Foxes is to make sure people are safe."

Coy gave a single bark, as though he wanted to pitch in.

The three men nodded hesitantly. Maybe they didn't like being told their responsibility by an outsider.

"Too many people are drunk," Flat Dog said.

Sam thought at least one of these Kit Foxes was boozy, and another seemed feeble with age.

"Two drunks have already gotten into a fight," Sam said, "and one is dead, Yellow Horse. I call upon the Kit Fox Society to enforce order here, so that no one else gets hurt."

Now the men nodded in agreement.

Beckwourth stepped up and said, "I'll help out."

After a hesitation, Sam said, "Good."

Peanut Head came out of the shadows and said in English, "Me too."

The feeble man said in Crow, "Is he a Kit Fox?"

"No," said Sam in the Crow language. Then in English, "Peanut Head, go with the old fellow and help him."

IT WAS A long night.

Sam marched around the camp as a guard. He broke up three fights. No one else died, but one man was bloody, and one broke an arm.

For a while Sam watched people play the gambling game with the fox bones in the hand. They sang the songs wildly, but nothing worse.

He kept an eye on Peanut Head and the old man. He checked regularly with Flat Dog, Bell Rock, and Beckwourth.

About midnight Plays with His Face staggered up to Sam. "Thank you," he said, "you are a true guardian of the people." The chief was still drunk. He walked off, threw both arms out, and loudly snorted like a buffalo. "I am a bull," he shouted. "I want a cow."

People nearby laughed.

Sam saw lots of couples go into the bushes hand in hand. Crow marital tolerance was being tested tonight.

Once he saw a teenage girl leave the hand game and make her way into the bushes. An older man slipped out of the crowd watching and padded quietly behind her.

Sam eased along behind both of them. The girl squatted, probably to pee. The man seized her by the hair and threw her on her back. She screamed.

Sam clubbed the man with the flat of his tomahawk. When the rapist crumpled, Sam pushed him with a foot onto some cactus. He howled.

"You're the one needs to get pricked," said Sam.

Then he led the girl back to the game. She glanced toward the creek, walked on to a lodge, and ducked in.

When the rapist came back picking needles out of his skin, he wore a huge scowl. He walked right past Sam without recognition. Apparently, he didn't even know who had pushed him onto the cactus.

"I seen an adventure at the crick myself," said Beckwourth.

Sam looked at him questioningly.

"A pair, them over there, was doing the deed on the bank. They picked an undercut place, I guess. The bank caved in, and they went for a swim."

"Cooled them off, I guess," Sam said.

"And shriveled him up," said Beckwourth.

Coy howled at the moon, a shivery sound.

By three or four o'clock, according to the Big Dipper, most people were in their lodges. A dozen or fifteen men were passed out on the ground, and a handful of women.

Sam and Flat Dog checked again on the sentries watching the ponies. One of them was drunk, another drunk and unconscious.

Sam took their names and sent them to their tipis. The camp police could deal with discipline later. He and Flat Dog took guard duty.

Coy slept. Sam waited irritably for the sun to come up. When it did, it looked like the broken yolk of a rotten egg oozing across the hills to the east.

Sam stewed.

The next watch arrived.

As he and Flat Dog walked back, Sam grumbled, "I want to sleep long enough that I don't have to see the damage this morning."

Thirty-seven

"I COME TO thank you," said Plays with His Face. "You acted as men for the people last night."

He was a different man today, clear of eye, firm of step. Sam saw a wily fellow, and a force to be reckoned with.

"We are Kit Foxes," said Sam, indicating Flat Dog too. "We did what Kit Foxes are pledged to do."

Julia handed cups of steaming coffee to each of the three men, and another cup filled with sugar. They were seated around the cold ashes of the center fire in her tipi.

"Our friends helped too," said Sam. Bell Rock, Beckwourth, and Peanut Head weren't there.

"I will thank them personally," said Plays with His Face. He hesitated, then gave Sam a glance that pretended to be rueful. "Last night I did what a leader must not do. I set down my vigilance.

I thought only of my own momentary pleasure. You saved me from a great embarrassment, perhaps from humiliation."

"We did what is our duty," said Flat Dog.

Plays with His Face nodded.

This entire exchange was ceremonial, political, but for all that something might come of it.

Someone scratched at the tipi door flap. Julia let Bell Rock in. He sat, accepted coffee, and heard Plays with His Face repeat his words of thanks.

The chief addressed Bell Rock. "You are our relative, and a medicine man from the village of Rides Twice. Flat Dog is from the same village. I know his father and mother, Gray Hawk and Needle." He turned his eyes to Sam and hesitated, searching for the right words. At last he settled on direct ones. "I don't remember you."

The chief would not have said it, except that Sam's skin and hair were white.

Flat Dog answered for Sam. "He is the husband of my sister, and the father of this girl."

They all looked at Esperanza, who was making a cat's cradle with her yarn.

This much of an introduction would have been given to any Crow.

Bell Rock spoke up. "He is Joins with Buffalo." Plays with His Face took in the fact that this fellow of warrior age had gone on the mountain for a vision and earned a name. "He has given a sun dance." Bell Rock let a moment pass. "I vouch for him."

Plays with His Face appraised Sam. A sun dance was a major ceremony. This trapper, then, was no ordinary man, no ordinary Crow. But not everything was explained here.

Flat Dog understood. "My brother and I, we have come because Joins with Buffalo cannot return to our camp." He paused to think of words. "Five summers ago the son of Rides Twice"—Flat Dog could not speak the name of the dead—"fought with Joins with Buffalo. Because of my sister, Joins with Buffalo's wife."

Plays with His Face sipped at his sweet coffee as he brought back the incident. "I heard the story," he said.

Everyone waited for his next words.

"You are welcome in my village," said Plays with His Face directly to Sam. Then his gaze widened to include all these guests. "At any time you are welcome."

Bell Rock said, "Then these young men with strong bow arms will join in the hunt next week, and bring back meat for the needy."

"Very good," said Plays with His Face. "The old ones, they always need meat."

Everyone smiled.

The chief said, "Thank you very much for the coffee. Bitter and sweet, like life." He stood and made his way through the door flap.

Sam spoke to Bell Rock. "When are we going to do the pipe ceremony?"

"*After* the hunt," said the medicine man.

"Don't rush off," said Flat Dog. "You're safe now."

Sam said, "I don't feel that way."

Thirty-eight

RISING OVER THE ocher buttes and cedared ridges of the Wolf Mountains, the sun burned excitement into Sam's eyes. The earth etched itself crystalline. He loved the world this morning.

The herd scattered itself in dark clots across the broken plains.

On the ridge next to Sam some young men peered through the sagebrush at this winter's sustenance. They were select Kit Foxes, assigned to creep as close to a cluster of buffalo as they could from downwind and slay fat cows with their silent bows. For a few minutes, while arrows whisked quiet death through the air, the buffalo would keep grazing. They were smug beasts, the lords of the plains, afraid of nothing, disturbed by little.

Which was their weakness. Until one saw a movement that violated his sense of propriety, they would stand and die.

The young hunters on the ridge draped their bodies with the skins of coyotes and wolves as disguises. They stuck big branches of sagebrush in front of themselves as cover. The chase was a thrill, but these men could feed a lot of people before some bull raised his snout into the air, sniffed something he didn't like, chuffed a warning, and thousands of buffalo rumbled toward the horizon.

Elsewhere at the head of this valley, as far as the eye could see, bunches of animals fed on grass, and other select young men crept forward, ready to do the same job. Behind them, out of sight, the rest of the hunters stood with their mounts, ready for the chase.

Sam slipped off the ridge and padded back to Paladin. He grinned at Flat Dog, Bell Rock, Peanut Head, and Beckwourth, who stood holding the reins of their horses in one hand, their rifles loaded and primed in the other. Their assignment was easier and more fun. Nothing was as exciting, to Sam, as running with a herd of buffalo, and he hadn't ridden in one of these huge, tribal hunts since he was a pork-eater.

Peanut Head, the current pork-eater, had never been near a big hunt like this.

Sam spoke quietly, his breath making huffs of steam in the dawn chill. "It's dangerous as hell, don't forget that for a second. You go down, you get trampled.

"Trust your horse—drop the reins and let him run. He'll take care of himself and that way take care of you. When you're ready to close in for a shot, guide him with your knees. He'll understand."

He looked Peanut Head in the eye. "You're a good horseman. You'll do fine."

Then he had another thought. "Buffalo may charge your horse. Mostly they just run like hell, but sometimes one charges. Don't do anything but keep your seat. Your gelding won't let himself be gored. The dodge he makes may be a tad sudden. Just stay in the saddle."

"When you get close, shoot low behind the front leg," added Flat Dog. "The brisket. Only shot that does it."

Flat Dog's eyes gleamed at Sam. Some things never got old.

* * *

GEYSERS OF DUST. Clods of dirt and dung flying. A thousand of the great beasts—hell, ten thousand or a million, who knew?—stampeded forward like the biggest, wildest river in the world.

The buffalo were a million bellowing voices and four million clattering hooves of thunder. Next to them a steam engine would have sounded like a tinkle, and Niagara Falls like the bleat of a lamb. It was as loud as having your head inside ten exploding kegs of gunpowder.

The roar, that above all exhilarated Sam.

Still, if a hoof hit you, it would feel like getting struck by lightning.

Paladin caught up with the tag end of the herd. Now she was edging herself close to a running animal—she knew this game and loved it. Coy sprinted alongside. Somehow, Sam had never understood how, the little coyote darted around in the midst of the herds and never got stepped on.

Sam was losing his mind. He had lost track of his fellow hunters. Though he was shouting, he couldn't hear himself. Safety, sanity, good sense, all were blown away like leaves in a tornado. The chase wasn't just all that mattered—this rampage was the whole of the world.

Paladin brought Sam alongside a charging buffalo. He tried to see whether it was a bull or a cow, but in the torrents of dust he could barely tell front leg from back. The mare pulled half a length ahead, giving Sam a perfect angle on the brisket.

Sam lifted his rifle, held as steady as could be in this tumult, and fired. The geyser of white smoke was lost in the clouds of dust. The buffalo staggered, and Sam hoped the critter was mortally hit. Coy skittered to the beast for a sniff.

As the men ran with the herd, the women came behind and butchered out the meat. By tomorrow morning hundreds of meat racks would hold slabs of meat up to the sun to dry. The camp dogs would feast on the scraps too small to bother with. The tribe would rejoice in having food for another Rocky Mountain winter.

At full speed, surging up and down with the galloping mare, Sam poured powder from his horn into the barrel of the Celt. He plucked a cloth patch out of his belt, where he had tucked half a dozen for a quick grab. He spit one of the lead balls out of his mouth, set it on the patch in the muzzle, and used his ramrod to send the ball home and seat it against the powder.

He looked around. Paladin was bringing him up on another target. Quickly, he poured priming powder into the pan. The Celt was ready.

He urged a little more speed from Paladin. She brought him alongside, and he aimed. Just as he was about to pull the trigger, the world flipped upside down.

Paladin staggered, fell, and got instantly to her feet.

Sam went flying. The earth slammed the breath out of him. His eyes were filled with bobbing snouts and pounding hoofs. His nose was rank with the odors of buffalo and dung. Dimly, as much as he could do anything, Sam embraced these sights and smells, his last.

Coy planted himself next to Sam and barked ferociously.

Paladin took a place just upstream of Sam in the mighty, four-footed river. She whickered, she neighed, she screamed. She reared and flashed her hoofs. The river parted and flowed around the three of them.

Sam tried to sit up and couldn't. He would have lain down to die, mashed into the grass and dust by a thousand hoofs, except it wasn't right. Paladin and Coy were trying to save his life.

Suddenly, Peanut Head loomed over him on a mount that was terrified and jumping every direction. The rider leaned down and extended a hand. Sam grabbed it.

Peanut Head tried to pull Sam up behind him on the saddle. When Sam was on his feet, though, he lunged for Paladin's reins and grabbed them. He weaved a little—he was still woozy—but somehow he got into the saddle.

He looked around. It was like when he crossed the raging Siskadee—dangers everywhere and no choice but desperate action.

Sam spurred Paladin to follow with the flow of the herd. Peanut Head trailed them.

Sam let out a shriek, part triumph, part exhilaration, part terror.

* * *

WHEN THEY HAD worked their way out of the herd and let it go past, Sam said to Peanut Head, "You saved my life."

"Paladin saved your life," said Peanut Head. "I picked up what was left." His face darkened. "Besides, it was all my fault."

Sam looked at him questioningly.

"I knocked you off."

Sam waited.

"I was riding just behind you, thought I'd watch you and learn. A buffalo turned—God, they turn fast and sudden—lowered his horns and came at me hard. My horse did a crow hop sideways, a huge one, twenty or thirty feet. His front quarters bumped Paladin and knocked you off."

Sam's feelings raged. *You son of a bitch, you almost killed me*. But he made himself think. He could see how that might happen. He said carefully, "Let's go look for my rifle."

They found the Celt mashed into the earth. The stock was cracked. When Sam picked her up, a piece the size of a forearm bone came off in his hand. It had splintered off right beneath the engraved plate that Jacob Hawken had made for Sam in St. Louis ten years ago. CELT, the plate said in fancy letters. Coy sniffed the dirt that stuck to the barrel.

Sam held the rifle to his shoulder. "Guess I can fire it, more or less," he said. "Glue it for now and have it fixed when I get to Taos." He lowered the rifle, and Coy sniffed at the dirt on the barrel.

He looked after the herd. "We've missed most of the fun," he told Peanut Head, "but let's see if we can get a straggler or two."

Before he touched his spurs to Paladin, he said, "I oughta have told you. When you run buffalo, stay way clear of the other hunters. Because of just what happened."

His nerves were still popping like corn in a hot pan.

Thirty-nine

THE COALS GLOWED fiercely in the fire pit, and by their glow Sam could see the knees of other men in the sweat lodge, Flat Dog, and next to the fire pit, Bell Rock. Their bodies and faces were lost in the darkness. Though he went into the sweat lodge at every rendezvous, Sam had not sat in the darkness of the womb of Mother Earth with Bell Rock since he got his pipe, seven years ago.

Sam's new pipe lay in front of Bell Rock's knees, wrapped in a deer hide. Bell Rock had insisted on making it himself, as a gift.

The medicine man dipped his gourd in the bucket of water, lifted it over the red-hot coals, and began to pour the sweat.

Steam and heat sprang like genies from the lava rocks and swirled around Sam. He felt as though he couldn't breathe. He told himself to relax, and as had happened many times before, his lungs found air in the moist, hot steam. Bell Rock apparently intended to pour this ceremony very hot.

He began with a ritual prayer, asking blessing for the unborn, for all children, for all mothers, for the elderly, for young men who might go on the mountain seeking a vision, for all sun dancers, and for all the people. Three times during this prayer, he poured more water on the coals. The steam was blistering. Sometimes Sam wanted to lie flat, where it was cooler. *But this ceremony is for me,* he reminded himself, *and I must be strong.* He sat straight up into the heat, made himself breathe, and in his mind echoed the words of Bell Rock's prayer, sending them up to Father Sky.

Bell Rock poured again and then sang, "Sun, we are doing this for you! May we live until next winter!"

"Aho!" exclaimed the other men in the lodge and the helper outside—thank you. "May we live until next winter!"

Then he called for the helper outside to open the door. Cool, crisp night air flooded the lodge. Sam lay down and relaxed. Round one was over.

When the door was closed and Bell Rock began to pour round two, he said words that broke the power of the pipe originally given to Joins with Buffalo. He condemned the Blackfeet who stole that pipe, and asked that whoever now claimed possession of it walk the black road of conflict and strife.

This second round, with seven pours of water, wasn't as aggressively hot as the first.

With the door open before the third round, Bell Rock unwrapped the new pipe. It was surprisingly simple, but beautiful. The bowl of red pipestone was intricately carved as the shaggy head of a buffalo, "to remind you who you are." The stem was short and plain.

"To be plain is good," said Bell Rock. Many Crow pipe stems were long and decorated flamboyantly with brass tacks or feathers. "I have modeled this pipe after my father's. He always said he carried a short pipe to remind himself that only a few things matter in a man—that he exhibit the true virtues. A man need not think of doing more than that."

Bell Rock looked pointedly at Sam. "I want to bring up a difficult topic. I think you worry about who you are, a white man or a Crow.

My advice to you is, throw away such foolish thoughts. You are a man. Like the pipe stem, you come from the earth. Like the red bowl, you are the blood of the buffalo. You walk the earth, you want what a man wants. This pipe will help you. Through it the powers will listen to you. Through it your heart will be true, your thinking simple and clear. The pipe will help you walk the red road. You are neither white nor red—you are a man seeking to keep your feet on a good path."

Now Bell Rock called for a few embers from the big fire outside. Then he took off the sage leaves that capped the pipe and lit it with an ember. He drew deeply from the mouthpiece, and the ember glowed. He blew a cloud of smoke out, and brushed the smoke across his head and shoulders. He held the pipe high over his head, then handed it to Flat Dog.

When Sam held the pipe and smoked, he thanked the powers for this pipe; for the events in his life that had brought him to the pipe; for his Crow relatives and friends; and for the love that had brought him a daughter. He uttered several other prayers for family and friends, and then asked for something that was peculiarly on his mind: "I feel uneasy here at this great gathering. I sense that my life is in danger. I ask for awareness, readiness, and courage. I ask for my days here to be safe."

Then Bell Rock handed the pipe to the attendant outside and asked for the door to be closed. The last round was hot and intense. Nothing existed for Sam except the eloquent songs and fervent prayers.

At the end of the fourth round the three men emerged into night air that felt like ambrosia.

Sam looked up and down the river. Hundreds of campfires flickered in front of hundreds of lodges belonging to several villages. One of the villages was led by Rides Twice. Sam had enemies there, and certainly wouldn't walk into that camp.

"Let's go," said Flat Dog.

They ran to the river and jumped in. As the hot steam had kept Sam's breath in, the cold river snatched it out. They all laughed and dipped themselves, getting every inch wet. Coy stood on the bank and barked at them. Then they ran back to their clothes.

"You are the honored guest of Plays with His Face here," said Bell Rock. "What are you afraid of?"

"Rides Twice has lots of relatives. If any one of them finds me alone, an arrow would be a great favor to the chief."

"While you are here," said Bell Rock, "we will make sure that someone is always with you. Myself, Flat Dog, or Peanut Head. You'll never be alone."

Forty

"WHAT NOW?" ASKED Peanut Head. He, Sam, and Flat Rock were broiling buffalo steaks, while Julia nursed the baby and the other kids slept.

"The women of the camps will dry the meat on the racks," Sam said, "and they'll make some of it into pemmican."

"How's that done?" Peanut Head seemed like a man to solve problems more with his muscles than his brain, but he had plenty of questions. And for some reason he always seemed to be on edge.

"Short version—grind it, render the fat into liquid, throw in some berries, and put everything together in a hide casing."

"How long we staying?"

"The camps will break up in a few days."

"Then we'll go trapping?"

Sam nodded. "Work the Big Horns, go to Taos for the winter."

"Fitzpatrick has the Big Horns," said Peanut Head.

"He doesn't like Crow country as well as he used to."

Sam asked Flat Dog, "You coming?"

"Yes," said his brother-in-law, "for the trapping part."

Peanut Head nodded to himself.

"We'll be sweating most nights," Flat Dog told him, "if you're interested."

The youth flexed his muscles and thought. "Back in Georgia my ma gave me more religion than I have any use for."

"Hell," Flat Dog said with a chuckle, "I got twice as much as most people."

Peanut Head cocked his head curiously.

Coy nosed up against Sam's leg and simpered.

"Julia made me marry her in the church and get baptized," Flat Dog said. "I say my Hail Marys in Spanish. She prays with her rosary every morning."

"That would be a *lot* more religion than I have any use for," said Peanut Head.

Flat Dog said, "You can put it in terms of languages. My religion in Spanish, my work in English, and my life in Crow."

"What do you see in Catholicism?"

Sam supposed Peanut Head had been raised an anti-Catholic Protestant, like himself.

"Christianity is a lot of big stories, maybe true, maybe not. The churches actually remind me of some place special, like the sweat lodge does. Difference is, in the sweat we pray to the four winds, Mother Earth, and Father Sky. Those are real. The Trinity, maybe not."

Peanut Head shrugged his big shoulders.

Sam said, "I'm going to the river for water."

Flat Dog stood up. "You don't go alone anywhere, especially at dusk or dawn, like this."

"I'll go with him," said Peanut Head.

* * *

PEANUT HEAD STOPPED twenty paces from the river, spread his feet wide, set the butt of his rifle on the ground, put his hands on the muzzle, and took a lookout stance. Sam smiled at him and trod on through the cottonwoods. Coy followed Sam but stopped halfway to the water and looked back at Peanut Head.

At the bank Sam knelt. The sun hadn't touched the river yet, and the mist made mushroom clouds over the water. He looked around before he dipped the kettle. He loved this time of morning. It seemed to him the way the world ought to be, fresh and new. The way it was in the Garden of Eden, if that story was true. Sam's father had showed him a favorite glade at their home near Pittsburgh, and they called it Eden. When he came west, Sam thought he would be an Adam. He would leave the tired Old World behind and start a new life, a whole new way of being.

He was no longer so innocent.

He stood up, holding the kettle, and caught his balance on the bank. Just then his head exploded. He didn't even know he pitched into the water.

FLAT DOG TRUNDLED along with the second kettle. He wondered why Sam hadn't reached into the tipi for it. Ahead he saw something very odd. Peanut Head raised his rifle. Soundlessly, over the swoosh of the river, he cocked it. What was the youth aiming at? A fat goose on the water?

Then horror flushed through Flat Dog. He dropped the kettle and flung his rifle up. Fear swung the barrel beyond Peanut Head, and Flat Dog needed a second try to steady the front sight on—

He saw the white smoke burst from Peanut Head's gun and heard the explosion. Sam fell into the river, and Flat Dog saw blood fly from his head.

Flat Dog centered on the murdering bastard's back and pulled.

Peanut Head flew into a sapling and crumpled to the ground.

As Flat Dog ran by him, he saw Peanut Head was hit in his lower spine. Flat Dog kept sprinting.

Coy marked the spot on the bank, barking furiously.

Sam lolled on his back in the river, a long plume of red seeping downstream from the floating ends of his white hair.

Flat Dog dropped his rifle, jumped in, hefted Sam up, and set him on the bank.

Crow men came running with bows, clubs, and some firearms.

Flat Dog inspected the wound frantically. Sam's head was a mass of blood on the right side, and his ear was mostly gone.

Flat Dog lifted Sam high and clambered onto the bank on his knees. He stood up with a humph and ran toward the camp. As he passed Peanut Head, two warriors were bending over the body.

"What?" snapped Flat Dog.

"Bad," said one of the warriors.

"Good," said Flat Dog. He called back over his shoulder, "Bring the son of a bitch to my lodge."

Coy loosed a tirade of barking at Peanut Head.

Flat Dog ran. Coy trotted behind, his head turned back and barking fury.

Flat Dog didn't know who the healer was in this camp, but Julia had acquired some skills. "Bring a robe," he yelled.

The moment she spread it, Flat laid Sam down on his back.

Esperanza came out of the lodge and stared at both her fathers, gape-mouthed.

Julia washed the wound and probed it with her fingers.

Sam didn't care—he was unconscious.

Flat Dog knelt opposite Julia by Sam's head.

"I think maybe it gouged the bone but didn't touch the brain," she said. She probed some more. "Maybe . . ."

"Will Papá be all right?" squeaked Esperanza.

Julia looked at her daughter, then at Flat Dog. "You can never tell with head injuries."

Esperanza went to Flat Dog and put a hand on his shoulder. "Father," she said, "help Papá."

Forty-one

"I CAN'T FEEL my legs," said Peanut Head. He was on a blanket a few steps from Sam.

Flat Dog slapped him with words. "Your spine is severed, and you're gutshot. By me."

He glared down at the son of a bitch. A dozen Crows looked on, men, women, and children.

"Dying," said Peanut Head, "shinin' times."

Flat Dog made a laugh that sounded like an axe cracking into wood. "That ain't all you're going to do."

Coy lay next to Sam, head on his paws, mewling.

"Why?" Flat Dog's word was sharp.

Soft and simple: "The bastard killed my father and my uncle."

Flat Dog slapped Peanut Head hard in the face.

"What are you talking about?"

"Elijah was my uncle."

Flat Dog said again, "What the hell are you talking about?"

"Micajah was my father."

"Oh."

These next words Peanut Head barely squeezed out. "The murderer Morgan bragged to me about how he did it. Righteous, he called it."

Flat Dog sniffed but said nothing about Peanut Head calling Sam a murderer. Instead he remembered: Micajah the drunk. Micajah the giant. Flat Dog saw the resemblance now. That's what had always nagged at him about Peanut Head—he was Micajah in miniature.

Bell Rock came up at a trot, his eyes pleading.

Flat Dog turned away from Peanut Head slowly and knelt by Sam's head. He barely heard Julia telling Bell Rock about the head wound.

"There's a man good at stopping a fever," Bell Rock said. "I'll go get him."

She carefully put a poultice on the angry rip on the side of Sam's head. "It's going to be a long time before we know anything," she told her husband.

Flat Dog nodded. They both looked at Esperanza, sitting on a log and staring into space.

"He might not wake up for hours, or days. He might never wake up."

Flat Dog pursed his mouth. "Right now there's things to take care of."

THREE YOUNG MEN helped Flat Dog carry Peanut Head on a blanket. They were as gentle as they could be. Flat Dog didn't give a damn how much pain they caused Peanut Head, or how much damage they did. He just didn't want the ass to pass out.

On the far side of the river, on the far side of a dry hillock, they set Peanut Head down.

"Listen," said Flat Dog.

The wounded man's eyes more or less focused in Flat Dog's direction.

"I'm leaving you this tin cup of water. Not to ease your pain. To make you last longer and suffer longer. Drink it when you want to."

He looked up at the sky and around at the hills, paying no attention at all to the three young men watching.

"What's going to happen to you is like this. The ants will come first. You'll feel them crawling, crawling, nibbling, nibbling. Then the ravens. They'll peck at you, picky here, picky there. They like blood, they like innards, and they'll go good for your gut wound. People say they like the eyes sometimes too." He paused, looked straight into Peanut Head's eyes, and smiled. "I hope so.

"After that the coyotes. Even if you can still move your arms, they won't give a damn. They like cripples. They'll eat your guts out good.

"The bears? No telling. If they find you soon enough, they'll chase the coyotes off. Ain't nothing they don't eat, if it's meat. Legs, arms, everything.

"And here's the good news. When the bears are done, the ravens will come back. They like to peck the last flesh off the bones, and they leave the carcass pretty clean.

"Last, the ants will come back and finish off every little scrap." He paused, savoring it. "All that will take a month, maybe. Then the wind will sing a little song through your ribs, moan through your eyeholes, whoo through your mouth cavity, through your brain chambers, your whole skull. After a while it will dry your bones, parch them all the way. That's when you start turning to dust."

He stood up.

"Savor every moment," he said.

Peanut Head moaned.

Flat Dog waved for the young men to follow him. As they approached the river again, one of them said, "You make a good comrade and a bad enemy."

"Thank you," said Flat Dog.

Forty-two

"There were signs," said Flat Dog. "He shot near Sam when we were hunting antelope. He knocked him off Paladin during the buffalo hunt. Signs we might have seen."

Julia poured them both cups of coffee and sat next to her husband in front of the fire.

"You want to hear the story?" asked Flat Dog.

"Please," said Julia.

The children were asleep. Esperanza, who seemed stuporous, had taken a long time to drift off but was gone at last. Man and wife were sharing black coffee at the center fire of their lodge, their sugar being gone. To the side of the fire lay Sam Morgan, still unconscious, his head wrapped with blue cloth intended for a shirt for Flat Dog, now drenched in blood.

Flat Dog looked at her questioningly.

"He's starting to get feverish. We're doing our best against it."

Flat Dog looked at his brother-friend in the shadows, and through his prone form into the past.

"The first year I went beaver hunting with Sam, there was a fellow trapper named Micajah. He was a river man, burly like Peanut Head but half a foot taller and fifty pounds stouter, the kind they call half horse, half alligator. For a reason I didn't understand, whenever he saw Sam, he'd tell him, 'I'm your friend—I really am.' And he wanted Sam to perform this ritual with him. It came from back in the States, among the river men. Two men would swear eternal friendship by shooting whiskey cups off each other's heads.

"But Sam would never do it, just wouldn't, not with anyone. Gideon stood in for him, which was allowed by the river man code."

Julia knew Gideon well, from the time Jedediah Smith's men crossed to California. That was when she met Flat Dog.

"So Gideon did the ceremony a couple of times in Sam's place. Big deal to Micajah.

"Sam finally told me why. Back in the States, when he was boating to St. Louis on a big river, Micajah and his brother tried to rob Sam and Abby."

Abby, Sam's friend the madam, was also in California now. Julia had heard endless stories about her beauty, cleverness, and spirited disregard of morality.

"Sam and Abby fought back, and she killed the brother. Elijah, his name was.

"When Sam ran across Micajah out here later, he was worried, thought Micajah might sneak-attack him.

"But Micajah said he didn't hold Elijah's death against Sam, said he and Elijah were drunk or it wouldn't have happened. 'Friends forever,' said Micajah.

"That seemed to work out fine as long as Micajah was sober. He was crazy when he was drunk. Which meant rendezvous.

"Anyway, after that, when we came across each other out here, Micajah was always going on about that one thing—what happened was forgotten, and now he and Sam were friends. Always he wanted to prove it in that one particular way.

"Eighteen twenty-six rendezvous, Micajah wouldn't stand for anything but to do it again. 'Friends forever,' he said, drunk as a skunk, 'us three against the world.'

"Gideon stood in for Sam like before. But Sam could see something was wrong—Micajah was riled up about something and hiding it. That's what Sam saw in his face.

"Well, Gideon's shot was clean—the cup flew off—Micajah's turn. Sam was bad scared. Just as Micajah pulled the trigger, Sam jumped forward and knocked the barrel of his rifle up."

Flat Dog pursed his lips and looked at the past.

"Mightily insulted. Outraged—that's what Micajah said. He ranted, 'My honor cries out to be satisfied.' Nothing would do but for him and Sam to fight.

"Seemed no one had seen that mean face but Sam, or else they didn't think much of reading a man's mind in his eyes in the twilight.

"So Jim Bridger says they must fight until one couldn't go on. No weapons, no eye-gouging, definitely no killing." Flat Dog sighed. "Bad for Sam—Micajah was big as one and a half of him. Anyhow, as they fought, the big bastard went to his boot and pulled a knife. Slashed Sam's ribs with it. Then the giant rolled on top of Sam and started strangling him. The man was monstrous strong—Sam didn't have a chance. I was about to interfere."

Flat Dog hesitated, remembering. "Sam slipped out that little knife he keeps hidden in his hair and cut the bastard's throat."

He looked at his friend, so silent on the blanket that even his breath was inaudible.

"And now these seven years later it comes back to kill him. Sneak-kill him."

ON THE FOURTH day Sam Morgan rolled over. "Thirsty," he said.

Julia gave Esperanza the cup of water to take to him.

After a couple of hours of sleep he sat up, and Julia got him to sip some broth.

The next day Esperanza brought him her yarn. She made a cat's cradle and slipped it onto his hands. He made a diamond pattern and passed it back.

The day after that he walked to the fire in front of the lodge and sat all day. In the twilight Sam walked around the camp of Plays with His Face. Though he had to sit down several times, he managed the full circle.

Over a breakfast of broiled strips of buffalo a few days later, Flat Dog raised the issue. "Most of the camps will ride out tomorrow," he said. "Rides Twice day after tomorrow."

The friends looked at each other, the dilemma in their eyes. Sam glanced sideways at Esperanza, who was shaking a buffalo hoof rattle vigorously. *Another winter and spring without my daughter.* Then he reminded himself. *This time I got extra months with her.*

Julia poured all three of them coffee and put the pot back on the center fire. The tipi was cozy against the morning chill.

Sam felt the side of his head. "What's here?"

"The scalp wound will heal," said Julia.

"And there's a little bit of an ear left," said Flat Dog. "Looks like a piece of gnarly root."

Sam decided to take a nap.

That evening Flat Dog said, "Plays with His Face has offered you sanctuary."

Sam pursed his lips.

"There are good women in this village. You are a man of many honors."

Sam nodded. "I need to catch up with Tomás."

"You don't even know where he is," said Julia.

"I need to find him." Simple as that.

"You figure he'll go in to Taos for the winter?"

Sam grinned. "There's a waitress he fancies."

"So you're on your own?" Flat Dog said. His expression said he didn't like it.

"I'll go to Taos," said Sam.

Two days later, when they left this camp on the Little Big Horn, no one crossed the river to see the remains of Peanut Head. They knew what was left.

The villages of Rides Twice and Plays with His Face were headed across the Pryor Mountains. Rides Twice would ride up the Big Horn to where it became the Wind River, and up that to the winter camp the people had used for generations. Plays with His Face would ford the Big Horn River, which was easy at the low-water season, and go up the Stinking Water to the river's hot springs. Sam knew the place. Nearly thirty years go, John Colter, the first of all the Rocky Mountain beaver hunters, came to the village there, a lone white man wandering the country of Crows. The people still remembered him, and how he invited them to come in to the fort at the mouth of the Big Horn to trade.

Sam saddled up Paladin and put his mule on a lead. Coy pranced around eagerly. Sam would ride along the eastern edge of the Rockies, where the plains rose to meet the peaks, all the way past the North Platte and South Platte to Boiling Fountain Creek, where he would rest and drink the healing waters. Then on across the Arkansas and over the Sangre de Cristo range to Taos. He would arrive before Christmas. Tomás would attend the vigil at the church on Christmas Eve, just as Paloma had always done.

"Damned dangerous," said Flat Dog. He was already mounted and ready to take his position as a Kit Fox alongside the train of pony drags. "You're not strong yet."

Sam guided Paladin over to Esperanza. She jumped up. He grabbed her, gave her a hug, and set her down. He lifted a hand to Flat Dog, Julia, and their sons.

With a touch to Paladin's flanks he was off.

Coy looked back, whined, and trotted after Sam.

Forty-three

TOMÁS'S TRIUMPH HAD come nearly three months earlier, the day rendezvous broke up. It was a nice, hot glow. Sam Morgan, the man who was not his father, had asked every brigade leader if Tomás was with his outfit. All of them answered no. So Mr. Morgan was now riding out with Mr. Fitzpatrick and his brigade, plus Flat Dog and the Crows, bound north.

Tomás was going the other way. His ruse was simple and it had worked. He was not working for any of the brigades. He had chosen to become a free trapper. With Old Bill Williams and a gaggle of other men who preferred freedom to high wages, plus Walkara's Utes, he was headed south. That's where his sisters would eventually show up, maybe in Walkara's camp, maybe in Taos or Santa Fé. He would find them. It was a much better mission than going after a pipe glorified by superstition.

He threw hitches on the load his packhorse would carry and

helped the other men get ready. They would be off within the hour. And he was glad, damn glad, that Baptiste had decided to go with him. The Frenchy smiled in his slow way and said, "I have a yen for Taos."

The only fly in their ointment was Joaquin. The drunk said, "I go you, fin' wife, fin' son, I go you."

"We'll toast our toes in Taos," said Tomás. "They'll freeze their asses in a lodge with snow piled head deep on the side to the wind."

"You're hoping to toast your thing in Xeveria," said Baptiste.

Tomás grinned. "I'm counting on it."

His grin wobbled a little. He was worried that half the men in the outfit, even Joaquin and Baptiste, might be looking forward to Xeveria. This Taos waitress liked dancing, drinking, and presents, and had special ways of rewarding any man who showed her a good time.

"Let's not fortheget that we need to take some fur to have pesos to spend in Taos," said Baptiste.

"Don't tease me," said Tomás. "Let's not fortheget that my sisters come first."

They rode south toward the Uinta Mountains, a country they knew had plenty of beaver. Old Bill, by seniority, led the free trappers as much as they were willing to be led. Walkara rode beside him, Tomás, Baptiste, and Joaquin several horse lengths behind them. Farther back came a throng of free trappers and their families, and on the flanks of the outfit the young Ute warriors.

It was on a scorching hot noon about a week later when the horses pulled up a rise, the Siskadee slugging along to their left, well below. Old Bill suddenly raised his left hand—halt. When the dozens of people stopped, they drooped.

Baptiste and Tomás eased their mounts up beside Old Bill and Walkara to see ahead. Joaquin piddled up behind.

A band of Indians. A whole village, riding straight upriver toward them. All at once they all stopped and waited, stretched across the long flat.

"Blackfeet," said Old Bill. Tomás wondered how he could tell at such a distance. The partisan motioned the outfit forward.

In a couple of minutes, when most of his men were visible, he halted them again. He watched and then spoke to Baptiste directly. "Let's go, the four of us." He gave Tomás an eye. "Keep your mouth shut," he said, "and your hands off your weapons."

Tomás nodded.

"Unless I make a move," finished Old Bill.

Tomás thought, *I am smart*, but he didn't say it.

IN AN HOUR both outfits were making camp. The leaders had smoked the pipe and made flowery declarations of friendship each knew was hypocritical. Then the Blackfeet chief said, "We want to trade."

The mountain men set up hard against a bluff. You never trusted Blackfeet. The camp was well away from the river, but better to have a dry tongue than a bloody head.

Seeing the doubt on Tomás's face, Old Bill said, "There be enough un us. They act like good little Indians." His smile was ironic.

"That's what we hope," said Baptiste. The Blackfeet warriors outnumbered the trappers at least five to one. But their guns were inferior fusils, and the trappers carried heavy-caliber mountain rifles.

"They don't have much taste for losing blood," said Old Bill.

Baptiste said smoothly, "That means they won't attack unless they think they can surprise us, kill all of us, and take everything."

Old Bill said, "Your partner here know what way the stick floats."

Joaquin laughed like this was the funniest line he'd ever heard.

Tomás and Baptiste set up camp. Joaquin puttered around half-assed, laid down, and passed out.

On a word from Old Bill, Tomás and Baptiste drove the horses into a little side canyon and rope-corralled them. These two would have first watch on the herd tonight.

Making the last tie, Tomás said, "Let's ride over and see their camp." He'd mostly trapped the southern mountains, and hadn't gone far enough north to encounter Blackfeet before.

On the way Baptiste told Tomás a little story. "When the Rees attacked Ashley's men on that beach—"

Tomás nodded. His father, or rather Sam Morgan, had been there. Fifteen mountain men died there.

"Right when the firing started," Baptiste went on, "there were several trappers still in the Ree village, dallying with the women."

Tomás looked a challenge at him.

Baptiste shrugged. "They died. Friendship, even love, they don't fend off bullets. Our friend Joaquin would have been up there diddling himself to death."

But it wasn't the Blackfeet women who caught Tomás's eye. It was a certain medicine hat pony, one with markings almost identical to the mount Tomás sat on, Kallie. Staked next to a painted lodge, his white hind end gleaming in the afternoon sun, was his stolen gelding, Vici.

"I got to get out of here," Tomás said.

Baptiste followed his eyes to Vici, looked at Kallie, and nodded. Any warrior who saw the two mounts together might catch on.

Back in the trapper camp Tomás steamed. Kallie was corralled with the other animals. He watched the Blackfeet crowd around the trade blankets. *What am I going to do? How am I going to do it?*

He stood behind the trade blankets and watched Old Bill and the other trappers bargain. The women were trading buffalo robes for all the booty offered by manufacturers in the States and England. Blankets were welcome. Cloth was treasured. Bells and beads struck the feminine fancy.

The men were less keen. They traded for tobacco, knives, powder, and lead. But they wanted American flintlocks, weapons with finely rifled bores. The trappers had none to trade.

What am I going to do?

The sun's heat irritated Tomás. His uncertainty frustrated him. As soon as he started to simmer, he saw something that made him boil. A warrior rode Vici right up to the trade blankets, dismounted, and held the reins while he looked over the merchandise. Clearly he prized this horse. Instead of turning him out with the herd, he would stake him by the lodge. He would keep him close at hand all the time. Probably Vici was the fellow's buffalo horse, and Tomás knew he was damned good at that. Or he was the bastard's war-horse.

Tomás fumed. *I know what, but I don't know how.*

Forty-four

TOMÁS WATCHED THE camp from the top of a big boulder against the rock wall above the Blackfeet camp. He was taking every precaution. He had waited a full day to slip away from Old Bill and Walkara's outfit, even from Baptiste, and he took his time making his way upriver to catch the Blackfeet. You never knew, they might put out extra guards the first couple of nights away from the mountain men. Now Kallie was staked on some grass by a nameless creek more than a mile to the west, and Tomás was in position, flat and still.

No risks, he reminded himself for the hundredth time, and mocked himself in his mind. *How do you get this done without huge risks?*

The camp was going up in a huge circle on the west bank of the Siskadee, what they called the horns making the opening to the east. The lodges were a swarm of women setting up for the night. A melee of kids and dogs ran around in the middle of the circle. The men were attending to their horses, putting up tripods to hold their medicine bundles, or doing other small tasks. They all looked tired from the long day's ride under a relentless sun.

The horse herd was on good grass where the creek angled into the river. Even from here Tomás could see figures moving around, sentries on duty. He wished he had his dad's—whoops, Sam Morgan's—field glass. Then he could spy out everything better.

Even with the naked eye, though, he could see what he really needed. Vici was staked next to a lodge on the north side of the circle. Since the lodge was near the horns, his owner was an important man. Not owner, thief.

What else do I need to know? I have enough to act. Tomás liked action and despised hesitation.

He slid down the back side of the boulder. The shadows in here were cool. He fished some jerked meat out of a pouch and chewed. He washed the meat down with a swig from his flask. He pictured the situation as clearly as he could. Vici would be next to that lodge until the camp moved out tomorrow morning, except for two times. The bastard who stole him would take him to the river to drink in the twilight, and again first thing in the morning.

Maybe Tomás could figure where Vici would drink. The bank was too steep in some places, the water too swift in others. *Maybe that will be my chance. And maybe I will kill the thief.*

Sam Morgan said killing was something you always regretted. But Tomás was finished with Sam Morgan's advice. *You steal from me, I smash your head.*

IN THE TWILIGHT Tomás floated down the Siskadee. He'd shoved a cottonwood off a sandbar, one with dead branches and leaves, and now drifted along behind it, feeling clever and sneaky.

He had everything worked out. A long chance, maybe, but he liked it. Nabbing Vici by the river might be easier than cutting his rope next to the lodge.

He carried his pistol high and dry behind the cottonwood foliage.

He'd left his rifle concealed near Kallie, well up the creek. He felt mixed up about that. He hated to be without the gun, but firing a shot would draw a furious buzz of Blackfeet warriors around his head.

Bobbing around the last curve, he saw the entire village spread out on the bank well ahead. It was a beautiful sight, truly, the lodge poles spiking up dark against the glowing western sky, mirror-image triangles of the hide tipis below. Fires flickered in front of the lodges, cooking stews, now that the sun was down. Figures flitted across the circle. He reminded himself, *At least a hundred of them would love to kill me.*

The root-ball of the tree caught gently on a spit of sand that stretched out from the curve. The leafy top, where Tomás clung, began to swing out, rotating downstream of the ball. He let go and found his footing. Keeping close to the moving tree, body well down, pistol up, he beavered his way to the sandbar.

The banks for the next couple of hundred paces were high, or at least tall enough to hide a man. Not until the creek flowed in would they drop. In a few places it would be easy to lead a horse down to the water. Tomás had picked out the one with quickest access from where Vici was staked.

He waded carefully, one hand propped against the dirt, the current pushing against his legs. The spring rise had undercut the bank here, and now, at low water, the roots of trees gnarled their way out of the slanted earth and into his face. They were a nuisance.

Tomás had not realized that the river would make so much noise, sloshing against the cut bank. He would have to use his eyes, not his ears.

There—that was the break in the bank he'd spotted. And he was lucky. A cedar clung to the bank on the upstream edge. He could hide in the cave made by its roots, half invisible.

He slipped inside and squatted down in the water to wait, tomahawk in his hand. That would be more useful than his pistol here. Spot your quarry, step out from the roots, and make one clean throw. At seven paces Tomás could clip the corner off a playing card. This was a good distance for him.

He crouched down and waited. His butt got cold, so he stood up and bent level from the waist. He waited. He held on to a root with his left hand and waited. Waited. Waited. He hadn't known he would feel so shut away down here—he could hear nothing, could see nothing but the small inlet in front of him.

He also hadn't realized he would be so cold. Wait, wait, wait . . .

Vici's muzzle was what he saw first, straining against the lead. He slurped up water greedily, like he'd been dry for days. The thief stepped alongside his neck on his upstream side and rubbed his mane, turning his back to his danger.

Tomás grinned. It was good to see Vici, and this attack was beautiful.

He stepped through the roots and cocked his arm.

Vici raised his head, looked at Tomás, and gave a friendly whicker.

The thief turned sideways, his eyes inquisitive.

The tomahawk bit into his shoulder instead of his back.

The son of a bitch let out a whoop like a pack of coyotes and charged.

A dozen, a score of war cries screeched up from the camp.

Goddamn it.

Tomás shot the ass. His chest bubbled red, and he fell backward into the water.

Vici trotted upstream, coming to his friend.

Tomás jumped onto him.

A half-dozen dark figures popped up on the bank.

Tomás turned Vici toward the middle of Siskadee and slapped his behind.

The gelding jumped forward. Tomás glanced back, saw a whir of something dark, looked back and . . .

A stone war club hammered him in the forehead.

He fell off Vici, backward into the dark water, and down, down, down.

Forty-five

HIS TONGUE WAS big and sticky in his mouth, like a slug. *Probably I will choke on it.* Tomás moaned.

A voice threw words at him the way a boy hurls small rocks. If it was a human language, Tomás didn't recognize it.

He lifted his hand to point to his mouth, angled his head up to meet the finger, and growled at the pain.

He had never felt anything like his damned head.

The voice laughed a little.

Carefully, gently, Tomás raised a hand to his head. Gingerly, he touched his hairline and felt something sticky. He looked at the fingers. A dark substance, probably his own blood, dark as his life was now.

He turned his head.

The pain was a muzzle blast.

He let time pass. Then he cupped his hand and barely touched the area.

There was a cannonball sticking out of his head.

No, it had skin on it, and hair. From the size and shape he guessed it looked like half an orange.

He felt heat coming from his right side. He rolled that way. His head swam through a big rapid, flipped, and crashed.

Later, whether seconds, minutes, or hours he didn't know, Tomás woke up again. Now he felt the heat on his face.

He made out the embers of a huge fire in front of him, and in the glow of the fire a man, probably the strange voice, probably a guard.

The night was black. Tomás wondered how many hours he'd been out cold. He thought back to the river, remembered blearily, and got a vague picture of a club whacking him on the head.

The guard reached forward, grabbed something on the ground, and pulled.

Tomás's neck bulged forward, and his head clang-clang-clanged.

As he fell into a well of darkness, he heard the same laugh again.

When he opened his eyes, he saw the guard still leering at him. *Maybe I wasn't out long that time.*

Now he saw it—a rope running from his neck to a tall, thick post.

He put things together. The Blackfeet had built this fire as the center of their dance circle. They'd whooped their triumph over this enemy. Tomorrow they would tie him to the stake and start a fire around his feet.

He'd heard plenty about it. Dying brave, the Indians called it. Show how much pain you can endure without complaining. Show how long you can last before you die. Sometimes, the stories said, a woman would come close, pick up a burning twig, sharpen the other end, and jab it hard into your flesh.

Then he realized. *Tie me to the post tomorrow? Hell, I'm already tied.*

The rope snaked away from his neck.

They'll shout and mock me as I die.

Tomás shuddered. His thoughts were jerked meat, old, dry, and tough.

He tested his hands. They were tied together at the front of his breechcloth. *Maybe they're still giving me a chance to piss.*

While he felt bitterness at this thought, he smiled wryly inside. *You made a mistake.*

He wiggled, paying attention to his arms and legs. He was naked, except for the breechcloth.

He trundled some more thoughts through his mind, and soon he resolved on something. *We're going to do this my way.*

He had one tiny advantage. His father, or rather Sam Morgan, kept a couple of blades on his person, hidden where enemies wouldn't find them even if they stripped him. Surprising weapons in very surprising places. Sam didn't tell anyone about them.

In Santa Fé, Tomás had a blacksmith hammer out concealed weapons for him. He wore his breechcloth on a rawhide rope as thick as his finger, and it tied in front. From one of the dangling ends of the rope hung a flat, short blade covered with rawhide, its lower half sharp as any knife. From the other end, also covered with rawhide, was a finger-length awl.

These weapons fell beneath the flap of his breechcloth and outside the girdling part. No one knew about them, except his fa—

Don't lie to yourself. The words were lances. *You can't do much, not with this head. Hardly anything.*

He breathed the cool night air in and out.

But I have a chance.

Very slowly, he pushed his breechcloth aside. Very gently, he slipped the rawhide scabbard off the knife blade. With as little movement as possible, he sawed at the rope binding his hands beneath the breechcloth.

He hesitated for a moment. He hated this. The situation was so . . . There was no give to this reality.

I have a chance.

Words in a strange language flew at him fast and furious. The guard stood and glared.

Tomás pretended to try to push the inner part of his breechcloth aside.

The guard laughed and sat back down.

Tomás sawed a few more strokes, and the rope gave.

The guard put predatory eyes on him.

Tomás took out his thing, covering it with his hand, and pissed.

The guard grunted.

Tomás rolled over, away from the guard. His mind teetered like a boat on roiling waters.

He waited, but the man said and did nothing. *Amazing how much better my head feels.*

He untied the rope holding his breechcloth. With as little motion as possible, he seized the neck rope hard with one hand. With the other, in several fierce swipes, he cut it.

Free.

He lay perfectly still.

He quivered.

In his mind he tittered.

Nothing solved yet.

He put his mind to it. *I need to get the bastard within reach.*

He made himself ready for the wooziness and rolled back toward the post, the fire, and the guard.

He lay still for a moment to recover.

Then he snapped words at the guard. "Hey, you, shit-eater, look at me."

The guard rose to his knees. If the man had no idea what Tomás was saying, he understood the tone perfectly.

Pretending that his hands were still tied together, Tomás jerked his breechcloth away and exposed himself.

This was a mortal insult.

The guard jumped and threw himself headlong at his prisoner.

Tomás braced his elbow on the ground. The guard's body weight punched the awl deep into his gut.

Tomás's head flashed furious lights, and he blacked out.

Forty-six

SOMEONE, SOMETHING SCRAPED on him.

Breath flooded back into his lungs. *How long was I breathing in itty-bitty pieces?*

"Let's get out of here," someone said.

Arms pulled him up, someone shouldered him. A picture of an angel hovered in Tomás's mind.

"Damn glad you're a shrimp."

An angel wouldn't call me a shrimp, he thought, irritated. *Whose the hell's voice?*

The Voice apparently didn't give a damn about him. His head bumped on the angel's back as they walked. It hurt like hell.

Tomás dimly noticed the circle as they passed between lodges.

His head banged. It was a drum, and this devil was beating it.

Strong arms spun him—whoopsy-doo!—and he landed with a *whumpf*. He was belly down on a saddle.

Quickly, a rope lashed around him several times and was hitched tight.

"I don't give a damn what happens, just stay on Vici."

Vici?

In the edge of his eye he saw the angel or devil swing up into his own saddle.

"How did you get Vici?"

"He came to me."

"What angel or devil are you?"

"Jean-Baptiste Charbonneau, at your service."

TOMÁS CHEWED ON the jerked meat. He tried to crunch teeth into flesh without moving his head. He felt like he'd been thrown off a mountain and landed on his skull.

The meat was stringy and tough. He wanted coffee. Hell, he wanted whiskey. He swigged creek water from a flask. He poured the water onto his head and wiped at the sore spot. The hand came away pink.

"Why did you follow me?"

Baptiste shrugged. "You followed me."

For a moment Tomás woozed toward a memory. His head rocked like a boat on choppy waters.

"Your dad and I rode into Canyon de Chelly. You followed us. Warned us about Nez Begay."

Tomás brought back the pictures of that night.

"Too late," said Baptiste with a grin, "but you warned us."

Tomás remembered Nez Begay pointing a rifle at himself and Sam Morgan.

"Maybe we better get the hell out of here," Tomás said.

"We already got the hell out of there," said Baptiste. "You rode all night, face down."

Tomás remembered the bumping, the feeling of being rapped in the head over and over, and the mad dreams. He grinned. He would have shaken his head, but he knew how that would feel. "Where in hell are we?"

"We rode into the river and then up the creek. We picked up Kallie. We came on up the creek a long way and then crossed the divide to Black's Fork. Eventually, they'll find the tracks where we came out of the water. We'll be to hell and gone by then. If you can ride."

"What's the hurry?" Tomás teased.

"Maybe we like Joaquin's jokes?"

"I need a few minutes."

They were quiet. After a while, Baptiste said, "You've been wanting to kill a man, now you did. How's it feel?"

Tomás floated his mind back. At the time he'd lost consciousness too fast. Finally he said, "Fantastic."

Forty-seven

"I AM SICK of this stuff," said Tomás.

Baptiste looked up from his knees. He took a few more strokes with his skinning knife on the whetstone. The beaver was flopped in front of him, drowned. He reached out and applied the tip of the knife to the right place.

"Every day, up a creek, down a creek. It is boring."

Baptiste quoted Sam Morgan as he worked. "You will learn to like trapping. When you ride upstream in the predawn light, the mist is still on the surface—"

Tomás took over in a mocking tone, "It is like the breath of the water."

"You find just the right set . . ." Baptiste plunged on.

"From your own sense of being like a beaver."

"You set the trap well, you bait the stick . . ."

"And you ghost your way back out of the cold, mysterious world of the water."

Baptiste held up the hide. "Result," he said in his own words, "the beaver loses his precious coat, so that there may be felt hats."

"And what," said Tomás, "is there to recommend all this labor?"

Baptiste turned half-serious. "Well, when you've skinned the animal, scraped the hide, and stretched it to dry, you have a plew worth six dollars. That's a week's wages in a town."

"In a town," said Tomás, "you have many friends, you have good food, you have whiskey, you have women."

Baptiste rolled the skin and tied it behind his saddle with another one. "I like eating beaver tail," he said. Most evenings he cooked the tails covered with hot coals.

He stepped up into the stirrup. "Trapping is a craft," he told Tomás, "a dollar, a way to live."

"Beaver stinks. You stink," said Tomás. "We stink."

Baptiste clucked his mount downstream, toward the camp. "What do you want to do?"

Tomás said, "Quit."

THEY TOLD JOAQUIN he couldn't come along—they'd see him in Taos. They said goodbye to Old Bill. The next morning they set their ponies' muzzles south along the river. Baptiste said, "How are we going to make a living?"

"Let's just live."

"All right." Baptiste mused. "Where are we going, exactly, and how are we going to spend our time?"

"I want adventure," said Tomás. "I want action."

Baptiste just looked at him sidelong.

"Also, I am mad to find my sisters."

"I can see that much. So why don't we start with Walkara?"

* * *

COLD LITTLE BUBBLES squirted up through Tomás's gut. "We're riding into the village of a damned slaver."

Baptiste smiled. "You said you wanted adventure."

Regardless, it was too late now. A half-dozen riders were on their way to take the strangers prisoner, or take them to the chief's hospitality, as the case might be.

Steely faces pointed at them. Tomás recognized two of Walkara's brothers, made sign language greetings, and said "Walkara" twice.

One of them corrected Tomás's pronunciation, though Tomás couldn't hear the difference. Funny how the faces never got less steely. Into the village they went, their status unclear.

At the sight of the two trappers Walkara's face burst out with joviality. "I am glad to see my beaver-man friends." He was also glad, according to his protestations, to have a chance to practice his English, and his Spanish, and with Baptiste even his Shoshone. He told Tomás and Baptiste they were guests of honor, and invited them to a multilingual smoke of the pipe. "Afterward we will have a feast," he said.

Then, studying Tomás's face, he asked Baptiste, "Why does your young friend look so relieved?"

Baptiste said, "I think he was afraid you would kill us."

"Kill you?" Walkara laughed and slapped his knees. Then he gave a devilish grin and said, "That would be bad for business."

Tomás didn't think he was kidding.

They smoked. They ate. They shared their only jug of whiskey with Walkara and his brothers. Late that night, Walkara showed them that his wives had put up a small tipi for their comfort. His last words to them that night were, "You are men without women. This is not good. While you are with us, perhaps you will look with favor on some of our beautiful women."

When they were stretched out in their blankets, Tomás said, "You think he means women for a night or women for long term?"

"Either one," said Baptiste.

Tomás slept at a simmer.

* * *

AT BREAKFAST TOMÁS put it to the chief. "Your brother-friend Pegleg has my sisters. I want them."

Baptiste leapt in. "I apologize for my young friend. Though he—"

Walkara interrupted, laughing. "The man who never quits!" He seemed to take thought, and shook his head. "I still don't know where they are. Pegleg has not returned. Maybe the three of them are living in a tipi in a beautiful place in . . ."

He asked Baptiste a question in Shoshone.

"Wedded bliss," Baptiste told Tomás.

Tomás frowned at that. "I am afraid he will trade them to men who will use them badly."

Walkara shrugged. "Anything is possible. Not all husbands are as good as Utes, and Comanches are especially bad. So . . . Here's my idea. I will tell you where I think Pegleg might have gone. I will even tell you without asking for anything in return for the information, since you come to us as paupers." He paused dramatically. "If I were them, looking to trade those horses, or the buffalo robes, or perhaps even the women, I go to the new fort the Bent brothers are building."

Tomás and Baptiste looked at each other quizzically.

"You heard about the fort," teased Walkara.

"Vaguely," said Tomás. There were reports of it at rendezvous. William Bent and his brother Charles were known as traders all over the southern plains, and now they were constructing a fort on the Arkansas River, below the Purgatory, within range of the Arapahos, Cheyennes, and Comanches.

"What fort?" said Tomás.

"It will be very big," said Walkara. "Those Bents, they plan to do very big trading."

"And you think Pegleg went there."

Walkara shrugged again. "Even I want to see this great fort. A man could trade anything there. To anybody. For months, in and out of that fort, you could trade. Go to Cheyenne, come back. Go to

Comanche, come back. Since Pegleg is not back yet, I think he is still there."

"You really think so?" asked Tomás eagerly.

"Yes. And now I make you a proposition. I will lead you straight to the fort myself, with enough of my young men to make us safe against enemies. I want to see it, and I want to show you what a good friend Walkara can be."

Tomás and Baptiste gaped at each other.

"The season is a little late," said Walkara, "for a long trip. I suggest that we start today."

Forty-eight

Tomás was exhausted and exhilarated. He couldn't believe they'd ridden so far so fast. They loped the horses more than they walked them. Every rider had two or three mounts and switched a couple of times during the day. They did not cook but ate pemmican. They barely took time to make fires, but rode from before sunrise to after sundown. Tomás had never seen anything like it.

And now they could see the fort in the distance on the north bank of the river. Relaxed, they walked their mounts ceremoniously toward Bent's big house.

Walkara put on one of his devilish grins. His favorite mood seemed to be devilment, not all of it in fun.

"Now is the time for me to apologize," he said. "I've been having a bit of fun with you." He looked frankly at Tomás.

"What do you mean?"

"Your sisters are not here."

"No?" Tomás was pissed off.

"No. They are in California."

"They *what?*"

"In California. Or maybe they have started back by now."

"What the hell are they doing there?"

"Pegleg decided to go to California to buy horses. People say horses in California are as common as leaves on trees. Your father once brought back a herd from there."

Tomás didn't need any more Sam Morgan stories. "They're buying horses?"

"Well, I don't think they'll actually pay for them."

Tomás couldn't speak for fear of yelling.

Baptiste said, "This is the second time you led us on a wild-goose chase."

Walkara shrugged. "My brother wouldn't want this hotheaded young man following him to California. And I like your company. And I wanted to go to rendezvous. And to visit Bent's fort . . ."

"You son of a bitch," said Tomás.

Walkara laughed. "I only have a little fun with you. Now let us enjoy ourselves at the fort, no?"

It stretched in front of them now. The outer walls were adobe, and though they were unfinished, the place was going to be huge, about sixty paces long.

A courtyard was partly enclosed, with a big fur press in the center. Rooms lined three sides, two stories high.

"Hell, it's a small town all by itself," said Baptiste.

"I have never been in an American town," said Walkara.

Neither had Tomás.

WALKARA STRUTTED AROUND the trade room all agog. He stroked each of the dozen rifles. He pinched several Hudson's Bay blankets.

"Look at these," said Baptiste. He pointed to a row of handsome coats sewn from light blue blankets.

"I have every kind of cloth you might fancy," said the man who introduced himself as William Bent, though the Indians called him Little White Man. Bent fingered a bolt of calico, another of wool.

"Your wives would appreciate these," he said, indicating the display of pots, pans, and other metal utensils.

"I want some of this," said Baptiste. It was blank paper. "And a bottle of that ink." Little White Man handed him the materials.

"Notions," said Bent, pointing to needles, thimbles, buttons, thread, and yarn.

"Here's a treat for you," Bent told Walkara, and handed the chief a dried apricot.

"Eat it," said Baptiste. "Dried fruit."

Walkara bit off half, tasted, and gave the remainder back to Little White Man, who made a face. The trader turned on a big smile, though, reached into a barrel, and offered Walkara a slice of dried apple. The chief nibbled a bit, popped all of it into his mouth, chewed, and shrugged his shoulders.

Baptiste held up a piece of chocolate, raised an eyebrow at Bent, and indicated the chief. "Sure," said the trader.

Walkara took one bite and said, "I want more. How much?"

Bent gave him a handful. "From a friend to a friend," he said.

Walkara started to pop all the chocolate into his mouth, but Tomás reached over and snitched a little. The chief laughed heartily and chomped the rest greedily.

"I have brought two dozen good horses," he said to Bent, "Ute horses. No other people have such fine horses. Maybe I trade you some."

"I have no doubt," said Bent, "that we can do business."

"Do you think," Baptiste asked Tomás softly, "it's Walkara the man who's excited, or the businessman?"

Tomás said, "It's the one who knows he can make enough profit to buy a hundred more horses."

Suddenly Tomás jerked to attention. A tall, rangy Indian with gray hair, a middle-aged woman, and a young woman had just stepped into the room, escorted by a clerk.

Tomás watched them cross the floor with the fascination he might have given the archangel Gabriel.

Baptiste coughed out a caution.

Tomás tore his eyes off the young woman, stepped close to Bent and asked, "Who are those three?"

The clerk got out strings of beads, and the older woman admired them with oohs and aahs.

Bent said softly, "That is the Cheyenne Yellow Eye, his wife, and their daughter."

"Who is the daughter?"

"Her name is Grass. She looks delicious, doesn't she?"

Tomás was too mesmerized to answer.

"Excuse me," said Bent. He picked up a large twist of tobacco from a pile of twists, strode across to Yellow Eye, greeted him in the Cheyenne language, and made him a gift of the tobacco.

Walkara had gotten the same treatment, and Bent was back in an instant.

Tomás asked, "Is Yellow Eye a chief?"

Bent's smile was hard to read. "No, but I'd say he's a man not to piss off."

"Will you introduce me to them?"

Bent gave him a lecherous grin. "Are you interested in Grass? She's probably available."

"Available?" If the Crow people were loose, the Cheyennes had a reputation for the opposite.

"Their daughter died, and Yellow Eye bought this one as a gift to his wife."

"Bought her!"

Bent spoke as though it was plain and simple. "Grass is a slave. To replace their daughter."

A slave!

"She's a pain in the ass, though. If she keeps up with that, she won't be a daughter long."

Trembling, Tomás said, "Will you introduce me to them?"

For a moment Bent looked taken aback. Then he said, "I'll do better than that. My wife is Yellow Eye's niece. If the three of you will join me at the head of the table in the dining room this evening, my wife will get her relatives to sup with us."

THE NEXT MORNING William Bent enjoyed telling everyone around the post that Tomás, son of the well-known free trapper and trader Sam Morgan, was infatuated with a slave woman. "And the way she looked at him," Bent went on, "I'd say there's likely to be fireworks."

At Yellow Eye's invitation, Tomás, Baptiste, and Walkara rode over to the Cheyenne camp, along the Arkansas River.

On the way Baptiste got up the nerve to tell his friend, "You need to talk easy to Yellow Eye."

Tomás said, "He looks like a difficult man."

Walkara laughed. "He looks like a damn devil!"

The oval of yellow that covered one eye, combined with the black line painted from the forehead across the nose to the chin, gave the Cheyenne a sinister aspect.

"Anyway, mind your manners," said Baptiste.

"Don't worry," said Tomás, "I am smart."

When they arrived, Yellow Eye's attempts at hospitality were defeated by his natural sourness. He responded to Baptiste's overtures in the Cheyenne language mostly with dark looks. Yellow Eye's wife stayed in the lodge, and their host made sure that Grass served them coffee, asked several times if they wanted more sugar, and refilled their cups repeatedly. Naturally, Baptiste said nothing about her. Just as naturally, and because he spoke no Cheyenne, Tomás paid attention to no one else.

In half an hour they took their leave. Tomás looked back at Grass, and she at him. For Tomás parting was like unraveling rope.

On the way back Baptiste spoke gently to him. "Your face is in a rage."

"Of course I'm enraged," said Tomás. "She's amazing. She's magnificent. And she's a slave."

"It's not what—"

"I can see what is going on. I don't need to speak Cheyenne to know slavery. The one who hasn't been a slave is you."

Baptiste said gently, "My mother was. My father bought her from the Hidatsas who abducted her. And though he was drunk sometimes and behaved badly, she loved him, and they made children together. They made a family."

Tomás glared at Baptiste.

After a few clops of horses' hoofs, Baptiste said, "It appears to me that Yellow Eye is exasperated with this girl. He was showing her off to you. Why don't you do something to impress her?"

"What do you have in mind?"

"Perform on Vici."

"Yes!"

WHEN THE SUN was low in the west, twenty or thirty Cheyennes gathered in the big courtyard of the fort. A dozen Arapahos, some Mexicans who were building the fort from adobe, and a few trappers also wrapped their blankets around their shoulders and waited for the show.

On the south side of the fur press was a circle of willow branches Tomás and Baptiste had cut that afternoon. They were now in the autumnal orange, and Tomás had taken the trouble to weave them into a giant wreath.

No one knew exactly what was supposed to happen, but Baptiste had spread the word enthusiastically, and Bent had added to the festivities by promising fiddling and dancing after the show.

Tomás dashed into the plaza at a canter standing on Vici's back, hands held high. The crowd hushed. Not only was the medicine hat an unusual and striking mount, no one had seen a man stand and ride a running horse without reins—most of them hadn't imagined it. Into the ring horse and rider charged, and once around. As the horse neared the entrance again, Tomás spoke, and Vici reared. Tomás did a flying dismount.

A few trappers clapped, but the Indians weren't used to this custom.

Now Tomás gave Vici a signal with his right hand. The pony went clockwise around the circle at a steady lope. Up went Tomás's arm, pointing the other way. Vici reared, pivoted on his rear hoofs, and circled in the other direction.

A man controlling a horse with gestures!

Men clapped, and women made the high trill of acclaim.

Tomás motioned like he was about to pat the ground. Vici came to him, extended his front legs, and ducked his head between them, like a bow.

The silence of the audience was awe.

Vici stood again, and Tomás hurtled onto him from behind. At a word Vici began a slow walk toward the circle entrance. On his back Tomás mounted into a handstand.

The crowd gasped collectively.

As horse and rider slid out of the circle, out the fort gate, and into the sunset, everyone cheered.

TOMÁS WOKE UP grinning. Grass's nose was about an inch from his. The rest of her flesh was even closer.

He also woke up with his ass and his feet freezing. Their covering of blankets wasn't enough. But he didn't want to budge. He wanted to hold her. He wanted her to sleep in his arms forever, and he wanted her to wake up and do everything again, all that they'd done until the stars said dawn was close.

He wanted to know where her mind was right now, in the land of dreams. Was she dreaming of him? Was she remembering their mad romp, time after time? In her mind did she move her lips against him? Her hips?

Or maybe she was a girl again, with her parents and in her village. She was a Comanche and grew up in a canyon called in his language Palo Duro. These were the only words, apparently, she spoke of any language except Comanche. Nor did she know sign language. When she was snatched away, somehow, from her family, she had been perfectly ignorant of the wider world.

But last night, with the help of the music and the dancing and the whiskey—last night they needed only one language. Their bodies were sensuous in the dance, electric in the kiss, and in their union an earthquake.

He planned to spend the rest of his life with her.

He imagined what it must have been like for her, being taken away. Who stole her, Cheyennes? Young warriors? Did they molest her? Or did they intend her, from the start, as a gift to Yellow Eye?

Or perhaps raiders from another tribe tore her away from all that she loved. Away from suitors, or even from a husband. (She had demonstrated beyond all doubt that she knew plenty about sex, and loved it.) Had those abductors abused her?

He wanted to know what had happened to her. He wanted to know how she had lived before then. He wanted to know everything about her life, every detail. Undoubtedly, after they went to see the priest in Taos and sanctified their marriage, they would ride to Palo Duro Canyon and meet her family and tribesmen. Maybe they would even stay and live there—who knew? Nothing mattered except that they would be together.

Grass's eyes fluttered open, and then popped wide. She grinned at him mischievously. The biggest thing he'd learned about her was that she loved to play.

Beneath the blankets their hands started playing.

Tomás heard footsteps.

Grass looked beyond his head and made a strange face.

Yellow Eye squatted next to them. In his hands he held two tin cups full of steaming coffee.

Tomás took the hint. He turned away from Grass, reached for a cup, gave it to Grass, and took another for himself. They lay under a leafless cottonwood, halfway between the fort and the river, in a place they thought would be private.

Yellow Eye said something.

Baptiste translated, "Good morning, I am glad to see you."

Tomás hadn't seen him until that moment.

"I hope you had a good night."

Tomás couldn't find his tongue.

"Did you enjoy each other?"

Grass spoke first—"Yes."

"Very much," said Tomás.

Yellow Eye sat and crossed his legs. He took another cup of coffee out of Baptiste's pot and sipped. He nodded to himself two or three times. Then he got a broad grin and said, "I trade her to you for that black-and-white pony."

Forty-nine

"DAMNED IF I'LL *buy* her!" snapped Tomás.

Baptiste said mildly, "She wants you to."

They walked the horses on. Since Tomás wanted to talk and felt an urge to keep Vici close by, they were going to sit by the river. They got off and let the mounts drink.

Baptiste said, "What are you thinking?"

"Seeing her back in the Cheyenne camp. With her captors."

Baptiste shook his head. "They were prepared to accept her. You are too, I think."

Tomás's eyes flashed fire at Baptiste. "Maybe instead of telling me to trade human beings like chattel, you will help me make a plan."

Baptiste shrugged. "All right," he said.

* * *

IT ALMOST DROVE Tomás crazy. Yellow Eye allowed Tomás to see Grass once a day, in the evening. First he and Baptiste took dinner with the Yellow Eye family, and Baptiste translated their awkward conversation. When dark fell, Tomás stayed for courtship in a proper Cheyenne way. But after the two of them stood by the door flap of the tipi for an hour or so, the blanket wrapped all the way over their heads, Yellow Eye would call, "Daughter, it is time to sleep."

Those words infuriated Tomás. He went away every night, back to the barracks room in the fort where visiting trappers slept, stomping his feet. What really made him mad was that Yellow Eye seemed willing to stall forever.

Walkara grew weary of waiting. On the morning he and his young men left for his village, packhorses laden with trade goods, Walkara found Tomás and Baptiste to say goodbye and give them some information. "Pegleg, he went to California in the month *junio . . .*"

"June," grumbled Tomás.

"And he comes back, maybe, so he said, in *diciembre*."

"December."

"To Taos."

"Taos?" said Tomás. He and Baptiste looked at each other.

"Naturally, Taos. He will sell many horses and bring much trade goods back to our people. The women will be very happy." Walkara gave a lascivious grin.

"You have led us on a merry chase," said Tomás.

"You were easy to fool, and a lot of fun," said Walkara. "Goodbye, my Mexican friend, my French-Canadian friend. I look forward to see you soon."

Everyone else went on with their business. The men who made adobe bricks from mud and laid them into walls worked on enclosing the fort. Bent entertained an Arapaho group and made a sizable trade. Baptiste hinted that they might as well go to Taos early, as it would be more entertaining than this outpost.

"I love Grass," he said.

"And you like to hate her father," said Baptiste.

"He's not her father," snapped Tomás.

Baptiste raised his eyebrows.

For another week Tomás lived only to wrap himself in that blanket with Grass in the evening. Unfortunately, it had to be standing up.

Once in a while Yellow Eye would taunt Tomás. At dinner he would say easily, "A father expects a suitor to show that he wants a woman." Or, "If you give nothing for her, she thinks you don't want her."

Twice he asked Tomás to show him Vici's wonderful abilities again, but Tomás refused. Yellow Eye always had the manner of a man in no rush.

The "father" never let them do their courting more than a few feet from the lodge. And at the end of that week he told Tomás that the Cheyennes would pack up their belongings the following day and ride back toward their winter camp. That evening Tomás was glad he and Grass were unable to communicate with words. They spoke only with their hands and bodies.

Tomás gave them two days' head start. Bent had told him where the band spent the cold months. Though he didn't know where Sand Creek was, Tomás had no difficulty sneaking away from the fort and from Baptiste and following something as broad as a lodge trail turning north, away from the Arkansas River.

Fifty

TOMÁS TOLD HIMSELF not to worry about the dogs, but his nerves danced a jig of fear.

The camp faced a big half-circle of creek, with a high bank on the far side. Tomás had waded downstream for a long way. He was in the thigh-deep water in the shadow of the bank, and any noise he made would be less than the swishing of the current.

Now he stood absolutely still again and looked around. The sentry who stood on the bank downstream was silhouetted against the moonlit sky, a dark shadow pointed away from the invader. The sentries on the far side of camp weren't visible from here. He'd spent all of last night and today watching the men who guarded the camp, so he knew where they were.

Nothing in the camp stirred. As the year grew later, dark came earlier, and people were inside, gathered close around their center fires, having a last talk before sleep.

Earlier Tomás crouched on the creek bank and watched the lodges go dark, one by one. From that distance he couldn't pick out the one that belonged to Yellow Eye. He wanted the whole camp asleep before he made his move.

Which was now. He reminded himself that the wind was wafting gently in from the west, so the dogs couldn't smell him. He'd been around the Cheyenne camp enough that they knew his odor anyway. Nothing was holding him back except that jig.

He stepped easily out of the creek and shivered—his wet leggings were icy almost to his groin. He looked back at the sentry. Still facing the other direction. He ran lightly across the open ground to the shadow of the nearest tipi. Again he looked back at the sentry. The man was looking away from the village, not into it. *Keep it up*, thought Tomás.

He padded quickly to the shadow of the next tipi, and the next. This was Yellow Eye's lodge. He slipped around to the south side and looked for the promised marker.

It was there. A strip of red ribbon poked from under the lodge cover. To Tomás it was a beacon, lit by Grass.

Yellow Eye was awake. Tomás heard it now, the rhythmic gasps of people making love. *If you can call what an animal like Yellow Eye does making love*. The thought of Grass lying near them, having to hear, irked Tomás. He wondered how often she had to put up with that.

He cursed. He asked himself if he should wait until the couple was asleep. Maybe they would hear him. Maybe they would see the movements.

To hell with it. Tomás didn't want to sit beside this lodge for a long time waiting—too dangerous, and too disgusting. Besides, Mr. Sam Morgan said what worked best in any attack was just plain daring.

Right while they're doing it, he told himself.

He knelt beside the strip of ribbon and got out his patch knife. It was always his sharpest blade, and he had spent his last afternoon back at the fort putting the best possible edge on it.

Mr. Sam Morgan, I am the daring one. He put the knife tip to the buffalo robe about a foot above the bottom and sliced.

The damn hide was tough, and the cutting seemed to take forever. Tomás listened to the sounds of sex and told himself that he was safe until they turned to silence.

Stroke, stroke, stroke—and his knife jerked through and hit the ground.

A hand grabbed his!

His heart stopped.

Then it beat fast—the hand belonged to Grass.

She slid her whole arm out, then a shoulder, followed by her face.

In the moonlight it was a spectacularly beautiful face.

She wiggled, but she couldn't get through.

Tomás turned the knife blade up, braced his hand on her ribs, and sliced upward.

She wiggled. Not quite enough. He cut again.

The sounds at the rear of the tipi got louder, gasps becoming grunts.

Both shoulders came through.

Tomás grabbed Grass under the arms and heaved. Slowly, wriggling, she squeezed out. Just when her hips cleared, the grunts turned to cries.

Tomás and Grass scrambled to their feet. They dashed headlong toward the creek—*to hell with everything, run.*

She hesitated when he splashed into the creek, then followed. Without a word he pointed upstream and waded.

After less than a hundred paces (what would have been genuine paces on land), Tomás grabbed her forearm and stopped her. The northern sentry stood still, a black line against a half-dark sky. He was looking toward them.

They stood as invisible, Tomás hoped, as the fish in the depths of the waters.

The sentry walked to the edge of the bank, which wasn't as high here. He peered in their direction. And peered and peered. Suddenly, he strode away from them, along the bank.

"Quick!" said Tomás.

He led Grass by the wrist. They worked their way to the bank, where the water was deepest and swiftest, and leaned back against it. *Maybe*, Tomás thought, *he won't see us*.

But this sentry was conscientious. He reappeared where the bank was low, twenty or thirty paces upstream. Tomás could see him studying the dark waters. Then he waded into the creek, holding his war club at the ready.

Tomás and Grass squatted down in the water and held their faces almost to the surging liquid.

The sentry splashed his way downstream knee-deep. Soon he passed them.

The man had seen or heard something. Tomás had no choice.

He motioned for Grass to stay where she was. Gently, he launched himself flat on the current and floated toward the sentry. Then he took several frog strokes to get directly upstream of the man.

Two steps away he stood up, knife in hand.

Hearing something, the sentry turned.

Tomás threw himself forward and buried the knife in the man's chest.

Fifty-one

THEY RODE VICI and Kallie upstream in the creek.

Tomás knew the Cheyennes would be furious when they found the sentry. He hoped the body would sink, and they wouldn't know what happened until well after sunup. The death would cause much more outrage than the theft of a woman.

"All we have," he told Grass, "is a few hours' lead and some tricks." Not speaking his language, she didn't understand. But she cooperated.

He headed north because they would expect them to ride south, toward the Arkansas. He stayed in the water because it would cover their tracks. After about two miles they rode onto the land at a stony place. Then they rode hard through the dark toward another creek Tomás had spotted to the west.

All night and all the day they kept riding, weary beyond weary in their saddles. When they bivouacked the second night, they built no fire, ate only jerked meat, took only the briefest moments for love, and slept the sleep of the dead.

TOMÁS EXPECTED TO honeymoon at the fort. Bent would have no part of it.

"You killed a sentry?" he squeaked. His voice, naturally high, got shrill when he was emotional.

"I had to," Tomás said.

Bent said something to Grass in Cheyenne, and it wasn't polite.

She threw words back at him, and he threw some at her. Finally, Bent turned back to Tomás. "She's proud that you were willing to kill a man to get her." He looked from one to the other. "Which shows that you're both idiots."

He thought a minute, fuming, and told them to follow him to the trade room. There he got out some sausage-shaped containers of pemmican and handed them to Grass. "Yellow Eye and the rest will be here today or tomorrow," he said. "I can't save you from them, and wouldn't if I could. I have to live with them. So get the hell out of here."

"What do I owe you for the pemmican?" asked Tomás.

"Nothing. It's worth it to get rid of you."

Bent followed them to find Baptiste.

The Frenchy was glad to see them, but not at all surprised.

Tomás told him their story.

"Past time to get gone," Baptiste agreed.

Quickly, they were packed and ready to ride.

"Where are you going?" asked Bent.

"Taos," said Baptiste.

"I'll tell them you rode west toward Walkara. Now get out of here."

"I think it is immoral to take a woman by trade, like she was livestock," Tomás declared.

"And not immoral," said Bent, "to kill a man to get her?"

Fifty-two

SAM MORGAN APPROACHED Boiling Fountain Creek carefully. The creek leapt down the eastern slopes of Zebulon Pike's big mountain. At one spot, before the steep slopes turned into rolling hills, the creek bubbled up in about a dozen springs of fizzy water. It was carbonated, said the doctor who had trekked out here with the army exploring expedition, and claimed that it was a remarkable tonic for the digestive system. Generations of Indians could have told him that. Cheyennes, Arapahos, and Utes came from a hundred miles around and more to drink the cold, medicinal waters. For the last decade or so, the beaver men had done the same. Sam liked to say, "That water eases my digestion and smooths the feathers of my spirits."

Since Boiling Fountain Creek was a goal for pilgrims, it was considered sacred ground, and neutral, all comers welcome.

Which did not mean that a lone white man would be entirely safe here.

White man—Sam was sick of the term. Out here in the mountains it meant the beaver trappers, half of them not white but French Canadian, Delaware, Iroquois, or Mexican. And even the white ones were making a new generation that blended white and red. Whenever anyone said "white man," Sam immediately thought of Esperanza, Azul, and Rojo, with spritzes of different blood in their veins, and was terrified about their futures.

Now Sam tied Paladin and the pack mule, eased up to the ridge, lay flat, and studied the Boiling Fountain Creek thoroughly with his field glass.

He stood up and said to Coy, "Empty. Not a soul here."

He grinned. Just what he had hoped for. Now, as the cold months approached, the Indians would be setting up their winter camps. Trappers of these southern Rocky Mountains would be finishing their fall hunts and heading for Taos. He could be alone. True, he had ridden south for nearly a month without speaking to another human being, Coy's comments being cryptic. Yet he hoped for more of the same. Since he first came to these springs six years ago, he'd yearned to spend time here with no one but Coy. The place stood big in his heart.

In fact, he told himself with an inward chuckle, maybe he would stay forever. This country, the headwaters of the South Platte River and the headwaters of the Arkansas, what the mountain men called South Park, was the finest land he knew in all the mountains. For some reason the big fur companies didn't bring their brigades here, but left it to the free trappers like Sam.

South Park was lofty. It spurted clear, cold creeks down every gully, and beaver were plenty. Buffalo, elk, deer—game was as abundant as corn in a planted field. There was grass enough to feed even the vast horse herds of California, and good timber. In summer the high country would keep you cool. In winter, if you didn't want to go to Taos, you could camp next to one of a hundred hot springs. The steam would keep you warm and the grass bare of snow. If you went crazy, you could take a bath any time.

He set up camp in a good spot, filled his belly with fizzy water, gathered firewood, and set out to make himself at home for a week or more. His plan was to shoot a fat buffalo cow tomorrow morning—the beasts dotted the hills only three or four miles down the creek. Then he would cut the meat into strips and spread it out on racks. The drying would need four or five days, probably. And what would he do while the meat turned to jerky? *Lounge and drink mineral water and do, or not do, exactly what I feel like.*

On the second day of the drying he took a notion to build a sweat lodge. He cut willows along the creek, tied them into an upside-down bowl, and covered them with his blankets. Besides housing some sweats, the lodge would also come in handy if it snowed.

He sweated most of the afternoon. It wasn't that he wanted to ask the powers for anything special. He just wanted to perform the ritual, to pray and chant. He supposed Catholics went to mass for no particular reason sometimes. Just before the early sunset he finished the last round, dipped himself in the freezing creek, hurried back to the fire, and warmed himself with rare steak cut from buffalo back strap.

That evening he played the tin whistle for hours.

The next day he spent part of the morning walking with Coy, and part of it looking into his kaleidoscope. It crossed his mind idly to wonder about the answer to the old Mexican gentleman's riddle—what *was* the meaning of life?—but he didn't feel like chasing after any answers now.

That afternoon he spent in the sweat lodge again, praying and singing. In the evening he gorged himself and then played music.

And so went every day. He ate, he tended to the drying meat, he walked, he sweated, he smoked his pipe, he ate, and he played music. Having the pipe felt damn good.

About the fifth day he asked himself, *What am I doing?*

He answered, *Not thinking*. For some reason that seemed funny.

On the sixth day the meat was dry enough, but he decided to let it stay on the racks. He was in no hurry.

In the sweat lodge that afternoon, when he was smoking his pipe between rounds of steaming, he had one sudden, thunderous feeling:

he ached for Tomás. Before he could correct himself—wasn't he headed to Taos specifically to find Tomás?—he went on to the next feeling: he had a huge pang for Esperanza. And for Meadowlark. Or was it Paloma?

Words came into his mind: *I want a family.* That was the realization he was fishing for.

I want a real family.

He started to shiver. Family—children of mixed blood—every kind of trouble.

He stopped the shiver, told himself to stop stirring words through his head, closed the lodge door, poured water on the fiery rocks, and asked the powers of the east, south, west, and north for a family.

Fifty-three

THE NEXT MORNING Hannibal MacKye rode into camp with a big grin. "Thought I might find you here."

He'd ridden up from Taos for two weeks. They'd done this before, spent some days here at Boiling Fountain Creek before heading down to New Mexico.

This time it was different. Sam shook his shoulders to throw off his discomfort.

Hannibal staked his horse and walked straight to the meat rack. "It's ready," he said, and helped himself.

Sam filled a second cup with coffee for Hannibal.

"I brought something," said Hannibal, and spooned sugar into both cups. Sam had hardly tasted sugar since rendezvous.

He shook his shoulders again, and the bad feeling still didn't go anywhere. "What's the news about Paloma?"

"I left her at the shrine of the Virgin of Guadalupe."

So she'd made it.

"The holy sisters," Hannibal went on, "said they'd take care of her from there." He felt silent for a moment. "She was near the end of her time."

Sam jumped up and walked away. *I knew it,* he said to himself. *Why am I upset?*

He and Coy walked up the creek for half a mile or so and came back. Hannibal was still munching on jerked meat.

"Thank you," said Sam.

"She was my friend," said Hannibal.

They lay around idly the entire day. Sam thought he could turn into the best idler in the Rocky Mountains

Finally he said, "Has Tomás turned up in Taos yet?"

"No."

"Pegleg Smith?"

"No." Then Sam had to tell Hannibal about Lupe and Rosalita getting abducted, and himself and Tomás trying to find them, and at last getting word that Pegleg had them.

Hannibal twisted his lips. "What a world," he said, "where your friends take your sisters to be slaves."

Other than that, they scarcely talked. There was no need.

The last thing before they fell asleep, Hannibal said, "Sounds like we better cut this short and get back to Taos."

Sam thought about how far his friend had ridden. He consulted his own mood. "Two more days here," he said.

Fifty-four

"YOU SEEM DIFFERENT."

The cold wind had died down, and the sun had warmed the day up halfway. The motion of Paladin felt good. Sam thought and said, "I relaxed. Spent a week not thinking."

"You mean not remembering?"

So much to remember. Right now especially Lupe and Rosalita, angry Tomás, and even Peanut Head, the reason for his mutilated ear. "Yeah, not remembering," he said. "Also not picking things apart in my head."

"That'll help."

Coy sprinted ahead, and a prairie dog ducked down a hole.

"And not fretting."

Hannibal raised an eyebrow at him.

"The kids."

Hannibal knew about the fight, and Tomás's disappearance.

"For a long time the past kept kicking my door in. My mind was in the dregs with Meadowlark. Or with Paloma. Sometimes with Jedediah." He mused and moved with the horse. "There's a lot of past, but it's not pounding on my door right now."

They rode.

Sam thought about asking and then couldn't believe that over eleven years, he'd never asked. "You ever have a long-time woman? Kids?"

"Women, only in passing. Kids, not that I know of."

"Because they'd be mixed blood?"

"Actually, I think the world needs all the mixed bloods it can get."

"Mulattoes aren't accepted back in the States. I doubt French Canadians are in Montreal."

"Hell, we'll just outbreed the purebloods. You're doing your part."

Sam squeezed out a chuckle, but it wasn't real. "I'm worried about the kids. You know what Milton Sublette told me at rendezvous?"

Sam looked across at the northern end of the Sangre de Cristo Mountains to the west. More than two hundred miles to Taos. "The Methodists are working up to send missionaries to Oregon next summer. Come out with the supply train to rendezvous, travel on from there."

He watched the hilltops for a moment. "Ten years ago I swore to the Crows that white people would never come here. Now they're on the way. Not that I believe they'll stop in these mountains, nor in the deserts. They'll go on to land they can plow. But white folks are going to traipse across this country like ants on a mission. Then they'll fill Oregon up."

"Also California," said Hannibal. "The Californios expect it. Half of them would rather be part of the States than Mexico right now. They're sick of *el presidente* in Mexico City."

Sam nodded. He knew. "So what about Esperanza, and Tomás, and Azul, and Rojo? And Jim Bridger's kids, and Joe Meek's, and all of them? We've left a trail of half-breeds wide and long as the Missouri

River. What will the missionaries say when they see them? What will the housewives say?"

They rode.

"They'll treat them like dirt," said Sam, "just like they do back in the States."

Hannibal said nothing for a long while. Then, "A man's happiness is in his own heart."

They rode.

Finally, Sam said, "Not all of us are strong as you, Hannibal." Clop-clop, clop-clop. "I'm not myself."

This turned Hannibal's head.

Sam plunged onward. "I feel like an in-betweener. I'm not white, haven't been for a long time. I'm not comfortable in boots, nor pants. I don't see things their way. Don't like whatever big whoop-de-doo they've got going back there—factories, jobs, products, more factories, more jobs, more products. It puffs out money like a steam engine, but it burns up people."

Clop-clop, clop-clop.

"I don't believe in their God. The four winds, Father Sky, and Mother Earth make a lot more sense to me than those stories about Jehovah and sin and hell to come."

Sam whistled, and Coy came trotting back.

"I'd rather be a Crow, which I can't be either." Now he was surprised at the bitterness in his own voice.

Clop-clop, clop-clop.

"The kids are the same, all our children, all in-betweeners, all heading to be despised and scorned."

They rode so long Sam wondered if Hannibal had been listening.

Suddenly Sam started singing, and making up some of the words:

This world is not my home, I'm just a-passing through
I keep on searching everywhere, but that just makes me blue
The housewives shoo me off, and then they slam the door
And I don't feel at home in their world anymore.

They rode, looking at the empty hills. Finally Hannibal said, "If you don't have a home, you have to make one."

Sam thought on that.

Hannibal said, "Maybe I shouldn't have spoken up about following your wild hair."

They both grinned. "No," said Sam, "I won't ever regret that."

"It's lonely," said Hannibal. "The world is lonely. I'm lonely. You know how I got started wandering?"

Sam looked at his friend a long moment. "No."

"When I got my growth, I wanted to make my way in the world. Didn't have a dime to my name, but I could read, even read Plato in Greek and Caesar in Latin. Even if I was half Delaware, I was strong and willing.

"I went to work for John Bill Pickett's circus in Philadelphia, took care of the horses, learned to do the trick riding on them, even learned to train them in it. I was good, I could have been a star, but Pickett wouldn't let me. A white audience didn't want to make a hero out of any Injun, he said."

Hannibal looked inward for a while, or into the past.

"So I decided just to wander. You know the story of the Wandering Jew?"

"No."

"When the Christ was carrying his cross to Calgary, a porter mocked him and struck him. Fellow's name was Buttadeo, isn't that rich? Butt-a-deo, God's ass. Anyway, Jesus put a kind of curse on him. 'Wait until my return,' he said."

Hannibal gave a strange smile. "Somehow the Second Coming has been laggard in getting here, and it's not in sight yet. Buttadeo, he did what he could—became a Christian, got himself baptized. But the curse stuck. He grew to be a hundred years old and then, like a snake, he shed his skin, reverted to the age of thirty, and started over again.

"And he wandered. He was seen in Armenia. In Poland. In Moscow, Athens, Rome, Paris, even London—everywhere people saw the Wandering Jew, plodding on. Wherever he went, he would trade the story of his life for a little food and a place to sleep for the night. In each place people doubted him, and then tested him, and always found him to be the genuine article.

"Well, I figured, with all that time, Buttadeo got to understand life better than anyone ever did, and that seemed good. So I set off wandering, never knowing where I would go next. But I didn't trade the story of my life—instead I traded a little thread, an awl, a knife, and on like that. It worked out fine."

Amusement jumped between the eyes of the friends.

"I haven't gotten to a hundred yet, so I can't say I'll be able to shed my skin and start over. And I don't know that I understand life. But I have learned to enjoy it day by day."

"You ever going to stop wandering?" asked Sam.

"Maybe. I've thought about one place."

Sam waited.

"California."

Sam waited.

"When Europeans came to America," Hannibal said, "they called it the New World. Part of the deal, I think, was leaving the Old World behind, and all its miseries. The church and the nobility, between them, did a hell of a job of keeping ordinary men and women down. Lots of people who came to America, I believe, saw themselves as Adams and Eves in a new Garden of Eden. A chance to start over and do things right."

Sam grunted agreement.

"In some ways it hasn't worked out. People brought too many old habits with them and made the same old mistakes. But when I ride around California, it seems different. It started out ruled by the Spanish, but it's not anymore. At first the padres worked hard at making the Indians Catholics, but the missions are all closing."

"I heard that."

"No more saving Indians, or enslaving them."

"A big step."

"The Mexican government hardly even knows the province is up there. Spaniards are marrying Indians, creating a new race. Americans are starting to move in, which will make three bloodstreams in each person."

Sam saw a faraway gleam in his friend's eye. "There's possibilities in California. Life is good. No winter, just summer and spring. If people want to farm, they can raise maybe three crops a year. And, I don't know, there's something in the air . . . It makes me think it could be a new world. It makes me dream."

After a while, he added, "So if I stop wandering, I'll settle there."

Sam looked at him quizzically.

"That's a big if."

Sam thought, *Make a home*.

CAMP HIGH ON the Cimarron River: tonight they were at the foot of the pass that crossed the mountain to Taos. The next two days they would be high and cold. Right now Sam felt cold enough. The sun was far gone beyond the Sangre de Cristos. The blackness of sky and the rushing of the river made the night feel even more bitter than it was.

The fire crackled, and Sam put the coffeepot on.

"Two weeks with these same grounds," he said.

"Better than nothing," said Hannibal.

Sam would as soon drink the hot water straight, but he didn't say so.

He handed Hannibal a couple of strips of jerked meat and tossed one to Coy. The coyote looked at it, sniffed it, and looked off across the plains. Out that direction was maybe a thousand miles of prairie, and the Mississippi River. Sam said, "Maybe he thinks the food around here is lousy, and he'd do better out there hunting."

Sam and Hannibal grinned and chewed. Neither of them would complain. They had pushed the horses down from Boiling Fountain Creek, doing no hunting, not even gathering wild onions or picking berries and rose hips—all they did from dawn to dusk, through the short days of early winter, was ride. They were half cold and half hungry. "I want some *chile verde,*" said Sam.

"Taos lightning," said Hannibal.

"A room with walls and a ceiling."

"A woman. I want a woman."

Hannibal looked at Sam, but the white-haired man said nothing. He was thinking, *I hope I feel like having a woman.*

Then for some reason Sam thought of the kaleidoscope. He fished it out of his possible sack, pointed it at the flames, and gazed at a weird picture. "If hell has churches," he said, "the stained-glass windows look like this."

He handed it to Hannibal, who eyed the devilish art.

Sam poured bitter coffee for both of them. "I never did figure out that riddle of the old Mexican gentleman's. The meaning of life."

"No ideas?"

"Nope."

"I did worse than you."

Over the rim of his cup Sam asked a question with his eyes.

"I went back to the old man and presented him with what I figured out. Something like this." He handed the kaleidoscope back to Sam. "Every picture this thing makes is new, unique, and it will never be repeated. Like days. Every one brand, spanking new, beautiful in its particular way, and never to come again."

"Well?"

"The old gentleman just shook his head, laughing kind of soft."

Sam waited.

"So I gave him my second idea. There is no meaning. That's the secret hidden in the kaleidoscope. There is no, well, *meaning* to life. There's just . . . whatever is right in front of you."

Hannibal poured his coffee back into the pot.

"Now the old man did laugh. I felt a little irked at that, so I said, 'All right, you tell me what it is.'

"The old man shrugged. 'I didn't find any meaning,' he said. 'The man who gave it to me, I told him I couldn't figure it out. He said, "Me neither. I thought maybe you was smarter than me."'"

Hannibal let a moment pass, laughing at himself. "I said to the old man, 'So you were kind of tormenting me.'

"He said, '*Sí*, just like you will torment the next fool.'

"'One day will someone win this game?'

"'Oh yes,' said the old gentleman, 'the wise man who says, "I don't analyze life, I just live it."'

"Now the old gentleman lit his pipe, and looked at me through the flame. 'But maybe this wise man, I think, he will keep the kaleidoscope because it makes pretty things.'"

Coy howled into the dark night.

The night yelled back. "Hello the camp!"

Sam jumped up. He started to reach for his pistol and then thought, *I know that voice.*

"Hello the camp!"

"Hello yourself."

Tomás rode straight up to the fire. And on Vici. Sam wanted to hug him. He said, "Looks like you got a story to tell."

"More than one." He turned back and said, "Come out of the dark so they can see you."

Baptiste Charbonneau came up on his mount, and behind him an unknown woman.

"Mr. Sam Morgan," said Tomás, "Mr. Hannibal MacKye, meet Grass, who is my fiancée."

Fifty-five

"TELL US EVERYTHING," Sam said. "This beautiful young woman, Vici, everything."

"I'll translate," said Baptiste. "Grass is a Comanche, has made barely a start at English yet."

"It would be easier to tell stories," said Tomás, making a face at his cup, "over better coffee."

Sam grinned at him. He was glad to see his son.

"Let's see." Tomás's voice was a pretend shrug. "My horse? The Blackfeet take him from Mr. Sam Morgan, Tomás takes him back."

Sam gave him a mock evil eye.

So Tomás launched into the telling about Vici first, and the story was one big brag. How he and Baptiste slipped off with Old Bill, fooling Sam. How Tomás spotted Vici and stole him back, got caught, and was rescued by Baptiste. How they quit Old Bill and went hunting for Lupe and Rosalita. Walkara told them, maybe

Bent's new fort. Since Walkara wanted to see it, they joined up and rode over the mountains to the headwaters of the Arkansas and followed that river all the way to the big house the Bent brothers built.

"You should see the fort," said Tomás, "it is incredible. Right on the Santa Fé Trail and immense. A huge courtyard surrounded by two stories of rooms, stables, a corral . . ."

While Tomás talked, Sam quietly checked out the girl. She was very striking and very sexy. Probably Tomás felt like a tree struck by lightning and still burning.

"Civilization in the wilderness," said Hannibal. "First American Fur's big castle on the Missouri, now this one."

Sam wanted to sound like he'd been listening. "Guess everybody will be going there."

"We even," Tomás said, "sort of found Pegleg Smith. I don't fortheget him for a minute. Walkara, he teases with you, Mr. Sam Morgan, me, all of us the whole time. He says, 'They went to rendezvous. They went to Bent's Fort.' All the time he knows they are in the opposite direction."

Sam looked at him quizzically.

"Pegleg and some Utes went to California to steal horses and bring them back to Taos."

"Walkara played us along the whole time?" Sam was chuckling.

"The son of a bitch," said Tomás. "When we find Pegleg, Mr. Sam Morgan, my sisters better be with him."

Sam noticed that Grass was staring off into the darkness, probably bored by talk she didn't understand. "Grass," he said, and Baptiste translated, "we are glad to have you with us. How did you and Tomás get together?"

Tomás plunged in immediately. Grass said not a word, though she seemed intent on everything Tomás said. He told about the first time he saw her, how he impressed her with the circus riding, their electric union that very night, the courtship policed by her father, the offensive offer to sell her to Tomás . . .

Clearly Tomás was infatuated. Grass's gaze on him was intense.

Sam wasn't sure what it meant. Perhaps adulation. And she looked like she ached to touch him, which would have been terrible manners.

The story of how Tomás abducted her was dramatic, and Sam was glad Grass had been plenty willing. Then, suddenly, he heard the story of the sentry Tomás had to kill. The tone in the youth's voice was pride, plus something Sam couldn't read.

They talked for another hour. For whatever reason Tomás always called his father "Mr. Sam Morgan."

"Time for bed," Tomás said, with a hot glance at Grass. No doubt he felt good, being the only man of four to have a woman to warm his blankets.

When Sam rolled up in his blankets and buffalo robe, he had trouble getting warm. The night was bitter. These days fatherhood didn't seem heartwarming either.

Fifty-six

"I WANT TO stay here," said Grass.

Sam didn't care for the whine in her voice, but her Spanish was coming along fast.

Tomás said, "We must go to mass. This is the day to honor the Holy Innocents."

"I rather be with Xeveria," said Grass.

They were standing in front of the cantina where Xeveria worked, Tomás and Grass, Sam, Hannibal, and Baptiste. This was the plaza of the town Fernandez de Taos, three miles down the creek from Taos Pueblo.

"I have to work," said Xeveria, coming up. "You go on. I wish I could go to mass today." She looked sideways at her older brother, Gabriel. "But the boss . . ."

Tomás took Grass by the hand and led her toward their horses. She gave a last glance back at their friends.

"They're lucky," said Hannibal, "they get to ride."

Villagers were flocking up the road to the mission on foot. Though both the town and pueblo had churches, one priest, Antonio Martínez, served both, and he would celebrate this feast day's mass at the pueblo's church.

Sam, Hannibal, and Baptiste took an outside table, for the winter day was mild, and this place sat on the north side of the plaza in the sun. Coy curled up next to Sam, and Xeveria took their order.

"You suppose Grass knows Tomás spent the whole last year fantasizing about Xeveria?" asked Hannibal.

"I doubt it." Sam watched the waitress walk away. "I can see why."

"That woman," Hannibal said, "the way she smiles and wiggles and wiggles and laughs, you forget she's not beautiful."

"Many a mountain man," said Baptiste, "has forgotten she's not beautiful. Or so I hear."

Coy gave a little yip.

Xeveria's background was murky. Rumors said she'd been married, gone to Santa Fé, and come back alone. Her brother owned this cantina, and she helped make it popular with the *Americanos*. Now they shared a low adobe house, and Xeveria's part had its own entrance, said to be well used.

"Funny how the Mexicans and Taoseños are way different," said Sam, "except they both go to that mission."

The church San Geronimo had stood at the pueblo for two centuries, and Sam thought it was extraordinarily beautiful. This Mexican village was new and unappetizing to the eye.

"Oh, profane plaza here," said Hannibal in a silly way, "sacred plaza at the mission."

Xeveria brought their orders, for Sam and Hannibal *café* and *bizcocho,* a delicious local biscuit, and for Baptiste Taos lightning. As she walked away, she made her skirts swirl.

Hannibal went on, "Up there they drink communion wine, which purifies their souls. Down here we drink Taos lightning, which leads us into sin."

"Here's to sin," said Baptiste. They all clinked their cups.

This cantina was a good spot to watch the comings and goings of the feast day. Almost all the New Mexicans were at the mission. Sam eyed a few women as they walked across the square carrying jugs of water on their heads.

"Classic grace," said Hannibal.

Paloma has been gone for eight or nine months, thought Sam, *and I haven't looked at a woman that way since.*

Feast days, immediately after mass, turned into market days. Even now sellers laid out their blankets and arranged their wares. Here was a family from Picurís Pueblo, the husband with a hat made of aspen leaves. From San Ildefonso had come a man with a load of pottery jars for sale. An Apache wearing gaudy earrings displayed beaded belts and beaded moccasins artfully on a blanket.

In an hour or so, when the priest said the last words, people would flood from the plaza of the sacred to the plaza of the profane. Women would buy bright baubles. Children would play. Men would smoke their cornhusk cigarillos and gamble away their wages. People would gossip and laugh.

Tonight would be even better. The women would powder their faces with pale lavender, wrap themselves in their *rebozos*, wear their flashiest necklaces, earrings, and bracelets, and hang heavy crosses between their breasts. Men would cover themselves up to their mouths in their serapes. Musicians would tune their instruments. And all would converge on the plaza and turn a lazy New Mexico afternoon into a wild fandango.

The mountain men didn't care about the mass, but they felt damn perky about the party.

"What's the name of this fiesta again?" asked Sam.

"Feast of the Holy Innocents," said Hannibal.

"What's that mean?"

"The story goes, King Herod found out about Jesus from the three wise men, and he ordered all male infants in Bethlehem under two years old killed. Those are the holy innocents."

"Didn't want to take any chances," said Baptiste with a sly smile.

"It's all right with me that Tomás believes these things," said Sam, "but he drags Grass along too."

"Hell, Grass has gone to mass four days in a row," said Baptiste. "More than I've gone in ten years."

Sam couldn't remember the names of the saint's days that came in a row after Christmas, which his son called "the Nativity."

Suddenly Old Bill Williams stood above them. He was still tall as a scarecrow on a pole, and just as disheveled, but he'd found a hat that didn't let his graying red hair poke out the top.

Coy growled.

"Sit down, Bill," said Sam, "and ease the crick in the coyote's neck."

He did. Then he looked at them with a bright gleam in his eyes. "Buy me a whiskey, and I'll tell you something you want to know. Want to know bad."

"I'll buy you a drink on general principles, Bill," said Hannibal. He signaled to Xeveria. She brought Old Bill his drink, leaned down to rub Coy's head, and threw Sam a smile that seemed to be just for him. Hannibal gave Sam a knowing look.

Bill made them wait until the whiskey was in his gullet. Then, in a low and conspiratorial voice, he said, "Pegleg Smith just came in with about a hundred Californy horses. He's camped right down where the creek hooks hard left."

"WHERE IN HELL is he?" yelled Sam.

He'd sent Baptiste to the mission after Tomás—at least they knew where he was. Sam and Hannibal were looking for Joaquin. They'd assumed he'd be sleeping it off in the rooms they rented and, unfortunately, let him use. But he wasn't there. Maybe he'd sobered up enough to get interested in a woman.

"Joaquin!" Sam hollered.

Why in hell today of all days?

Sam barged into Young and Wolfskill's store, Coy at his heels. Ewing Young, a big man, measured them from behind a counter.

"You seen Joaquin?"

"Every barkeep in town has seen him," said Young, "no telling which one last."

Sam banged out of the store.

Hannibal came out of another building.

"Any luck?" called Sam.

"No."

Tomás and Baptiste came roaring through the street on their mounts. Grass rode behind them, but without the hell-for-leather enthusiasm.

"Tomás!" called Sam.

His son ignored him, and Baptiste followed Tomás.

Grass reined up and tied her horse at the cantina. Coy trotted down to her.

Sam clomped into another street of low, windowless adobe houses, cursing.

Coy sent up a flight of yips.

"Coy," called Sam from a block away, "come."

Instead the coyote sent up a whole herd of yips.

What the hell is wrong with him? Sam stomped toward the plaza. Coy trotted a few feet and out of sight. When Sam got there, Coy was lying next to Joaquin, who was talking to the Apache selling belts and moccasins.

"Joaquin, let's go!" said Sam.

Lupe's husband kept talking to his new friend.

Sam grabbed a hand and jerked him to his feet.

"Qué-é-é?" said Joaquin.

"Lupe," said Sam, "Lupe's here."

Sam got him up behind the saddle on Paladin, and they dashed for Pegleg Smith's camp, Hannibal and Coy on their tails.

PEGLEG LOOKED STRAIGHT into the muzzle of Tomás's rifle, and his eyes said he wasn't going to tolerate it. Sam noticed Pegleg's rifle leaning against a cottonwood, just out of reach. Baptiste stood off to one side, the butt of his rifle on the frozen ground.

"Tomás," barked Sam.

Coy barked too.

"Tomás, put that rifle down."

The youth didn't budge.

"Easy, Pegleg," said Sam, "there doesn't need to be trouble here." Which felt like a lie.

Lupe stood in front of the lodge flap, and Rosalita was halfway out, blocked by her sister.

"Tomás, put that damn thing down."

Joaquin mooned at Lupe from behind Sam.

Walkara strode up with several Utes, eyeballing the situation.

"Brother-friend," said Pegleg in the Ute language, "I need your help."

Instantly, Walkara pointed his rifle at Tomás. All the Utes did the same.

Tomás quivered. His barrel bobbed like he was going to turn it toward the Utes, then it quickly refocused on Pegleg.

Sam launched himself and shouldered Tomás flat.

The Celt, left standing, arced toward the earth. Hannibal grabbed it.

When Tomás hit the ground, the hammer of his muzzleloader snapped.

KABOOM!

White smoke surrounded Tomás's head.

Sam turned a tackle into an embrace.

Gradually, the smoke cleared. Tomás's black hair was gray. His face was white. As far as Sam could tell, nothing was red.

No one around seemed to be shot. Maybe Tomás's ball had killed nothing but weeds.

Hannibal said to the Utes, "I ask you to lower your guns." His tone said, "I'm only going to ask once."

They did.

"You son of a bitch!" Tomás yelled into his father's face.

Sam held him tight, half from love, half to keep him from attacking his father or someone else.

"You ass!" Tomás elbowed him hard.

Sam climbed right on top of him and held on until Tomás stopped wiggling.

Coy lifted his leg on a bush.

After a few moments Sam and Tomás got up slowly.

Sam looked at Pegleg and knew that he and his son didn't have long in this camp. Pegleg had his rifle in hand now, though all weapons were pointed at the ground. Pegleg had called Walkara "brother-friend." Sam's side was outnumbered.

"Hello, Lupe," he said. "Hello, Rosalita."

"Hello, Sam." Their smiles were tremulous.

"Pegleg, I'm sorry for the ruckus. We've been looking for these women for months."

Tomás snarled, "You enslaved me sisters—"

Sam turned and clamped one hand over Tomás's mouth and the other one behind his head, firmly. He looked hard into the young man's eyes. He whispered, "Shut up or you'll get yourself killed."

Sam turned back to Pegleg. "Can we talk about these women?"

"What right you got to say words about my wives?" said Pegleg.

Your wives!

Sam gave Tomás a look of warning, not that it would help.

Wives! That was a horse of a different color.

Sam remembered how tough this man was. He was said to have amputated his own leg.

"There's a story behind this," Sam said. "I ask a favor. Will you let me tell it?"

"Por qué?" said Lupe. *"No importa."* Why? It doesn't matter.

Sam tried to suss out this situation. He sure didn't see any wife rushing to Joaquin to greet her long-lost husband. Lupe and Rosalita stood behind Pegleg like they were backing him up. "May I tell the story?"

"You don't have a whole of rope here," said Pegleg.

Sam told briefly how Tomás, Lupe, and Rosalita had been slaves who came to Rancho de las Palomas, and were freed. How they adopted each other as brother and sisters. He left out the part about them getting married in a big ceremony at the church. Instead he told how the Navajos stole them from their husbands, he and Tomás found out about it, and for eight or nine months now they'd trekked from Santa Fé to high on the Siskadee and all the way to Bent's fort, trying to find Tomás's sisters and rescue them. He said nothing about Joaquin, nothing about the unborn child.

Not that there was an unborn, not anymore.

"You're talking about my *wives*," said Pegleg. His voice rasped with anger.

Lupe piped up, "I am with *this* man now. He is the one I love. He is good to me. And he is rich."

Lupe apparently didn't need to add to that.

Joaquin burst out, "Querida, I love you."

Lupe laughed. "What? You old drunk? Even now you barely walk or talk. You love only booze."

"Querida . . ."

Lupe stepped forward and slapped him hard. "You think I forget how you hit me?"

Joaquin stumbled backward, tripped over a root, and fell flat on his back.

"You hit me." She advanced and kicked him. "There, this is my revenge. You deserve it." She kicked him again. She laughed. "Kicks instead of kisses, like you gave me."

She walked back and stood next to her husband.

"Pegleg," said Sam, "I'm sorry for the disturbance. Seems clear the way things are. Maybe we can have a drink later."

"I want to talk to me sisters," said Tomás.

Sam took him by the arm and pulled him away, protesting.

Fifty-seven

EARLY THAT EVENING, as the sun dropped below the lines of the western mountains, vendors on the plaza folded their blankets and put away their merchandise. The people of Fernandez de Taos thronged to the plaza. Young, single men and older, married men, señoras and señoritas, old men and women, toddlers, kids, teenagers—everyone gathered, milled, and talked with animation in small groups. In the twilight, cigarillos glowed in the fingers of both men and women. Jugs of *aguardiente* were passed.

Most important, the musicians plucked out trial tunes on their instruments. Soon the music would sing, and all of Taos would dance. The sweet songs would make feet move, lift heads, set bodies to swaying. And later these bodies, inspired by the dance to move together, would join in another way, in alleys, in the willows, and in unfamiliar bedrooms.

Restraint? They cared nothing for that. Taos was a town in love with sensuality, in love with romance. Neither men nor women paid attention to the bonds of marriage, or any other bonds. And they were happily led in this path by Father Antonio Martínez, the priest at the Church of San Geronimo, who set the example by siring children hither and yon throughout the valley.

The trappers came to the plaza too, mostly the cantina run by Xeveria and her brother Gabriel, because they had money to spend. The commanding Ewing Young and his gangly partner William Wolfskill held court at one outside table, and men who had trapped with Young came and went. Some asked after Kit Carson, a fellow everyone liked and expected to see in Taos in the winter. "He sold his beaver here in October," Young told everyone. "Now he's trapping up on the Uinta."

At a table at the cantina's opposite corner sat trappers and traders too small for Young and Wolfskill to see as competition. Hannibal MacKye chatted with Baptiste Charbonneau. If Captain William Drummond Stewart had joined them, most of the education in the mountains would have come together in one dialogue; but Stewart was wintering far to the north with Broken Hand Fitzpatrick. Sam Morgan, pretending to watch the scores of people, subtly observed Tomás and his fiancée. Tomás, who now introduced himself by his birth name, Guerrero, instead of Morgan, held hands with Grass. The young couple said nothing. Silence can be sweet, it can be sullen. This one cast a pall on the company.

Joaquin wandered from table to table, cluster to cluster, family to family, joining anyone who offered him a drink.

All at once Sam jumped to his feet, and Coy gave a little yip. Sumner strode to the table, grinning broadly. Sam's friend always looked the dandy, but tonight he had outdone himself. He was outfitted in a moss-green suit that set off his black skin dramatically. His royal-blue beaver hat was the perfect complement.

Sam embraced Sumner in the Taos style, an *abrazo*. "You are some," he said. "Is that suit . . . ?"

"Silk," Sumner confirmed. He pulled up a seat. "Did you notice the silver thread in the weave?"

Everyone at the table murmured admiration for his outfit.

Sam was surprised at how glad he was to see Sumner. His trading partner had written in care of Young and Wolfskill that he would ride up for a few days to talk about the coming summer's business, but . . .

Xeveria arrived in a fever to ask the handsome black man what he wanted. "Pass brandy," Sumner said, his usual. In a flash she was back with the drink and Gabriel. She introduced her brother as though the new guest was royalty.

"You are a peacock," said Hannibal. "Everyone looks up to the slave who has made himself prosperous."

Sam introduced him to Grass. "Me fiancée," added Tomás.

Suddenly Grass interrupted. "When will dancing start?" As far as anyone could tell, dancing was what Grass liked most about Taos.

"It starts when it starts," said Sumner, "and it goes on forever. I intend to dance with every beautiful woman in Taos," he said, "and the fiancée of my friend Tomás is at the top of my list."

Since Grass looked puzzled, Sam explained the compliment to her, and she beamed at Sumner.

"Xeveria," he said as the waitress appeared. He grasped one of her hands. "Will you be able to get off work and do a little fandango?"

She gave him a flirtatious look. "For you, anything. My cousin is coming later to help tonight, so . . ." She twirled away laughing.

Shadowed figures moved by, and Sam recognized the profiles of Pegleg, Lupe, and Rosalita passing. He jumped up. "Join us," he said.

They stopped.

"Please," said Tomás. Lupe and Rosalita squeezed in, but Pegleg strode on to sit with Young and Wolfskill.

Sam called, "Gabriel," and the owner came. "What would you like to drink?" he asked the sisters.

"Chocolate," said Rosalita. Lupe nodded

"An entire pot," said Sam. He remembered making spicy Mexican chocolate with the two girls in Paloma's kitchen many times.

When the pot came, Sam poured Lupe's cup because one of her

arms was full of baby. Sam, Tomás, and Grass leaned close to look at the child.

"Beautiful," said Grass.

"Handsome," said Lupe. "A boy."

"Congratulations on your first child," Tomás said. Sam's son was capable of a courtly politeness.

Sam echoed, "Congratulations."

"His name is Thomas," said Lupe, pronouncing it in the American way.

"Tomás?" said the teenage Tomás, his voice sailing up the musical scale.

Lupe nodded, a moony smile on her face. "My husband, the one you call Pegleg, his name is Thomas."

Pegleg nodded. Sam hadn't known his given name until now.

Sam sat back down in silence and sipped his coffee. *Joaquin's son. Now Pegleg's.*

No one knew quite what to say next. Sam scratched Coy's ears and decided he had to hand out some news. "Rosalita, your daughter is with Ernesto's parents."

She nodded, dipped her head, and let her long hair cover her sad eyes.

Sam didn't need to tell her what happened to Ernesto—she'd seen it with her own eyes.

"She is well."

"My husband," said Rosalita, "he takes us to Santa Fé next, and will pick up my child. Our child."

And sell more horses. Sam also thought, *Maybe the prodigious drinker and brawler is ready to take on a family.*

Sam looked across the heads at Pegleg. The man who amputated his own leg was staring at Sam's table, his expression unreadable.

"You look wonderful," Sam told Lupe.

"I am good, and it is because of my husband," she said.

"Good man," Rosalita echoed.

"I want to tell." Lupe plunged forward with her story. "After the birth I got the childbed fever."

Sam blinked. That was what killed Meadowlark.

"Pegleg, he put me on a travois and hauled me all day to San Diego, to a *curandera*. I owe him my life."

"He saved my sister," agreed Rosalita.

"Good for both of you," Sam said, "and for Thomas." He sneaked a look at Tomás to see whether his son understood the bond between Pegleg and these women.

Suddenly the fanfare of a trumpet and fiddle put an end to all conversation.

TOWARD MIDNIGHT, ACCORDING to the Big Dipper, Sam left the fandango. He loved the music, and he liked to dance. Tonight he'd danced with Grass and Xeveria, with Rosalita and Lupe, and with women he'd never seen before. Everyone had danced with everyone, in fact. The most popular of the men dancers was certainly Sumner. This afternoon Sam had thought of dallying with Xeveria himself—he couldn't act like a monk forever. But once the black man appeared, Xeveria was his captive. In fact, Sumner could have had a harem.

Trailed by Coy, Sam headed for the creek. He needed a drink that wasn't whiskey, and he needed some peace.

The moon was bright, and turned the water to flowing silver. He knelt, plunged his face into the cold liquid, and drank. It tasted good. Bell Rock had told him once that mountain water captures those who taste it. "Once you drink of a mountain creek," he said, "you will have to come back to its sweetness again."

Sam had borrowed a cigarillo back at the cantina, and now he lit it. Though he didn't have his pipe with him, smoke was smoke. He offered it in a proper way to the four directions, the earth, and the sky. He said some words for the well-being of the children yet to be born; for all mothers, two-legged, four-legged—all; for the young, the old, the ill; for the men who would make the sacrifice of the sun dance or the vision quest in the coming year; for all medicine men of any religion; and last for the health, in body and spirit, of his family, his friends, all the men who hunted the beaver, all Indian people, all white people, all Mexicans, and all two-leggeds everywhere.

He rubbed Coy's head. From the far side of the creek he could hear the herd Pegleg had brought, clomps of hoofs, flabbers of lips, wheezes, all the nighttime sounds of horses. One thought came strongly to him—bedtime.

He rose and started up the trail toward town. Ahead he could hear voices. Though he expected them to be the exclamations of lovers, these were two women. After a moment he recognized them. And a man.

Then Lupe began to scream.

Sam sprinted.

Lupe was hollering bloody murder. Rosalita was shrieking helplessly. Sam saw that she had snatched the baby.

The dark figure slung Lupe, and she fell hard on her back.

The man jumped on top of her.

"Diablo!" Lupe bellowed. She seemed to hit him in the face.

Sam dived at Joaquin and hit him square in the trunk with one shoulder. They both rolled off Lupe and up against a bush.

Sam hit Joaquin as hard as he could in the face with a fist.

Joaquin's head lolled sideways unnaturally.

Sam looked at Lupe, on her knees now. "I already killed the diablo. He thought he owned me."

Rosalita wept piteously.

Lupe wiped some sort of blade on her skirt and tucked it back into the waistband. "I don't leave this job for Pegleg," she said.

Sam stood up from Joaquin's body. The neck grinned red.

Lupe walked over, cocked her foot, and kicked him as hard as she could between the legs. Joaquin was beyond protest.

Then she stomped off.

Fifty-eight

"I CAN'T FIND Grass."

Sam opened his eyes and looked into Tomás's face. He thought, *I've got plenty to worry about, and I don't need to be chasing women for Tomás*. But he blinked until he could see his lodgings, rolled out of his buffalo robes, reached for his blanket coat, and said, "Let's walk around together."

They had to walk without coffee—the town was still in bed, whether for sleep or for fun.

Sam took the search seriously. With Tomás fretting loudly at his side, he couldn't do anything else.

She wasn't on the plaza. A rap on Xeveria's door brought a sleepy "Qué?"

Sam asked the question, and Xeveria made a sound of disgust. "Go away."

Grass wasn't visible in any of the twisted streets and alleys.

"I'm worried that she's hurt," Tomás said.

"Probably not as serious as that," Sam said.

"You saying she is in another man's bed?" Tomás's voice was full of challenge.

"Haven't you been in someone else's bed?"

Tomás's face flushed. "She said she wanted to be with Lupe and Rosalita. I left her with them. But she didn't come home."

That gave Sam an idea. "Then let's go ask Lupe and Rosalita when they saw her last." He was thinking that there might be coffee at Pegleg's camp.

Sam chose not to take Tomás along the main path, where Joaquin's body probably lay frozen.

AT PEGLEG'S THEY were unlucky and then lucky.

No one was stirring. But the coffeepot still had some black brew in it.

Sam set to making a fire.

After a minute or so Pegleg's voice roared from inside the tipi.

"Making coffee," Sam said.

It was Rosalita who came out.

"Where is she?" Tomás cried, even before Rosalita got all the way outside the flap.

Rosalita pursed her lips and sat down primly on a log.

"Me fiancée," said Tomás, "where is she?"

"I don't know," Rosalita said.

Sam said, "We've only got one cup, we'll have to share." He handed it to Rosalita.

Tomás's sister took one sip, looking fearfully over the brim at her brother.

"You don't know?!"

"I will get some more cups," said Rosalita, "and some nice ground coffee."

She disappeared into the tipi.

When Lupe and Rosalita came back out, Lupe said firmly, "We won't talk about Grass. We don't know, we won't say."

Pegleg never did come out.

SAM BEGAN TO worry the next day, December 30. He was glad it wasn't another feast day. The four blowouts in a row starting on Christmas, plus the New Year's Eve celebration tomorrow night, that was plenty for him.

He and Tomás walked the streets again. They asked everyone they saw. They stopped by the cantina several times. They walked over to Pegleg's camp. He was packing up to go to Santa Fé, and was curt with them. Yes, he'd made a sale of some horses here, to Señor Fernandez, the *alcalde*. Yes, he was going to Santa Fé now, and expected to be back in about three weeks, without horses.

Tomás hugged his sisters goodbye, but he and Pegleg still didn't speak.

"It's not that odd," Sam told Tomás on the way back to town. "We haven't seen Hannibal or Baptiste in two days either."

"We keep looking," said Tomás.

At noon they found Sumner at the cantina, taking a breakfast of biscuits and coffee, and Xeveria sharing the table with him.

Sumner gave Tomás a knowing smile and said, "I haven't seen her." Xeveria just shrugged.

Sumner told Sam, "We need to talk business." Rideo Trading, their small outfit.

Sam looked at Tomás.

Sumner said, "How about sundown, today, here?"

Sam waited for Tomás, and his son shrugged.

"Yes," Sam told Sumner.

As they walked away, Tomás said, "I'm really afraid something has happened to her."

"Then let's go see the alcalde," said Sam.

* * *

A SMALL TOWN in Nuevo Mexico usually had no more government than a mayor, the man of paperwork, and a police officer, the man for dirty work, often the brother, son, or cousin of the mayor, or alcalde. If a dispute was large enough, the priest would get involved.

The alcalde of Fernandez de Taos was a gray eminence named Fernandez. Sam didn't know whether this Fernandez was somehow connected to the town's founding family or not. He lived in one of the town's few decent adobe houses. Sam presented their question to him, simply and politely.

Señor Fernandez, who seemed as thin and frail as corn silk, regarded Sam and Tomás for a long moment. "Morgan is your name?" he said.

"Sam Morgan."

"And your name again is . . . ?"

"Tomás Guerrero."

Fernandez raised an eyebrow at Sam.

"Sometimes he goes by Tomás Morgan," said Sam.

Fernandez rose and stepped into his own kitchen. Sam couldn't understand the soft words he said to someone.

Fernandez came back, seated himself, and said in English, "One minute."

In about five minutes a burly man of about forty barged in and pointed a pistol at Sam and Tomás.

"Thank you, Jacinto," said Fernandez. "The young man."

Jacinto reached out to grab Tomás.

When Tomás went for his own pistol, Sam wrapped his son up from behind. "This is not the time," he said softly. "I'll take care of things."

Tomás let Jacinto wind a rope around his arms quickly.

"Perhaps it will not be so easy," said Fernandez. "Tomás Morgan is accused of murder."

"Murder?!" exclaimed Sam and Tomás at once.

"Yes, murder. On the night of the Feast of the Holy Innocents. Of a peasant named Joaquin. We have a body."

"Accused by who?" snapped Sam.

"Señor Pegleg Smith," said Fernandez.

Jacinto jerked Tomás out the door. Sam's son flung a look of fury and fear back at him.

Fifty-nine

THE TOWN *JUZGADO* was a one-room shack on the back of Jacinto's property. Sam suspected it had once been a double privy, moved to a new foundation. Since it had no window at all, Sam and Hannibal could see Tomás only through cracks. The lock on the door was sturdy. Jacinto stood a few feet away, weapon in hand.

"The son of a bitch, he lies."

"Yes," Sam said, "I told you. Pegleg wanted to protect Lupe. Now he's got her out of town and he slapped you in the face."

"Viejo hediondo!" said Tomás.

Hannibal said, "I'm getting to where I don't see the humor in calling someone old."

"I sent Baptiste after Pegleg," said Sam. "He'll be back in a day or two and we'll know more."

"What do you mean?"

"Pegleg would have to testify against you. I'm the only one who saw what happened. I could bring Lupe into court. Pegleg wouldn't like that."

Tomás crashed his fists against the boards. "I am penned like an animal in this miserable shit hole," he yelled. "I will kill the bastard."

"Pegleg takes a lot of killing," observed Hannibal.

Sam added, "I think we can work something out."

HANNIBAL AND SAM decided to have their midday meal at Gabriel's cantina—the town offered few choices—and take some tortillas back to Tomás. Being in jail in New Mexico apparently deprived you of food as well as freedom.

Fifty paces from the plaza, as they were passing the house Gabriel and Xeveria shared, they saw Sumner coming out of Xeveria's door. With Xeveria behind him. And Grass behind her.

"I'll be damned," said Sam.

Sumner offered an arm to each lady, and they accepted. He walked toward his friends with a broad smile. All of them strode on to the cantina, everybody grinning, nobody saying a word.

They took a table. "I must help Gabriel," said Xeveria, and off she danced.

Grass gave them a proud smile. She held up an arm thick with silver bracelets.

"This answers some questions," said Hannibal.

"Fun," said Sumner. "Fun provides a lot of answers."

Grass put her head on Sumner's shoulder.

Sam told her, "Tomás has been looking for you."

"Where is he?" she said.

"In jail."

Sam explained.

"We'll make it turn out right," said Sumner.

"Tomás, he no listen to me," said Grass. "Maybe now."

"I think he will," said Sam.

"Let's go."

Jacinto was nervous about it, but he let all of them walk back to the hoosegow.

Grass grasped Sumner's arm as they made their way across the red sand and patchy grass. Sam was sure Tomás's eyes were fixed on the way she clung to Sumner.

When they got close, she said, "Tomás, where are you?"

"Here."

Sam indicated the crack his son was peering through.

She stepped close, holding Sumner's hand. "Tomás?" she said, searching for his face in the shadows behind the boards.

"Right here."

Sam could hear him seething.

"I have something to tell you."

"Do it."

She put her lips out, as though to kiss the crack where his face was.

She whispered, "You don't own me."

Sixty

"WHICHEVER WAY YOU figure whatever," said Baptiste, "I don't think it's right for Tomás to sit in the hoosegow until Pegleg gets back."

"Me neither," said Sam.

"Me neither," said Hannibal.

They were having coffee before Gabriel's first batch of *bizcocho* was ready.

"Then let's do something about it," said Baptiste.

About half an hour later three mountain men rapped on the door of the town policeman, Jacinto.

Very quickly, Jacinto came outside, hands high, three pistols pointed at him.

"I lost it," said Jacinto.

"You lost the key?" said Sam Morgan.

"I lost it."

"He sounds sullen to me," said Hannibal. "What do you think?"

"Sullen," said Baptiste.

"But we may not have time for him to look for it," said Sam.

"How many horses you think," said Hannibal, "two or three?"

"Make it three," said Baptiste. "After that a few weeks in Santa Fé would be good."

"Let's do it," said Sam.

Four mounts were tied out front, including Vici for Tomás.

Three pairs of hands trussed Jacinto's arms and legs and lashed him to the post in front of his own door.

"We don't have a lot of time," said Sam.

The three mounted and rode through Jacinto's yard, and his shouts, to the hoosegow.

"What's happening, Mr. Sam Morgan?" asked Tomás.

"Freedom," said Sam.

"Life, liberty, and the pursuit of happiness," said Hannibal.

"We're gonna bust you out," said Baptiste.

"How?"

Three ropes floated through the air and nestled around the outhouse. Sam eyed the thick log foundation, and the way the shack had been nailed to it.

"But there's a condition," said Sam.

"A condition?"

"Yes."

"What?"

The ropes pulled taut.

"You have to say, 'Thanks, Dad.'"

"That's stupid," said Tomás.

The riders looked at each other and eased the tension off the ropes.

"Thanks!" said Tomás. Loudly.

"'Thanks, Dad,'" Sam repeated.

Silence.

Then in a shout—"THANKS, DAD!"

"If I were you," said Sam Morgan, "I'd get right down flat on the floor."

The riders spurred their horses.

The shack popped off its foundation like a cork flying from a champagne bottle.

Four mountain men rode like hell.

The Never-Ending Song of Jedediah Smith

(to the tune of "Sweet Betsy from Pike")

We set out from Salt Lake, not knowing the track
Whites, Spanyards and Injuns, and even a black
Our captain was Diah, a man of great vision
Our dream Californy, and beaver our mission

(chorus)
Captain Smith was a rollickin' man
A wanderin' man was he
He led us 'cross the desert sands
And on to the sweet blue sea

We rode through the deserts, our throats were so dry
If we didn't find water, we surely would die
The captain saw a river, our hearts came down thud
The river was dry, and we got to drink mud

We rode through a salt plain, scarce a creature could live
The captain saw a village, said the Injuns might give
Our stomachs were aching—we smiled and said "Please"
Our tongues were surprised when they fed us on fleas

(chorus)

We was lost in that desert, no beaver, no creeks
Don't worry, says the Captain, we'll find water next week
He climbed up a hilltop to get a good look
And studied his Bible—was there a map in the book?

We parleyed with Injuns, we traded tobacco
We took gals to the willows, and made canyons echo
And only the captain, with morals full girt
Missed out on the fun—never lifted a skirt

(chorus)

Our Diah, oh he was a far-seeing man
He captained us clear to the Spanyard land
There we did gaze on the foam of the sea
And the Spanyards they threw us a big jamboree

It was grand, Californy, a life of pure ease
It was warm all year round, with a sweet-scented breeze
There was plews in the creeks and mountains to roam
Only one problem—we couldn't get home

(chorus)

Captain Smith, he stared at the mountains and snow
How to get over, he said, I know
Three good men I'll take, and hay for the mounts
We'll fight and we'll claw and come through when it counts

His words gave no hint of the desert beyond
The fierce sun, the hot winds—mirages, not ponds
We wandered but found only dry watercourses
And finally, half starved, we ate up horses

(chorus)

One terrible noon, a man fell to his knees
No more, he cried, just leave me—please
We shoveled the sand clear up to his chin
We'll be back, they promised, don't never give in

After three dusty miles, we came to a spring
We drank deep, we splashed—oh, water was king
Diah took back a kettle, good as his word
They knew then they'd survive—Die? that's absurd

(chorus)

They spied out the Salt Lake, and thought journey's end
Their hearts were for meat and whiskey and friends
When the camp saw them coming, they gave out a hoot
Got out the cannon and fired a salute

So the story went round, from white men to red
Jed Smith may be pious, but living or dead
He's a captain to ride with, a partner to side with
A leader with art, and a friend of big heart

(chorus)

On the Santa Fe Trail, it was four years after
The men came to trouble, they couldn't find water
Jed Smith rode ahead to find the Cimarron
He found the Comanch, their eyes hard like stone

Not a living man knows where his bones are a-bleaching
His flesh, it is dust that drifts in the haze
The life that he lived is all that needs preaching
The coyotes on the night wind are singing his praise

Historical Note

The time in history and places of this novel are as accurate as I can make them, and as truthful.

The Indian slave trade was just as it's shown here, and the relationship between the New Mexicans and Navajos as well. The treaty terms which Governor Armijo offers to Hosteen Tso and the Navajo, ridiculous as they seem, are based on an actual treaty of the time. Though the enslavement of black people in the United States is more than notorious, the enslavement of red people is acknowledged less than it should be; and it lasted long past the Emancipation Proclamation.

The rendezvous of 1833 and the state of the fur trade in that year, pivoting on the struggle between Rocky Mountain Fur and the monopoly, are also depicted accurately. The historical characters presented here—Tom Fitzpatrick, Joe Meek, Captain Stewart, Milton Sublette, Robert Campbell, and others—were in fact there and behaved as I have shown. Jean-Baptiste Charbonneau is likewise drawn from history.

Though Pegleg Smith's purchase of Tomás's fictional cousins is my invention, he and other mountain men did trade women in this manner.

I am grateful to many people for help along the way. Dick James is a true expert on the physical culture of the mountain men. Murphy Fox is a fountainhead of information about Plains Indians. Stan Hordes, former state historian of New Mexico, is a treasure trove of information about that state. Lana Latham is my invaluable supplier of interlibrary loan books. And my friends Clyde Hall and Heidi Schulman once again deserve my thanks.

The two people most crucial to my writing, this book or any other, are my wife, Meredith, who brainstorms with me and inspires me, and my editor, Dale Walker, who guides me, encourages me, and occasionally shakes his finger at me.